The Column of Burning Spices

The Column of Burning Spices

Burning Spices

A Novel of Germany's First Female Physician

BY

P.K. ADAMS

IRON KNIGHT PRESS

The Column of Burning Spices

ISBN: 978-1-7323611-3-3 (paperback)
ISBN: 978-1-7323611-2-6 (ebook)

Cover designed by Jennifer Quinlan

Iron Knight Press
25 W. Howard St
Quincy, MA 02169

www.pkadams-author.com
Twitter @pk_adams
Facebook P.K. Adams Author

Contents

Praise for
The Greenest Branch
and *The Column of Burning Spices*

"A fascinating portrayal of one of history's most remarkable women, Hildegard of Bingen—composer, mystic, theologian, and physician. The characters and settings come alive on the page, and by the end I felt as if I'd traveled in time to 12th-century Germany." – C.P. Lesley, author of *The Golden Lynx* and other novels.

"Hauntingly beautiful and meticulously researched. P.K. Adams writes about the Middle Ages like someone who has lived there. Hildegard's story is inspiring, and her voice feels so real that it's almost spooky." – Jessica Cale, author of *Tyburn*

"Had Hildegard been born a boy, she would likely have become an archbishop or even a pope. As it was, her reach spanned many disciplines and extended across Europe. If it's hard to believe that this larger-than-life character was a real historical figure, read *The Column of Burning Spices* for yourself, and follow the path of the very human woman who brought a feminine perspective to the Catholic church." – Paula Butterfield, author of *La Luministe*

"Every word of this book is beautiful. The phrasing, the description, the subtle historical details that pull the reader into medieval Germany. P.K. Adams' talent for writing brings Hildegard back to life in this exquisite tale of perseverance." - K.M. Pohlkamp, author of *Apricots and Wolfsbane*

Glossary Of Terms

A S CLOCKS WERE not in use in the Middle Ages, the passage of time was typically measured by the eight daily services of the Divine Office. The exact timing of these services was dictated by the rising and setting of the sun and therefore varied depending on the season. Here's a rough approximation:

matins - in the middle of the night, any time between midnight and 2 a.m.
lauds - at dawn (around 3 a.m. in the summer)
prime - first office of the day, around 6 a.m.
terce - mid-morning office, around 9 a.m.
sext - mid-day office, around 12 noon
nones – mid-afternoon office, around 3 p.m.
vespers - the evening office, between 5 p.m. and 7 p.m.
compline - at nightfall, around 9 p.m.

Anchorite monasticism – a form of monasticism popular in the Middle Ages characterized by complete isolation from the world for the purpose of practicing religious devotion. Most commonly, anchorite enclosures were attached to a church in the form of a wooden shack or a stone-walled annex. There were more women than men who practiced that form of monasticism, and they were referred to as anchoresses. Anchorite monasticism was in contrast to cenobitic (community-based) monasticism as exemplified by priories or abbeys, although sometimes the two co-existed in the same place. Hildegard's monastic life started out in an anchorite enclosure, but she moved away from it and toward a community-based life.

Holy Roman Empire – a complex of multi-ethnic lands in west-central Europe that lasted for a thousand years, from AD 800-1806, under the rule of Frankish and then German kings. The Kingdom of Germany was its core and largest part, but at different times it also included territories that are part of modern-day Czech Republic, northern Poland, western France, Switzerland and northern and central Italy.

Investiture controversy – a power struggle between the papacy and the secular rulers of the Holy Roman Empire over who should have the right to appoint bishops (by symbolically investing them with the insignia of their authority – a ring and crosier). It lasted some 75 years from the second half of the 11th to the early 12th century. It resulted in a state of civil war in most of the German territory as well as the appointments of several anti-popes by successive emperors in an effort to ensure a more pliable papacy that would allow them to preserve their investiture rights. The most acute phase of the conflict was ended by the Concordat of Worms in 1122, but attempts of kings to control ecclesiastical appointments continued intermittently for the rest of the 12th century and beyond.

Magistra – the Latin term for 'teacher', sometimes applied to leaders of female monastic communities who held a rank lower than abbess.

Rule of Saint Benedict (Lat. *Regula Benedicti*) – a set of regulations governing the daily life in the Benedictine communities. It covers both religious practices and non-religious activities like work, study, recreation, and meals. It was written by Benedict of Nursia (c. 480-550), the founder of the order. (Note: Benedict was only canonized in the year 1220, later than the events in this story).

Viriditas – derived from the Latin word for "weed" or "herb," it is a term coined by Hildegard of Bingen to signify the life-force that flows through the universe. It is directed towards healing and wholeness by imbuing all nature with greenness, vitality, vigor, and freshness, and is present in all creation, not just its animate parts. It can be perceived most immediately in the act of blossoming, growth, and development, but Hildegard also ascribed the property of *viriditas* to light, which causes all nature to take its proper form, and to love.

1

Abbey of St. Disibod, September 1143

I FOLDED THE letter and rose from my desk, intending to go find Volmar in the scriptorium to share the long-awaited news. It was a reply from Abbot Bernard of Clairvaux, to whom I had sent a chapter of my new book some months earlier in hopes that he would look favorably on my writing. He was such a famed cleric that I feared my effort would go unnoticed or ignored, but he had written back, and the response was positive. It stopped short of outright praise, for the ascetic French monk would have considered that an extravagance, but he told me I had a gift that it was my duty to nurture, and he sent me his blessings. It was enough. It would help pave my way for leaving St. Disibod and the monks who had made my life increasingly difficult, and to establish my own foundation. I could not wait to tell Volmar, my oldest and dearest friend.

But I did not make it halfway to the door of the surgery before it squeaked in its hinges, and Brother Fabian poked in his head. He had been scarcely more than a child when I had persuaded the late Brother Wigbert, my tutor and predecessor at the helm of the infirmary, to take him on as our assistant, but now his hair was threaded with gray.

"We have a patient with a hand injury you should see," he informed me.

Putting the thoughts of Bernard of Clairvaux aside, I followed him, immediately assuming the mantle of physician.

"Second bed on the right." Fabian pointed as we entered the ward. "He lost two fingers doing fieldwork. I washed the wound with warm wine and vinegar, but it does not look right. It's a few days old, and I fear corruption has set in."

The patient was a man in his thirties of strong peasant stock, but he looked pale and drawn as he held his left hand gingerly in his lap. The end of it was lightly swathed in a clean bandage, while a pile of dirty rags smelling faintly of barnyard lay on a nearby table. When I got closer, I saw that his face was covered with a film of sweat.

"What is your name, my good man?"

"Egbert, Sister. I come all the way from Weiler, near St. Rupert."

The name of St. Rupert was vaguely familiar. "Is it farther down on the Nahe?" I began to take off the bandage.

"Aye. Just at the point when it flows into the Rhine." His voice was strained, and he flinched when I touched the inflamed skin. The tips of his index and the middle fingers were gone, sliced clean off.

"Scythe?" I had seen this type of injury often, especially at harvest time.

He nodded.

"When?"

"Near a week ago."

"Had anyone cleaned the wound for you before you came here?"

"My wife made a poultice, but the bandages started smelling and getting warm. She made another, but it got worse, so I came up here with a merchant who was passing through our village on the way to Disibodenberg. He said you know how to treat such wounds."

I sighed. I could have treated it if he had come quickly and avoided his wife's ministrations. Judging by the smell of the old bandages, she had used animal dung, a practice that persisted in the countryside despite my efforts to make people aware of its dangers. As it was, the edges of Egbert's wound had turned purple-blue, a sign of dangerous corruption. If unaddressed, it would move up the fingers, the hand, and the arm, blackening them and killing him in an agony of fever and pain. The only way to stop the progress was to perform an amputation.

Egbert's lower lip wobbled when he heard my diagnosis, and I knew it was not from fear of pain—his livelihood was at stake.

"You are not the first man to lose a finger or two in this way." I sought to console him as I rinsed the knife in vinegar and ran it over the flame of a candle. "With time and practice, you will learn to use the remaining three as if they were a full hand."

After the procedure, which I completed swiftly, having been well trained in the art of surgery by Brother Wigbert, I cauterized the wound and made a poultice of mugwort, sanicle, and lovage to relieve the inflammation.

"You will stay here for three days so we can observe your progress," I said and directed Fabian to reapply the poultice alternating with plasters of betony to bring down the swelling, which would help the wound to start knitting. Luckily, there were still fresh leaves available at that time of year; their effect was stronger than that of ointments or salves made from dried ingredients in wintertime.

Leaving Egbert in my assistant's capable hands, I headed for the scriptorium.

On the way, I allowed myself a small fantasy of what my new life of freedom would be. I would be able to practice medicine as I saw fit, and write and share my work with whom I pleased. I had saved enough money from the income from our endowments, and from my medical guidebook that Volmar had copied and Ricardis had illuminated before they were sold to abbeys across the land.

But Abbot Kuno was an old man now; it was only a matter of time before Prior Helenger replaced him, and all of that would come to an end. Despite the convent's wealth and my reputation as a physician, I could only hope to relocate over the monks' objection if I had the endorsement of a great man of the Church. Abbot Bernard had unquestionably been one since he had helped to confirm Pope Innocent's right to the throne of St. Peter against the usurper Anacletus in the year 1130. He was now considered one of the most powerful clerics in Christendom.

The day had started sunny, promising long hours of good light, but banks of gray clouds were now visible in the east. That worried me because it meant that Volmar and Ricardis would have to strain their eyes. They created beautiful books that had made the convent rich, but it was hard work, especially in autumn and winter when darkness fell early, and they had to labor with stiff fingers in dim candlelight. But they never complained. Ricardis never looked less than enthusiastic, eager to show off the imaginative drawings with which she decorated each page.

The weather was still mild. Clouds or rain meant that the work would be more challenging than usual, yet as I approached the carrel we were renting in the scriptorium, I smiled. Ricardis and Volmar were bent over their work, light flooding their slanted desks under the round arch of a window. I considered them for a moment, my two most beloved people in the world. Ricardis was in the prime of her life at thirty, glorious with a cascade of black hair — covered with a veil outside the convent — that surrounded a smooth face that had lost nothing of its youthful rosy glow. She was no longer the plump girl I had first met at Sponheim, the result of the monastic diet, but her slimness gave her a more sublime look, like a saint fresh from under a painter's brush.

Volmar's chestnut hair had thinned somewhat, but it still curled above his ears in the way that I found hopelessly charming, and he still applied himself to every task with the passion I remembered from our childhood. I sometimes wondered if the passage of time had been as kind to my appearance as it had been to theirs — I had just turned thirty-nine, though I felt as vigorous as ever. Between the three of us, our *viriditas* was strong, and we were blessed indeed.

If only they got along with each other! That was the only thing that marred my happiness. Though he had never said it, I knew Volmar did not like Ricardis. I sensed that he found her attachment to me excessive, and her desire to please me and elicit frequent approval unseemly. I did not understand what bothered him so about her — she was devoted, beautiful, and talented, and I saw no reason not to indulge her need for recognition. She deserved it, and I gave my praise freely when she presented me with margins ornamented with floral motifs, biblical scenes, or imagery suggested by me to represent my own words. Her skill shone through the exquisite red, green, yellow, and blue hues, combined with gold leaf to create perfect harmony. I praised Volmar too, though he never sought it, and it pained me to think that he might be jealous.

God knew he had no reason to feel that way. I loved Ricardis like one loves an exotic bird with colorful plumage or a cherry tree in fragrant bloom. One gets used to such wonders over time; they still please, but they cease to thrill. Volmar was different. He had a place in my life that nobody could take, and each day I was amazed anew that he had once given up a post at the Cluny abbey and returned to St. Disibod to share this simple lot with me. Without him, who knows if I would have become who I was, or had the courage to reach for what was still possible?

Volmar heard me first. As he lifted his eyes, the crease of concentration on his forehead relaxed, softening his face. Today he was copying my notes for *Scivias*, a book I had been working on for the past few years, committing to parchment my thoughts on faith, redemption, and the mysteries of creation as my mind understood them. Not all mysteries, of course—for God would forever hide certain things from human comprehension—but the ones that were discernible to those who knew how to look at the natural world.

For a long time, I had struggled with doubts about making my thoughts known and risking condemnation from the men who ruled the Church. Then one day, when I was ill with a particularly strong headache, out of the shimmering light that hurt my eyes came the old familiar voice that seemed to resonate both within me and without, and it permeated my body like a warming flame. *Write the things you see and hear.*

So I did.

And then I sent what I had written to Bernard of Clairvaux.

Next to Ricardis's desk was a table on which she laid out the finished sheets to let the paints dry. I picked up the one with the image of the Holy Trinity, verdant vine entwined through the initial letter S of the text, and studied the figure painted in deep blue, surrounded by circles of blazing red and radiant white. That was how I had wanted the triune God to be depicted—the luminous outer disk symbolizing the perfection of the Father, the glowing fire the Holy Spirit, and the image of the Son encircled by both so the three were one.

Ricardis stopped working and trained her dark eyes on me. They shone with anticipation, and her chest swelled with bated breath.

"It looks better than I ever imagined it," I said appreciatively. Though my eyes were on the parchment, I could sense Volmar shaking his head, so subtly Ricardis probably missed it. I smiled to appease him, though he looked more concerned than angry. What was he worried about? He was the most brilliant man I knew, the abbey's authority on the finer points of Latin syntax, and his transcription refined my writing so it matched that produced by any man.

"I would have a word with you, Brother," I said.

We crossed the scriptorium and stepped out onto the cloister walk, where yellowing leaves crunched under our feet, blown over the wall by the strengthening wind. Volmar breathed in the ripe, earthy scent of the approaching autumn, welcoming the break as we began to pace the arcaded perimeter to the soothing sounds of water trickling into a marble lavatorium. It was a reminder—if I needed any—that with my convent still within the Abbey of St. Disibod, the monks were sitting on a pot of gold.

"I have something to show you." I paused under an arch and took the letter from the folds of my habit.

Volmar read the few lines—as in everything, Bernard of Clairvaux was spare in his writing—and his eyebrows rose higher and higher. He gave me a puzzled look of his hazel eyes. In sunlight, they were flecked with honey. At thirty-seven, fine lines had begun to appear in the corners of his eyes, but now astonishment had smoothed them all out. "You sent *Scivias* to Abbot Bernard." It was a statement more than a question, and there was disbelief in it.

"Only the chapter on the Trinity," I said, a contrite note stealing into my voice. "I made the copy myself." I held my breath. "What do you think of his response? He encourages me to continue."

He opened his mouth to speak, then shook his head helplessly. I knew what he was thinking. *The Trinity, of all things!* Bernard of Clairvaux had been involved in a long and infamous feud with Peter Abelard on that very subject.

"It seemed presumptuous" — I wrung my hands, though I could not bring myself to feel any regret over it — "which is why I didn't tell you earlier. I was afraid you would try to dissuade me."

"What you sent . . ." Volmar rubbed his forehead. "You didn't have Ricardis illuminate it, by any chance?"

I grinned as I shook my head, and his relief was visible. Abbot Bernard was famous for his fiery sermons as much as for the asceticism that went beyond the body and stretched to everyday objects, even the buildings surrounding him. Volmar had once heard him denounce the sumptuous church at Cluny, and the comforts of that abbey's cloister and its guest quarters. I knew he would not have taken kindly to receiving anything colorful and expensive. I had been careful to send him only the plain text.

The frown returned to Volmar's face. "You took a great risk. You know what clerics like Bernard think of women speaking on theological matters. Even with men's writings, they scrutinize every word for dogmatic conformity." I opened my mouth, but he spoke over me, his normally calm voice sharpening with an accusatory edge. "I thought we were going to keep *Scivias* at St. Disibod, not circulate it."

I lowered my head, feeling guilty for the first time. It was true that when I had first told him about my idea for the book, he had been wary. It was around the time the conflict between Bernard and Abelard had flared up again, leading to another trial of the hapless Parisian theologian, during which the abbot of Clairvaux persuaded the council of bishops to condemn him for daring to apply reason to the effort of comprehending the nature of God. After that censure, Abelard had retired to the Priory of Saint-Marcel-lès-Chalon, where he died less than a year later.

Bernard's numerous supporters were constantly on the lookout for heresy — or any departure from the orthodoxy, for that matter. What Volmar had worried about then, as now, was the charged atmosphere in the Church, so I had told him the book would be for the sisters' edification.

"Sending it to Abbot Bernard is not the same as circulating it," I countered. "Besides, you know there is nothing subversive in my take on the Trinity. It is about the imagery, not the essence. I use the senses and intuition rather than logical arguments."

"What I know doesn't matter," he replied, but the edge had not quite disappeared from his voice. "The Church is in a frenzy, and if you attract attention, there are many who would not rest until they found something with which to charge you, and they would be impervious to all arguments to the contrary."

Irritation began to rise within me, and I straightened my back. Lately, it seemed that Volmar disapproved of too many things I did. I appreciated that he worried about me, but I had to grasp opportunities without dwelling on the risks. I was responsible for a community of seven women, and our well-being depended on whether I had the courage to act.

Above the cloister, the clouds were fleeting across the sky, alternately flooding the quadrangle with sunlight and plunging it into a more somber shade. "I will be fine." I pointed at the letter he was still holding in his hands. "It worked out. He could have condemned me, but he did not. He gave me his blessing. With this kind of endorsement, the abbot will not be able to refuse my request."

"Your request?"

"To release us so we can relocate the convent."

His gaze darkened. We had not spoken about this for years. "Do not expect it to be easy," he warned me quietly, handing the letter back. Then he was struck by a sudden thought. "Is that why you wrote to Abbot Bernard?"

I took a moment to respond. "Partly, but I also wanted him to read my work."

Now that I had Bernard's acknowledgment, I was going to continue to write no matter how many men of the Church it offended.

Later that night, when everyone was asleep, I sat in the chapel, reflecting. It had been twelve years since I had made a pledge at the grave of our founder, Jutta von Sponheim, to leave St. Disibod. I was finally going to honor it. It did not escape me that Jutta's extreme asceticism — which had ended her life before its time, and which I had never been able to accept or justify — was most likely the reason Abbot Bernard had responded so favorably to me. He knew her reputation, and he admired her. It is curious the compromises life sometimes forces upon us. For under different circumstances, if I were not so desperate to move, I doubt I would have had much time for Bernard of Clairvaux.

I reached into the pocket of my robe for the little box with the lump of salt my mother had given me on the day we had arrived at St. Disibod twenty-nine years before. I opened the lid and gazed at the dazzling whiteness of the piece. Both my parents had long since died, as had my brother Roric and my sister Clementia more recently, the last threads connecting me to Bermersheim fraying and breaking. But this heart-shaped stone was still with me, hard and unchanged, a silent witness over the years to my sorrows and hopes. And now, perhaps, a triumph at last.

Of course, none of this meant that things would go smoothly with Kuno and Helenger. They had grown rich from their association with me, and I fully expected them to put up a fight. What I did not know was just how fierce it would be.

2

October 1143

MY FIRST TASTE of the challenge ahead of me came two weeks later, during my monthly supper with Abbot Kuno.

"You appear anxious tonight, Sister. I hope my table has not disappointed you." The abbot had thinned considerably in recent years, the fault of frequent bouts of gout, for which I was treating him with a solution of colchicum powder. Although he ate less these days, the food was still of the finest quality.

"The supper is exquisite, as always." I took a piece of a perfectly seasoned stewed lamb and followed with a sip of fragrant Rhenish wine from a silver goblet. Suddenly, the quiet defiance with which I had come to the meeting fell away, and I found myself hoping for the abbot's cooperation. True, it was not in his best interest for me to establish an independent house, but if I continued to attract endowments and patronage, and our parting was amicable, we might come to an arrangement whereby the abbey would benefit from some of it.

I cleared my throat as I realized how far ahead my thoughts had raced. *First things first,* I thought, reaching into my pocket for the letter from Bernard of Clairvaux. I needed to start by getting the monks used to my acquaintance with the man whose name struck fear and respect in clerics far more powerful than Kuno and Helenger—or so I hoped.

I was about to read it aloud—the abbot's eyes were far too weak by then—when he shifted apprehensively.

"Are you all right, Father?"

"Yes, pray proceed." His voice sounded hollow, emphasizing his frailty. He was almost seventy, with only a few wisps of white hair hugging his wrinkled skull. Liver spots marked his gaunt hands, and his fingers trembled slightly.

The sight and its implications—not just for him, but for me and the convent— scrambled my carefully prepared wording. "I have been writing for a while now—" I faltered, dropping the letter into my lap.

Kuno nodded. "The medical book."

"Not only that."

He raised his sparse eyebrows, as pale as his milky blue eyes.

I took a breath. "Since I was a child, I have suffered bouts of strong headaches, during which I have seen bright light, pulsing like a living thing, and heard a voice that has compelled me to write what my mind knows about the world and God's design for it—" I broke off. I was still reluctant to share this with other people. Except for Jutta, who was long dead, only Volmar knew—and Abbot Bernard, of course.

"These are matters best left to theologians."

"I would not presume to count myself among their number," I assured him, "for I do not know these things with my own faculties. God has given me the insight. It is"—I paused—"like being a string plucked by a musician that sounds not by itself, but by his hand."

He nodded. "Such experiences are not unheard of among men—and women sometimes," he acknowledged, measuring his words. "If genuine, they are a true gift from God, and they can bring great prominence to one so favored by Him. But in the interest of preserving the integrity of the Church and the purity of our faith, such a person must be subjected to due scrutiny by ecclesiastical authorities," he added, as if in warning.

I grasped the letter so hard I almost crumpled it. "I have taken a step toward that, Father. I wrote to Abbot Bernard of Clairvaux asking for guidance. He approves of my writing and expresses hope that I will continue." I read the lines to him.

Kuno ran a trembling hand over his face as if to clear away something invisible but oppressive. Suddenly his demeanor changed, leaving me wondering if it was because of the French monk's reputation or my initiative in writing to him. "Abbot Bernard is a troublesome monk who involves himself in affairs in which he has no business meddling." He grimaced. "French bishops have complained to the pope about him."

"Nonetheless, he is a respected theologian, and the late Pope Innocent owed him his throne," I countered. "At St. Disibod we have copies of his sermons, made by our own scribes."

"He is an ascetic who almost starved himself to death once." Kuno knew that this would resonate with me.

I did not like to be reminded of Jutta's final months—how she had died because of an infection caused by bodily mortification and her refusal of all food but bread and water— but I would not be deterred. "I am aware of his reputation, Father, but I still treasure his blessing and his encouragement."

"Very succinctly worded."

"He is a busy man."

The conversation had taken a chilly turn, and Kuno shifted in his seat again. "Who else knows about it?"

"Brother Volmar and Sister Ricardis. They are helping me with the manuscript, which is titled *Scivias Domini* — Know the Ways of the Lord. I had also confided in Sister Jutta on the day of my novitiate vows, and she, too, encouraged me to write."

The abbot looked skeptical. "Jutta was a holy woman, and yet she never presumed to write herself."

"Indeed not. But I think we underestimated her spirit's generosity because of her . . . other inclinations."

"I will be honest with you, Sister." The abbot leaned back in his chair heavily. "Women are not supposed to write books, especially on matters of theology. Do not misunderstand me" — he raised his hand to forestall my protest, which he must have guessed would be a reminder that he was profiting greatly from my writing — "you have many talents, and you have done valuable work for this abbey, but you are always pushing the limits of what is acceptable, leaving me with the task of justifying it to the monks."

I raised my chin defiantly. "You mean to Prior Helenger."

"This can bring serious consequences down on the abbey, perhaps our entire Order." He ignored the gibe. "The Bible admonishes against women's preaching."

That again.

But this time I was prepared.

"I am unlearned in the complexities of the Scriptures and therefore cannot be considered a preacher in any way," I said. "I know these things through God and not by the strength of my own reasoning, and thus I am not the author of what I write."

Kuno was silent for a while, his face inscrutable. "For what it's worth, I admire your argument," he said at length. "But if you decide to have these writings propagated, you will face such charges at every turn, so be prepared to make it again *and again*." Then his voice took on an ominous quality. "Abbot Bernard is known for making enemies out of friends through his obsession with denouncing heretics everywhere."

I was aware of that too.

"I assure you that there is nothing in *Scivias* that goes against the teachings of the Church." I reached for the wine goblet and took a long slow sip to hide a smile of relief. Even if Kuno was not enthusiastic about my writing and my new rapport with the abbot of Clairvaux, at least he did not seem determined to get in my way. It looked like the foundations for my move had been successfully laid.

I was wrong about that, as I found out less than two hours later.

I attended vespers in the church that night, as I usually did after our supper. When the service was over, I caught sight of the abbot whispering to Prior Helenger as the monks, still chanting, were filing back to the cloister through the connecting door. It was sufficiently unlike Kuno to break his prayerful concentration that it gave me pause. The whispering had been too brief to have filled the prior on my news, but somehow I knew that it was about just that. Despite his bodily frailty, the abbot's mind was still sharp. After he had thought it over, he must have drawn the only logical conclusion from our meeting—Bernard's favor would be my pass out of St. Disibod. I was sure that was what they were going to discuss.

Perhaps I should have gone back to the convent and left it at that. After all, the prior was bound to find out sooner or later. But I could not. I was overcome by a desire to know what they were planning to do, whether they would let me go or try to prevent it. The reassurance I had felt that the abbot was going to give me his blessing was gone. He would not have whispered like that to Helenger if the issue was not still on his mind.

19

I walked out of the church by the side door and stood in the nook between the wall and the protruding porch. It was fully dark, and the nook was shadowed. In my robe, I would have been difficult to spot unless someone peered in my direction.

I did not have to wait long before I heard footsteps inside the church, and the two monks emerged into the courtyard by the same side door. I held my breath, but they walked past me, talking in low voices muffled further by their cowls. I was right. The only reason the prior would be heading to the abbot's house this late would be for an important meeting. A meeting about me.

Once again, I thought of going to bed and letting things unfold as they may. They would have to inform me at some point of their opposition, and then I would fight them with all I had.

But it would be easier if I knew their strategy.

I am not proud to admit it, but I decided to eavesdrop.

One side of the abbot's house was abutted by the abbey cemetery, and the window of his parlor gave on to it. The autumn night was mild; it would not be a great hardship to be outside, and I doubted that they would be long about it. When the door to the abbot's house closed behind them, I made my way quickly but quietly to the cemetery. I crept up to the window.

". . . so that was true. It *was* her plan all along." I caught Helenger's words. His voice was indignant, and I could imagine anger blazing in his hard, ageless eyes. But what did he mean by "that was true"? I was puzzled, even though I should have known in that moment. Did a part of me suspect, but the truth was so terrible to contemplate that I preferred not to do it? To this day, I cannot tell.

"It would seem so," the abbot said quietly.

"But this *Scivias* —" Helenger sounded like he was speaking through gritted teeth. I had no doubt that when he had heard about my book, his bile rose and his face colored from the neck all the way to his tonsure. "I did not know about *that*." Again, the emphasis. "All that time I thought she had been working on those medical scribbles of hers. She had us all fooled!"

"Now, Brother Prior—"

But Helenger would not let him interrupt. "I have said from the beginning that it was a bad idea to let her into the scriptorium." In the old days, he would never have spoken like that to his superior, but Kuno was old and weak, and Helenger was increasingly dropping the pretense of respect.

"She is paying for the privilege," Kuno reminded him of the fee for the use of the carrel that he had imposed on me a few years earlier at the prior's behest.

If that was intended to calm the prior's temper, it failed. "We have brought this calamity onto ourselves."

In a slow and tired voice, the abbot repeated what he had told me about Bernard's hunt for heretics, as well as his warning that my female condition might expose me to such allegations if I started diffusing my writings outside the abbey.

"You should impose a ban on her sending and receiving all correspondence," Helenger suggested when he had finished, and I held my breath again.

"The Rule does not allow me to isolate a member of our community from the outside world without his or her consent. You know that."

This was how it had always been—Helenger pushing to throw me out of the infirmary, lock me inside the convent, and throw away the key, and Kuno proving to be my only bulwark against that fate. And yet, I had never felt that the abbot was completely on my side. He saw me as useful for the abbey's wealth and reputation, and that was the reason he had allowed me certain freedom, but there were boundaries he would not let me cross, and they were not expansive. At least, not to me.

Seeing that he was not getting what he wanted, Helenger changed his tack. "You should at the very least refer the matter of her writing to a Church authority. Abbot Bernard is a powerful cleric, but as far as hierarchies go, he is not very high."

"Do you mean the Archbishop of Mainz?" Kuno asked.

Helenger scoffed. "No, I mean the new pope. He is bound to come down on our side against a woman, and with that kind of a ban, she would have to comply."

I had not foreseen that, but it is often the way of things that momentous events in our lives assume a course that we least expected.

There was a long moment of silence, and my heart beat fast as I waited for the abbot's response.

Finally, he spoke. "Very well. I will write to Rome." Then he added, in a warning tone, "But then it will be out of our hands."

"I am not worried about that, Father." Helenger sounded lighter now. He was convinced he had stopped me.

He very well may have, I realized. Abbot Bernard's friend Pope Innocent II had died a month before and had been succeeded by Celestinus, about whom I did not know very much. For the past two weeks, things had looked good for me, but now the prize was slipping from my grasp.

I do not know exactly when Kuno's letter was sent, but it must have happened within the next few days. It set in motion a chain of events that none of us could have foreseen.

3

April 1145

T HE CAUSE WAS a mystery, but it was serious, and I was distraught. I had asked the sisters to leave me alone in the chapel and prayed all afternoon, even though I knew deep inside it was inevitable. The spring sun, pale and heatless, had sunk behind the abbey walls, and dusk gathered in the corners when a soft knock on the door broke the silence. Griselda entered.

She was one of my oldest companions. We had known each other since the age of eleven when we had met at a roadside inn her father ran for travelers. I was on my way to St. Disibod with my parents, but it was she, the daughter of an innkeeper, who had the stronger desire for the consecrated life. Yet she had no money for a monastic dowry, and it was only years later, after I had become *magistra* of the convent, that I was able to secure her entry. She was quiet and retiring, and happy with a life of near-anchorite isolation—she had never left the boundaries of the convent since she had taken her vows. I marveled at that kind of sacrifice. My family had hoped I would be that way when they had gifted me to the Church as a child. But that did not happen, and it never would.

"She is asking for you, says it won't be long now." Griselda's eyes were sorrowful.

I laid a hand on her shoulder, both to give and to draw comfort, for the coming hours would be a trying time for us. "I will stay with her for as long as it takes," I said. "Let Gertrude lead the evening offices."

"Is there anything I can do?"

"Just pray with the others. That is all she needs now."

Sister Juliana lay in a private room at the far end of the infirmary, accessible by a door located between the men's and the women's sides of the main ward. She was waxen-faced and tried to lift a hand when I entered, but it fell back on the blanket. Her *viriditas* was ebbing fast. A month earlier she had slipped on an icy patch in the yard—the winter had been unusually long that year—and broke a leg. I had set it, and for a while it seemed to be mending well, then Juliana had taken an inexplicable turn for the worse.

There was no fever, no sign of an infection, but she kept weakening and was soon unable to rise from her bed. I moved her to the infirmary and tried all manner of strengthening medicines—fennel and nettle tisanes; a tonic of oak bark and dried sage infused in wine—to no avail. Yet until the day before, I had still held out hope for a reversal. It was only that morning that the unmistakable signs had appeared—the unnatural pallor of the skin, its chill clamminess, and the eyes shining as if with a fever that was not there.

At noon Juliana had asked for a priest, and that was when I had gone to take refuge in the chapel. Now I was back with her, the only sister who had been at the convent longer than I, a quiet but reassuring presence for all those years. It was she who had taught me music and composition, gifting me a lifetime of joy which she had always denied to herself.

Ricardis was at her bedside when I arrived, a somber expression on her face. Nonetheless, she gave me one of her brilliant smiles before withdrawing from the chamber.

Juliana's eyes followed her until the door closed. "I never understood why she wanted this life," she said. "She is not humble enough for it and seems more interested in ingratiating herself with the world than with God."

I sat down on the vacated stool. "How are you feeling?" I did not want to talk about Ricardis.

"Better now." In the candlelight, Juliana's dull skin acquired an enlivening glow that made her look almost healthy again.

"I have been praying for your recovery." I took her hand. "If God wills it, you may yet walk again." I hoped my voice sounded convincing.

Juliana gave me a knowing smile. "Not this time." The serenity lingered on her features for some moments before dissolving like a morning fog. "I am ready and in no discomfort of body or soul."

I squeezed her hand lightly and felt the gesture reciprocated. Juliana turned her head and her gaze locked on mine. She hesitated briefly, then spoke in a low voice, "I had abandoned my loved ones in taking the vows all those years ago, but with you I was able to reclaim a small piece of what I had lost. It was a blessing I did not deserve."

"We all deserve comfort."

She laughed bitterly. "That is such an unlikely lesson for our sort . . ." Her voice trailed off. After a moment, she resumed, "It was a mistake, but it could have been much worse for me had you not arrived to guide us with wisdom. Monastic life can be so dreary . . . and lonely."

I nodded, unable to argue with that. Juliana had never had a true vocation; she had entered the convent as an act of rebellion against her parents, who had wanted her to marry an old widower with lands adjoining their estate. She had fallen in love with her father's groom and thought the monastery would give her the solace she needed. But that never happened, and she spent the rest of her life regretting that decision. She had told me the story one dark and desperate night many years before.

"I have confessed and asked God for forgiveness that I was never able to truly give myself to Him in this state," she resumed, "and for the sin of melancholy I was never quite able to overcome. But I did my best and was always mindful, even in my weakest moments, of your admonition to love this life as much as what is promised to us afterward."

"I know."

Juliana remained silent for a long while, the lines of her face relaxing and smoothing out again. "I was happier than I had ever thought possible for me after you became our *magistra*. I rarely showed it, but I was." Her countenance lit up with a desperate sort of intensity, and her voice strengthened momentarily. "Do not let them stop you! Do not be held back by the petty attacks of those who have neither the courage nor the imagination to go beyond the narrow rules to which they are bound. *You* are doing God's work. *They* only pretend to do it to satisfy their lust for power over human souls."

I listened, astonished. I had never suspected Juliana of such a depth of conviction. She had always kept to herself, and I had assumed she cared little about my squabbles with the monks. That was why this forceful, deeply felt plea mattered more to me than the recognition from the abbot of Clairvaux.

"It is not my place to judge them," I replied nonetheless. "They will answer for their deeds in due course, as will we all."

"But you mustn't let them keep you down!" she repeated, her grip on my hand tightening.

"I try not to."

"Will you promise me something, Hildegard?"

"If it is in my power."

"Promise me that you will take the sisters and leave this place. It has been a long time since I heard you talk about it — you have not abandoned the idea, have you?"

I shook my head. "No, but there is a lot that needs to happen before I can do it." Kuno's letter to Rome had not yet produced a response. It was not entirely surprising. The Holy City had been in turmoil for the past few years, both politically and because of the quick deaths of two popes in succession — Celestinus in March 1144 and Lucius the following February. We now had the third pope since the abbot had sent his letter. His name was Eugenius, and he was a former pupil of Abbot Bernard's, which raised my hopes again. But I had not heard anything yet, and all I could do was wait.

"There is one thing that keeps you here, one thing you are afraid to lose," Juliana said, and her eyes became soft.

I was stunned. Her words made me realize something I had not admitted to myself until then — as much as I found the delay and the uncertainty frustrating, a part of me was glad because that meant more time with Volmar.

"What you set out to do has required everything of you, and you have given it. Unlike me, you could have had the man you wanted, which makes your sacrifice so much greater than mine."

She had always known, then. I looked away, blinking at the prickling sensation under my eyelids.

"You have a mission to fulfill and a driving passion." Juliana's whisper reached me like a caress. "God gave you in abundance what He withheld from me. From that you will draw the strength you need."

I nodded, still unable to speak through the clenched muscles of my throat.

"But keep your eyes open, for danger sometimes lurks in the places you deem safest."

North of the Italian peninsula, the winter lingered. It was not until the middle of May that a group of five finely dressed men, two of them in ecclesiastical garb, crossed the Brenner pass, turned east through the thickly forested mountains of Swabia, and continued north along the Rhine toward Disibodenberg.

Late one afternoon, a messenger in mud-splattered clothes galloped through the town gate and up to the abbey. Brother Rainald, the fat and languid-faced porter, was in no hurry to open the doors, but when he saw the visitor's seal through the grille, his eyes widened and his movements quickened. He called for a groom to take the horse and ran to the abbot's house as fast as his short legs could carry him.

"Father Abbot!" He was nearly out of wind from the exertion. "A message from His Holiness the Pope has arrived for you."

In the next moment, Prior Helenger swooped in out of nowhere in a flurry of robes. In the commotion, Rainald delayed his withdrawal from the parlor until he caught the gist of the message. Then he ran to the infirmary.

"Emissaries from Pope Eugenius are on their way," he informed me, gulping for air. "They should be here tomorrow at midday, and they want to speak with you."

Rome, March 1145

I MAGINE THIS SCENE as I did when I first learned about it.
The pope stands in an arched window of his private apart-
ment at the Lateran Palace, gazing thoughtfully across the
courtyard with its bronze statue of the She-wolf. "Who is
this woman who rises out of the wilderness like a column of
smoke from burning spices?" he asks.

Beyond the arch of a nearby aqueduct, Via Sacra is nearly empty, its ancient cobblestones covered with a thick layer
of mud stirred by torrents of rain. A solitary man, his hooded
head bowed against the deluge, is pulling on a horse's bri-
dle to try to get his cart out of a rut. To the south, the round
shape of the Basilica of Santo Stefano is visible through the
fingers of mist enveloping the Caelian Hill. The pope turns
slowly back toward the small assembly gathered around a
marble table near the hearth fire. The flames are brisk, duti-

fully kept up by a servant against the gloom and chill of the soggy afternoon.

Bernardo da Pisa—Pope Eugenius, the third of that name to occupy the throne of St. Peter—has a habit of quoting biblical verses when something puzzles him, as if to summon divine inspiration to provide him with clarity. He called the meeting to discuss the singular case of a Benedictine sister from a small Rhenish abbey, whose fame as a healer and writer has reached the Holy See.

What Eugenius knows thus far is difficult to make sense of. Some prominent churchmen have spoken highly of her medical skills and her leadership of the women's convent. Yet there have also been cautionary voices, like that of her own abbot who wrote to Rome a year and a half earlier— when Pope Celestinus was still in office—concerned that her writings on matters of Christian doctrine might scandalize the Church. He urged the Holy Father to examine her case.

The new pope is a small man with a gentle face framed by a curly graying beard, and he wears the simple robe of his Cistercian Order. He looks the picture of benevolent calm, even as the task at hand is anything but easy. The breadth of the accomplishments ascribed to Hildegard of Disibodenberg intrigues him, but he is the guardian of the integrity of the Church's teachings, and it is his duty to ensure that anyone who speaks on matters of faith acts on divine inspiration and not as an agent of darkness.

"My great friend and teacher, Abbot Bernard of the monastery of Clairvaux, mentioned in one of his letters that he had encouraged Sister Hildegard's writing," he tells the gathering as he seats himself back at the table, "but this office also received an inquiry from her superior, Abbot . . . ah—"

"Kuno, Holiness," his private secretary offers.

"Thank you, monsignor. I am notoriously bad with names." The pope smiles apologetically, and his guests laugh politely. "Abbot Kuno of St. Disibod in the Rhineland wrote to our predecessor asking him to investigate the case, but the request has languished as we are still busy healing the wounds of the schism that tore our Church under Pope Innocent." He sighs heavily. "And relations with the Romans demand our constant attention, of course."

Heads nod sympathetically. Eugenius had only ascended to the papacy the previous month, and the Roman rebellion that had been raging since 1144 was showing no signs of abating.

"The abbot cites the biblical warning against women who do not learn in silence," the pope resumes, "yet Hildegard's reputation as a physician cannot be ignored, and neither can Abbot Bernard's opinion."

He sends a meaningful look toward his advisor Archbishop Albero of Verdun, who inclines his head, signifying understanding. Bernard of Clairvaux is not just Eugenius's friend and mentor; the pope is pinning high hopes on his help with yet another urgent and sensitive matter, that of a new threat facing the Holy Land. Another crusade is necessary, and Eugenius is going to ask Bernard to rally Christendom in its support.

"I called this meeting to gauge how the matter is seen at the court of the Archbishop of Mainz." The pope directs these words to the middle-aged cleric who sits on his left. Bishop Eberhard had been the late Archbishop Adalbert's closest advisor for nearly twenty years, and has come on behalf of Adalbert's successor, Heinrich, to apprise the Holy Father of the archdiocese's affairs.

"Archbishop Adalbert, may God rest his soul, was a friend of Sister Hildegard's, Your Holiness," Eberhard replies. "He had given her the veil and often spoke of her wisdom and strength of character. A story he was fond of telling was of how she had almost singlehandedly saved her abbey from a marauding mercenary band shortly before the Treaty of Worms was signed. She organized an effort to dig a defensive ditch and stationed townspeople with bows and arrows along the wall. That ad hoc army was as well trained as a group of boys playing at battle, but the posture worked, and the attackers retreated. Hildegard was still only a novice then."

The bishop pauses as eight pairs of eyes round with disbelief. "It is true," he assures them. "I have heard it told around the court by others as well, including Rudolf von Stade. Archbishop Adalbert corresponded with Sister Hildegard regularly in the last years of his life, even asking her for spiritual advice on a few occasions."

"Did he acquaint himself with *Scivias Domini*?"

"He did not live long enough to see it." The bishop shakes his head ruefully. "She wrote to him last summer, promising to send a copy, but he died before it arrived, leaving that and many other matters unfinished."

The pope ponders this for a long moment. "Has it been circulated since then?"

"Besides our copy at Mainz, which Archbishop Heinrich had just started reading when I was leaving for Rome, there is at least one in Trier; I know of it from the abbot of St. Eucharius, who ordered his best scribe to make a copy for their library. There are probably others I am not aware of because it is being discussed widely."

"Is it? And what are the opinions?"

"Positive, overall, but I have heard concerns similar to those expressed by Abbot Kuno." Eberhard shifts uncomfortably. "Namely, that a woman authoring a theological work could be guilty of heresy."

Eugenius grimaces. "It is certainly unusual and deserving of scrutiny, but why do so many people call things they dislike 'heresy'?" There is a note of irritation in his voice. "It only makes true dissent that much more difficult to detect."

There is a moment of silence, then the pope turns to Archbishop Albero. "I would like to read this work so I may issue my proclamation. With so much turmoil facing our Church, it is important to put such matters to rest as quickly as possible."

"Of course, Your Holiness." The archbishop's habitually composed features melt into an obliging smile. "I am sure someone in Mainz will be able to have a copy made for us," he adds, casting a glance at Bishop Eberhard.

"No." The pope shakes his head. "This requires a personal approach. Send an emissary to St. Disibod as soon as the Alpine passes are open. I want a trusted and experienced man to speak with Sister Hildegard where she lives and serves God to ascertain her devotion and gauge her motivations."

Albero opens his mouth to respond, but the pope raises his palm to forestall him. "I also want him to inquire about the basis for her healing successes — do they truly stem from the juices of the herbs she uses, or is something else involved? I have heard some of her outcomes described as 'miraculous', and while God can certainly work miracles, we must ensure that nothing untoward is happening where those herbs are concerned — no spells or other questionable practices. In other words" — he pauses emphatically — "I want a full report on whether her work, both medical and theological, is aligned with the teachings of the Church."

Another silence follows as the gathered dignitaries absorb the request.

"I will see to it, Your Holiness," the archbishop says. "Do you wish to inform Abbot Kuno of this visit in advance, or would you rather surprise him?"

Eugenius considers this. "Write to him on my behalf, but not until the emissary is on his way. We should give him a bit of notice, but not much. Which means" — he turns to Eberhard — "that there should be no communication about this from the archdiocese either."

But I found out well ahead of time. Bishop Eberhard was an old friend of mine, and he wrote to me in his personal capacity, not as a representative of the Archbishop of Mainz.

That was how I learned the details of the meeting in the papal palace.

I—torn from my family at a gentle age and intended to be shut away in a tiny convent—was on the mind of one of the most powerful men in the world.

I would have been delighted had I not been about to face the greatest test of my life.

5

Abbey of St. Disibod, May 1145

Brother Rainald was an old gossip, and the abbey was buzzing with the news of the impending arrival of the papal envoys before the day was out.

I, thanks to Bishop Eberhard, already knew about it.

I was assailed by a mix of emotions. I was both excited and nervous. Despite my best efforts, I could not rid myself of the sense of betrayal at the abbot's underhanded dealing. He had not told me about the letter to Rome, but he had not objected when I had sent copies of *Scivias* to Mainz, Trier, and Cologne in past year either. My book was now the subject of much debate around monasteries and ecclesiastical courts. Patrons were eager to pay for illuminated copies, a bounty in which Kuno was only too happy to partake. Our relationship, even after all these years, was still based on a calculation of cost and benefit rather than a bond of mutual respect.

On the night of the messenger's arrival, I went to the church for compline despite a raging thunderstorm. After the service, I sought out Volmar. When the monks disappeared inside the cloister, he came to sit with me in the pew. A lay brother began extinguishing all but a handful of candles, and we sat in the incense-scented shadows as I related the contents of Bishop Eberhard's letter — the details of the meeting at the papal palace and the choice of Bishop Umberto Visconti, a Milanese prelate, as the envoy. He was to be accompanied by a Father Godfrey, who was Archbishop Albero of Verdun's secretary. Two soldiers — including Bishop Umberto's younger half-brother Donato, a Milanese knight — would escort them.

Volmar took the news in stride. His calm had a soothing effect on me, but my frustration was not gone yet. "My reputation has been attracting interest from candidates desiring to join this abbey," I said, trying to keep the bitterness out of my voice. In the previous ten years, the number of monks at St. Disibod had doubled, but the convent had not grown; once again, we had no room to accommodate new entrants. "It has brought them a prosperity beyond what they could have achieved by themselves." This time a note of anger stole into my words. "I thought the abbot would recognize that; instead, he went behind my back and treated me like a heretic."

"I don't think he did that out of malice. It's not like him," Volmar said. "His duty, first and foremost, is to the Church, and you have laid claim to that which has been the domain of its men. He wants to ensure that your activities are sanctioned, and I hope they will be." He turned to me, and the soft light from the candles reflected the specks of amber in his eyes.

I looked away. "But what if they pronounce against me?" I maintained good relations with many bishops and abbots, but I could not discount that possibility. There were never any guarantees in Church politics; allegiances and favors changed more frequently than spring weather in the Rhineland. I smiled sardonically as a fresh evening breeze smelling of moist earth wafted through the still-open doors from the courtyard, where all was still and quiet after the storm.

"They will not," Volmar stated with a certainty that was both reassuring and a little irritating. He always chose to look on the bright side, while I tended to worry. "Remember that Pope Eugenius is a Cistercian, like your friend Abbot Bernard." In the deepening dark, I heard a smile in his voice.

I hoped he was right. I had exchanged two more letters with Bernard of Clairvaux and had sent him more excerpts from my book, and although his replies had been short, they were always encouraging. The pope would have to have good cause to publicly disagree with his former teacher, and he would not find that in *Scivias*.

"Let's prepare a copy for them to take to the Holy Father." I was buoyed once again by a sense of opportunity — if the pope approved of my writing, *nobody* could stand in my way.

"We have two copies that are almost done, one of which is illuminated."

"The plain one will do — in the spirit of the Cistercian preference for simplicity." I chuckled softly, and Volmar echoed. For a moment, we were children again, complicit in an adventure.

"It will be ready by the time they arrive," he said.

I threw my head back and inhaled the last of the incense mingled with the scent of May blossoms. "Then I will be ready too." I smiled into the dark.

The emissaries arrived in the afternoon of the next day, their traveling cloaks covered with mud and road dust. As soon as the porter brought the news, servants were ordered to set the table in the parlor for an early supper, and the abbot and the prior went to meet the newcomers in the courtyard.

When I first saw them through an infirmary window, they had just dismounted, their horses whinnying as they were led away to the stables. I considered the two clerics — the bishop tall and thin, the monk a head shorter and rather corpulent — although I could not hear the words with which they greeted their hosts.

Introductions completed, they were led toward the guesthouse, followed by the two men of the escort. The one of lower rank wore a simple padded gambeson, and as he strode with his efficient soldierly gait, he was intent only on his path. But the knight Donato looked around as he slowly followed the others. His hand rested casually on the hilt of his sword, and the coat of arms on his cloak looked like a coiled blue snake swishing to the rhythm of his step.

An hour later, I was summoned to join them.

With only a day's notice, the abbot had managed to direct his cooks to prepare a feast fit for the pope himself. Bowls of steaming fish stew in lemon and rosemary sauce, platters of cheese and white bread, and squares of warm gingerbread filled the parlor with a sweet and spicy aroma that made me momentarily forget why I was there. But the look on our hosts' faces brought me quickly back to earth. Kuno's expression was serious with a tinge of what I thought was guilt, though perhaps it was just weariness, for he seemed exhausted. Helenger, by contrast, had the look of someone who could barely contain his excitement. His handsome face — his skin taut and nearly wrinkle free despite his fifty-eight years — was aglow. Some internal fire sparkled in his eyes without endowing them with even the slightest touch of warmth.

"Sister, may I introduce Bishop Umberto of Milan and Father Godfrey of Canterbury?" The abbot gestured across the table as I took my seat, and I saw that the trembling of his hand was more pronounced. "They have been sent by His Holiness Pope Eugenius to look into the matter of your theological writings." I locked my gaze on his, both to convey that I knew he was responsible for it and to challenge him to admit it, but he looked away. "They will stay with us for a few days but would like to start their inquiry today."

"I will answer any questions to the best of my ability and with full honesty of the heart," I said, and studied them as they inclined their heads. Their faces were hard to read — whether by nature or from force of habit, I had no way of knowing — and betrayed no emotions that might indicate how they felt about their mission.

Just then, a knock on the door announced a lay brother arriving with a flagon of the abbey's best wine. After the toast, the guests attacked the stew with great appetite, outdoing each other in praising the food and the drink. They, too, knew a good vintage when they tasted it.

At first, the conversation revolved around the expectations for this year's harvest, which the emissaries believed would be abundant based on the frequent showers they had encountered along the way. I agreed with that view, for my herb garden had been yielding some of the best early crops in years, and the clerics proceeded to query me about the medicinal properties of various plants. From Bishop Eberhard's letter, I knew that it was more than just polite curiosity. I had already noticed Bishop Umberto's swollen knuckles and the way he absentmindedly rubbed his joints as he spoke, and I offered to treat him with aconite oil. He guardedly accepted the offer before bringing the conversation around to the main reason for his visit.

"Your writing activities have come to the attention of His Holiness the Pope, who is most anxious to acquaint himself with *Scivias*," he said, and the abbot's expression remained unchanged.

In addition to being tall and reedy, Umberto was in his fifties and exuded a pious air that made him resemble Helenger. However, there was a softness in him that the prior did not possess, and his tone was respectful, which raised my hopes that the pope had chosen a fair man to carry out his mission.

"I am humbled to learn that my poor work is of interest to the Holy Father, for I do not think it deserves it," I replied.

"I understand that you have experienced certain visions since you were a child?" he asked neutrally, causing the prior to turn to me with a sharp frown. The outer edges of my mind registered that reaction with surprise, not because Helenger would be incapable of questioning anything I said, but because it meant that Kuno had not told him about it.

Facing the bishop, I once again described the light I had seen during my spells of headaches, the voice that spoke to me from within it, and the vivid images that stood before my mind's eye. I explained that I had feared the world's judgement for a long time, but ever since the voice had commanded me to write, I was no longer afraid.

He listened intently while Abbot Kuno seemed to doze off. When I finished, the bishop assured me that he would relate my words faithfully in Rome. "We would also request a copy of your book," he added, "so its content can be examined against our faith's dogmas." He said it mildly, but the message was unmistakable. *Scivias* would be inspected for heresy.

I smiled obligingly. "You will find that while I apply logical reasoning to my writing on medicine and nature, I treat matters of Christian doctrine differently, and I have never condoned Master Abelard's dialectic approach." I spoke the last words with emphasis, knowing that the section on the Trinity would come under particular scrutiny. "The fact that a revered theologian like the Abbot of Clairvaux has found no fault with my interpretation is proof that my writing is consistent with the orthodoxy. I will include a copy of his letter with the manuscript."

"Your Excellency may incur papal anger by bringing such writings to the Holy See," Helenger interjected before the envoy could respond. "They are inappropriate, and their very existence violates the Church's teachings."

The bishop looked momentarily disconcerted under the prior's glare, but he rallied quickly. "His Holiness expressed his desire to read the book that he may form his own opinion about it, Brother Prior. And he is not given to fits of anger," he added coolly.

The subtle chastisement was lost on Helenger. "Whoever heard of a woman writing in the first place?" he continued querulously. The inquiry was not going the way he had expected, and his frustration was visible. "It is well known that they are not capable of abstract thinking; their views count for less."

"It *is* unusual for a woman to occupy herself with the activities of the intellect," the bishop conceded, "but we have come on a fact-finding mission, not to sit in judgment on Sister Hildegard."

I barely dared to breathe as I listened to this exchange, taking heart from the fact that even if Bishop Umberto would be no defender of mine, he seemed a dutiful diplomat unwilling to step outside the boundaries of his remit.

"But she is determined to continue with the abomination!" Helenger pointed at me like a child telling on another. "Apparently one book is not enough, and she has an appetite for more!"

My insides twisted painfully. Recently, I had started writing a book of meditations on everyday living. For the first time, a suspicion of being spied on formed clearly in my mind. But it could not be; only Volmar and Ricardis knew . . .

"My instructions are to gather information about *Scivias Domini*." The bishop's voice broke through my jumbled thoughts, and there was a hint of irritation in it. He was finally becoming impatient. "We are not authorized to inquire into anything else."

But the prior would not be deterred. He reached for the argument I had been expecting all evening. "In his first letter to Timotheus, St. Paul says, 'I do not permit a woman to teach, but she must be in silence'. Nowhere is this warning more relevant than when it comes to matters of theology, for if women's interpretations were to be given any weight, what would stop them from claiming the right to become preachers?" His voice rose dramatically, prompting the abbot to stir in his chair.

A look of discomfort on the bishop's face suggested that the words had struck a chord.

"It was never my intention to assume the mantle of a preacher since I am—as Brother Prior is fond of reminding everyone—a mere woman," I assured him. "I am also an anchoress." That last word echoed strangely and uncomfortably in my ears; I had purposefully not used it since Jutta's death. As a matter of practice—if not the convent's charter—it was no longer accurate, but I had to defend myself with all I had. "The knowledge I share is the fruit of the intuition God has bestowed on me, not of my own reasoning." I saw Helenger gearing up for a rebuttal, and I spoke a shade more loudly to forestall him. "It is the divine grace that banishes the darkness of my senses and makes clear those things they cannot perceive because of their weakness." Inwardly, I reflected that it was none other than St. Augustine, one of my least favorite theologians, who had made divine grace a central point of his teachings.

"It is presumptuous, and the Holy Father will surely condemn it." Helenger sent the bishop a challenging look even as he spoke to me. "Until you came along with your notions, I had never heard of a woman writer. You want to be the first to be recognized as such, but you will not," he added complacently, his confidence rising again.

"You are right, Brother Prior. I am not going to be the first." I held his gaze levelly. "That distinction belongs to Hrotsvitha."

"Who?"

"Hrotsvitha, a canoness at Gandersheim Abbey, who wrote poems and plays about Christian martyrs."

"I have never heard of her." He shrugged dismissively.

"That does not make the fact of her existence any less true."

The prior reddened. "I hope Your Excellency will report to the Holy Father the extent of the contempt Sister Hildegard has for The Rule of our Order and for the laws of nature."

A silence descended on the room, and I suddenly felt alone. The only person who could back up my claim was Volmar, but he was not there. It was he who had first told me about Hrotsvitha, whose *Martyrdom of St. Agnes* he had read at the Cluny library years before.

"The *magistra* is right," a new voice spoke up unexpectedly. "Hrotsvitha of Gandersheim has been dead more than a century, but she left written works, although not all of them are of a religious nature." It was Father Godfrey, the English monk. He was quieter and had a more scholarly air than his senior companion, which did not prevent Helenger from giving him a look of profound resentment.

The church bell began its summons to vespers, and Abbot Kuno awoke with a start. "Is there anything else you want of Sister Hildegard, my lord bishop?" he asked, feigning attention throughout.

"Yes, as a matter of fact," Umberto replied. "St. Disibod's infirmary has a fine reputation for its healing outcomes, and I wish to see for myself the care it offers to the sick."

"It will be an honor to show you around, Your Excellency," I assured him, warming at the praise, "and you, Father." I turned to Godfrey gratefully.

Instead of returning to the convent for vespers, I went straight to the infirmary. The evening had left me with an uneasy feeling, and to push it from my mind, I decided to ensure that all was ready for the inspection.

They arrived after terce the next morning. I introduced Sister Elfrid as they had already made Brother Fabian's acquaintance when I had sent him with a vial of aconite oil for Bishop Umberto the night before. At my inquiry as to its efficacy, the bishop stretched his fingers as if he only now remembered his affliction. "It stung a little at the application, but since then, I must say I haven't felt the usual aches."

Despite his words, there was some reluctance in his admission — the Church will always be mistrustful of herbal healing — and I refrained from commenting further, letting the cure speak for itself. Instead, I showed off my shelves of medicine jars and bottles, and cupboards stocked with clean linen. I answered questions about the humoral theory, sparked by a large diagram sent to me as a gift by Bishop Seward of Uppsala, who was learned in medicine and natural philosophy. Then I took them to the recovery garden, where ambulant patients were encouraged to take the air and to walk for exercise.

"Do such practices work?" the bishop asked skeptically. It was a familiar reaction.

"They certainly do, Your Excellency. Not only do patients recover faster, but the melancholy humor that is often overabundant during illness diminishes without a need for bleeding or purging." I had never been a proponent of either method, popular though they were among barbers and monastic physicians alike.

Back inside, I led my guests to the ward occupied by a dozen patients, including a man injured during spring plowing, two people with the wasting disease, a child with a stomach ailment, and a young woman with a burn covering her right arm. The clerics wanted to know the details of her case — how had I been treating it, and what was the prognosis?

"Grussalen was cleaning up after cooking when she tripped on a piece of wood and fell into the hearth," I explained, then turned to the patient. Seeing a bishop's robe, she tried to sit up, wincing. "How are you feeling today, dear?"

"I am better, Sister, and the pain is less, but I have to be careful not to touch it to anything or turn onto it," she replied, wide-eyed at being the center of attention. "If I do, it hurts a lot still." The very thought of it made her breathe faster.

"She was lucky the fire had already been put out, but the hearth was still hot enough to give her a bad burn. It is blistering now and will leave a scar, but fortunately there is no infection that might cost her the arm."

"And what treatments have you ordered?" Father Godfrey asked, eyeing the linen bandage covering the limb all the way to the shoulder. The tips of her fingers were poking out of the dressing, and a shiny substance covered the intensely red blotches.

"We are applying lavender oil three times a day; it has cold and wet properties that make it ideal for treating burns."

"Does that bring you relief, mistress?" the monk asked Grussalen.

She nodded timidly. "When I first arrived here, I thought I would go mad with pain."

Just then, a weak infant's cry reached our ears. The clerics looked around, and I pointed to the door that led to the private room. "A peasant woman delivered a babe yesterday morning after two days in labor, with Sister Elfrid's help." I acknowledged my assistant. "But he was sluggish and wouldn't take the teat, so we brought him here to be fed goat milk, which his family cannot afford." I did not add that I'd had to fight with Helenger, who was against allowing a woman fresh from her childbed into the abbey precincts. Kuno finally overruled him on the condition that the mother and child be kept in isolation, and the woman not allowed to set foot in the church. "We are often called upon to help with complicated births."

Bishop Umberto looked uncomfortable. "I hope you have not turned Brother Fabian into a midwife too." He attempted to cover his unease with a joke.

"Just Sister Elfrid, who had practiced the trade before she took the veil." I smiled in acknowledgment of his effort, valiant by clerical standards. "Childbirth is a medical matter. The women value our work, for the need is great."

"Hmm." The bishop grunted, and I took that as a cue to head toward the exit.

"I will take you to my workshop now."

He followed me with visible relief, but as we stepped outside, our attention was drawn to a commotion near the church. A pair of peasants stood near the door, surrounded by a group of monks. Filippo, Umberto's other man-at-arms, was among them.

When he saw us, Filippo broke away and walked over rapidly, a worried expression on his face. "My lord bishop, we have received the most disturbing news," he said. "Those men have found a body in the woods. They say the dead man looks like a knight, and one of them remembers him arriving with our party yesterday."

6

May 1145

Bishop Umberto gazed at the soldier in astonishment. "With our party? But how can that be? We are all in the precinct." He looked around, frowning. "Are we not?"

"There must be a mistake." Father Godfrey was equally puzzled.

"Perhaps not, Father," Filippo said. "Signor Donato was absent from the guesthouse this morning. I didn't make much of it, for I thought he had gone to the town, but he has not returned yet—" he broke off, blanching. "He is not with you either."

A shocked silence fell as we turned toward the abbot, who was approaching from the direction of his house, accompanied by a young monk who was apparently appraising him of the situation. Kuno proceeded slowly, propping himself on a walking stick. "How far away was the body found?" he asked when he joined us. Despite his frailty, he projected an aura of efficiency I could not help but admire.

"Not even a league. At the edge of the woods, right after the high road turns north."

"Was it a robbery?"

"They say it looks like it." Filippo gestured toward the peasants, who still stood with the monks near the church door, their expressions fearful. "He was finely dressed and alone, an easy prey to outlaws."

"We must inform the officer of the law and send men to bring the body to the abbey so it can be identified," the abbot said.

"Father, if I may," I interjected. "I think he should be left where he was found, so I can examine him."

"He has no need of a cure, he is dead!" Helenger exclaimed, arriving at just that moment. His outburst immediately attracted scandalized glares—Donato was, after all, Bishop Umberto's brother.

"If his death was indeed due to foul play," I went on, "there might be clues on the body that will be destroyed if he is moved."

"It is the job of the officer of the law to investigate unexplained deaths," Helenger insisted.

Kuno thought for a moment. "Signor Donato was a guest of this abbey, so I will allow Sister Hildegard to join the inquiry. Provided it *is* him," he added, glancing at the bishop, who had paled but had not spoken yet.

"What can she discover that Lotulf cannot?" the prior protested.

"Maybe nothing." I turned to face him. "But I have dealt with many injuries over the years that required investigation into their cause in order to treat them properly, and that experience may prove useful. Besides," I added, giving voice to a growing misgiving, "outlaws are not common in these parts; we have not had a complaint in more than two years."

"I think His Excellency needs to sit down." Brother Godfrey eyed his companion with concern. "This is a terrible shock." Indeed, Umberto now looked like he might collapse at any moment. Beads of sweat stood out on his forehead. "I trust you will let us know when . . . the body . . . is brought back, so we can pay proper respects and prepare it for burial."

"Of course." The abbot nodded with sympathy.

Godfrey led the bishop back to the cloister where they were lodging in a guest cell. When they were out of earshot, Kuno sighed. "What a sad development to have to report to His Holiness." Gazing over the abbey wall, he added, "If it is not outlaws, I hope we do not harbor a killer in this town."

As we awaited the arrival of Lotulf, Disibodenberg's officer of the law, I made a calming drink for Bishop Umberto. I found him sitting on his bed, pale and breathing with effort. "This will soothe your nerves," I said.

The bishop eyed the cup suspiciously. "What sort of concoction is this?" he asked, politeness leaving his voice for the first time. "I am a man of the Church and will not be subjected to heathen treatments."

"And I am a woman of the Church and would not subject you to anything that would imperil the health of your soul." I sat in a nearby chair; there was no point in arguing with a man in shock and in the first throes of grief. "It is only a mix of chamomile, valerian, and lemon balm infused in wine. Lemon balm grows freely in many gardens across the land and is known as an herb of good cheer, its pure essence given to us by God to help blunt the pain of hardships in our lives," I added gently.

Umberto's hands were shaking. He gazed at them, resting on his chasuble-covered knees, perhaps willing them to stop, but they would not. He looked up at me, his face full of despair.

I offered the cup again. "It will soothe you," I repeated. "You will feel better, I promise."

He hesitated a moment longer, then took it, spilling a little of the contents. He drank slowly, uneasily, as if half-expecting me to start muttering incantations. Then he returned the vessel without meeting my eyes. As I stepped outside the cell, I found Filippo waiting in the corridor to inform me that the party was ready to leave for the forest.

Father Godfrey joined us, along with two men with a litter to carry the body, and the peasants who had found it. On the way, Filippo and Godfrey tried to remember the details of Donato's dress from the day before, recalling a jeweled brooch he used to clasp his cloak at his throat, a sword, a fine silver dagger, and a gold ring set with an emerald. When we arrived at the site, the sun was past its zenith but still strong, and the day was warm.

The peasants led us to the spot and stepped aside, looking on fearfully. The body was splayed on its back ten paces off the main track in the deep shade of the trees, surrounded by bracken. The cloak was pulled to the side, and a part of the coiled blue snake was visible, leaving me with no doubt as to the victim's identity. Still, for formality's sake, I looked at Father Godfrey, who nodded grimly in confirmation.

"How did you come across him?" I asked the peasants. "He would not be visible from the road."

"We were carting vegetables to the market and stopped here because Harmeric had to respond to the call of nature," the more confident of the two responded, pointing at his companion. "I swear we didn't do this." He seemed to shrink into himself as he clutched his hat to his chest.

"Nobody is accusing you, my good man." I softened my tone, realizing that the strain of the situation was affecting me too. "But I need to know if you touched or moved anything." I turned to the one named Harmeric.

"No." He shook his head vigorously. "I saw a man on the ground and called to him, but as he didn't respond, we hurried straight to the abbey. We didn't dare approach." He crossed himself.

Lotulf gave the body a cursory look from head to toe. "The silver brooch is gone and the dagger is missing. This is a clear case of robbery," he pronounced. "Shall we bring him back, Father?" he asked Godfrey.

"Let me have a closer look." I circled the corpse once, then did it again while lifting the feathery leaves of the nearby ferns. "When did you last see Signor Donato?" I asked Filippo.

"Soon after the compline bell last night," the soldier replied. "He said he was tired from the journey and wanted to retire early. I went to the kitchen to see if I could get more ale, and I sat there for a bit, chatting with the cook, but I followed Donato not long after, for I needed rest myself."

"Was he in bed when you returned to your cell?"

"I didn't light the lamp so as not to disturb him, but I believe so." He sounded hesitant. "Though now that I think about it, it was rather quiet, and he had snored mightily the previous nights we had shared quarters. I remember being relieved and hoping he would stay that way so I could go to sleep quickly —"

A horse's whinny from a clearing close by cut off his words, and everyone turned in that direction. It came again, higher pitched and with something pleading in its tone. The beast was standing alone in the small opening among the trees, tossing its head and pulling on reins tied to a trunk.

I turned to the two townsmen who came with us. "Would you find me several sturdy sticks, and bring the horse out to the main road?"

When they walked away, I knelt by the body and inspected the head, then pulled aside the beard to find a purplish bruise around Donato's neck. I looked up at Godfrey, who gasped and crossed himself. Lotulf frowned. Moving on, I examined the torso, covered with a shirt of mail over a leather tunic, and felt the fingers of the still-gloved hands. "Why would he wear mail if this was just a pleasure ride?" I wondered aloud. Lotulf and Filippo exchanged surprised glances.

The men brought the sticks, which I inserted into the ground near Donato's head and a few feet away, in the direction of the road. Then I went to examine the horse. It seemed nervous and had taken to pawing the ground and pulling on its reins again, but it bore no signs of violence. I checked the pockets of the saddle until my fingers rested on a leather purse in one of them. When I untied its strings, it revealed five marks of gold. I replaced the purse and returned to the body.

I asked the men to turn Donato over, and kneeled again to examine his back, running my fingers over the links of the mail where bits of purple aconite flowers were tangled among the metal loops.

"I am not sure what you are looking for, Sister." Lotulf stirred impatiently. "He was attacked by outlaws, killed, and dumped away from the main road. That is what happens when you go riding alone through the forest early in the morning —"

I straightened up. "He was not killed by outlaws. He was assassinated." I watched disbelief color his rugged features. "It happened somewhere else, and he was brought here to make it look like a random attack and robbery," I added.

"Where was he killed, then?" Father Godfrey pulled a handkerchief out of the folds of his robe and wiped his forehead as he realized the scope of this misfortune.

"Somewhere across the river." I pointed toward the bridge on the Nahe. "Also, a robber would not have left this on him." I pulled off the right glove, revealing the emerald ring still on his finger. "There is a purse full of gold in a pocket of his horse's saddle as well."

Godfrey opened his mouth, but no words came out.

"Maybe he had another purse on his belt and the killers took it for the only money he had on him," Lotulf persisted. "And they didn't notice the ring because he had his gloves on."

I felt the bruise on the dead man's neck. "He was strangled, which is not the usual method of outlaws who use knives or clubs. There are no injuries to his head and no stab wounds anywhere, although I cannot be certain until he is back at the abbey and I can examine his body and clothes." I paused. "He was strangled by a person of means — take a look at this." I pointed to the right side of the neck, and the men leaned closer. "There is a round mark where the assassin's fourth finger would have been." I imitated the stranglehold by holding my hands an inch above the neck. "He wore a large ring on his left hand."

The monk covered his face with his hands, mumbling a prayer, and Lotulf begrudgingly called my observation "interesting." "But what are the sticks for?" he asked.

"Ah!" I rose to my feet and led them to the clumps of upturned earth that the sticks marked. They were footprints hidden by the ferns and running on two distinct tracks, some barely visible but others quite deep and distinct. "The men who found Donato say they did not approach the body, so these have to belong to the killer. See how this track is deeper than the other? That is because he was carrying the body. The softer footprints show the path he took when he was walking away without his burden."

"How does that help us?" Lotulf looked skeptical.

I suppressed a sigh of impatience. Much of what I was doing should have been his job. "We must make a wax imprint of the deeper marks and show them around the town. Perhaps someone has seen somebody wearing boots with soles that would fit the mold."

"An excellent idea." Father Godfrey had rallied and was looking around with a new sense of purpose. "Can you tell how long he has been dead?"

I made a quick calculation. "He was alive at compline last night and the body is still rigid, so I would say since the early hours of the morning, before dawn."

"And he was not killed here?"

"No. He was attacked somewhere it rained last night; his back is wet, but the night was dry around here. I went to my garden just before prime, and there was no dew. Then there is this." I held out my palm to show them the long and narrow purple petals, oddly similar to a monk's cowl, I had found stuck in the rings of Donato's chain mail. "Aconite doesn't grow on this side of the Nahe. I use it to make medicine for achy joints, but I have to have it delivered from across the river." I paused, considering all of this, and there was only one conclusion I could draw from the evidence before me. "He was killed there and brought here to be found, then some valuable items were taken to make it look like he had been attacked by outlaws or perhaps someone from the town. But the killer left a lot of money behind, which suggests it was staged."

The silence that followed was broken only by the buzzing of forest insects around us that suddenly seemed to reach a higher pitch, and the air felt heavy with the deepening mystery.

"What do we do now?" Filippo asked quietly.

"We will take the body back to the abbey, and I will return with my assistant." I turned to the peasants and took two silver coins out of my pocket. "Would you stay here to guard these footprints until we come back, and gather some wood for a fire?" They accepted the coins eagerly and wanted to kiss my hand before I stopped them.

I walked to the edge of the woods with Filippo and was about to climb onto the wagon when he stopped in his tracks. "God's wounds!" he exclaimed, forgetting the presence of the clergy. "This is not Signor Donato's horse!" He stared at the beast that had been brought from the clearing.

"What do you mean?"

"This is not the horse he rode when we came here, though from a distance it looked similar enough. But his was a fine chestnut courser, taller than this one. He was proud of that horse and would not have gone anywhere without it."

"We never checked the stables," Father Godfrey murmured as we stared at the ordinary bay rouncey. My head was swimming in confusion. Why would Donato have left his horse behind and gone to the town to get a different one? I was familiar with St. Disibod's stables and knew that the horse we were looking at did not belong to the abbey. There could only be one answer, I realized. Donato wanted to slip out of the abbey without anyone knowing, and it was easier—and quieter—to do so on foot.

As the body, wrapped loosely in a shroud, was being loaded onto the wagon and secured with leather belts, I said to Filippo and Godfrey, "You must not discuss my findings with the bishop or the abbot until I bring back the wax imprints and examine the body further."

Moments later, our somber procession was on its way back.

The abbey was in an uproar by the time I left again for the forest, this time with Brother Fabian and an iron pot full of candle stumps. Those we melted over the fire, and with the peasants' help, Fabian filled several footprints with hot liquid wax. We brought the casts back to the abbey with time to spare before vespers. By then, word had already spread that Donato had ridden out on a different horse, and a questioning around Disibodenberg revealed that he had hired the rouncey there. The town gatekeeper also confirmed that Donato had left late in the night. Up at the abbey, Brother Rainald had not seen him leave, but he was known to fall asleep at his post at night. While he would have awakened if someone had tried to ride out, a man on foot could have easily slipped out.

Donato's body lay on a stone table in the coolness of the mortuary chapel in the church, where I had a chance to take another look at it before it was wrapped in a burial shroud. Before the overnight vigil commenced, we gathered at the abbot's house.

"My initial findings have been confirmed," I said. "There are no signs of stabbing or blows to the head, and the cause of death is strangulation. There are some bruises on his left arm, suggesting that he was pulled down from his horse. The fact that he had not drawn his sword means that he most likely knew his attacker."

I went on to describe my observations from the forest, noticing that Bishop Umberto's face blanched when he heard that Donato had been killed on the other side of the Nahe. I even thought I saw a flash of anger crossing his face. "I was able to secure these wax imprints of the killer's boots." I held out the yellowish cast for everyone to see. "These are sturdy riding boots, and the soles are finely shaped. It is hard to imagine a common bandit in possession of such footwear."

"Unless he stole it," Helenger suggested with a self-satisfied smirk, happy to throw a wrench in my theory.

"That is possible." I acknowledged him with exaggerated politeness. "However, if we consider that the killer wore a ring and left Signor Donato's emerald ring and a purse of gold behind, I think we can confidently reject the idea that this was an opportunistic murder motivated by greed."

Abbot Kuno sighed heavily. "So this was planned." It was more of a statement than a question.

"It does appear so, Father."

"But who would want to kill Donato?" Father Godfrey spread his arms helplessly. "He was such a brave and gallant knight, well-liked in both Milan and Rome."

"He may have had a secret." I voiced a suspicion that had been growing in my mind since finding out that Donato had ridden out on a horse that was not his. "That secret took him out of the abbey in the dead of night to meet someone across the Nahe. Whatever he had been up to must have gone wrong, and he was killed, brought back here, and a robbery was staged — rather clumsily."

The sound of a chair being pushed back with force made everybody turn to Bishop Umberto. He looked wildly around the room, his face red with anger or — perhaps — shame. "Of course this was an accidental crime! My brother must have felt like taking the air on a spring night and hired a horse in town so as not to disturb anybody within the abbey. Unfortunately, he fell prey to a bandit in search of profit," he said loudly and emphatically, ignoring all the evidence I had presented. But he sounded strained.

"Your Excellency!" Abbot Kuno was aghast. "A knight in the service of the Holy Father was deprived of his life most foully. Surely, the perpetrator must be found and brought to justice!"

"He may have gone anywhere by now; there is no point chasing after him throughout the Rhineland." Umberto turned to his companion. "Father Godfrey, we are returning to Rome as soon as my brother is buried."

And with that, he left the parlor before any of us could react.

Donato was buried in the abbey cemetery the next morning. During the Mass, I observed Bishop Umberto discreetly. In addition to the pain caused by the loss of his brother, another emotion was visible on his drawn face; each time he raised his eyes from the coffin, they were full of terrified astonishment mixed with something I had already noted the evening before — shame.

After the funeral, the abbot invited the emissaries to his house again, where I gave them a copy of *Scivias* for the pope. The atmosphere was tense, but while the bishop was grimly determined to cut the visit short, Father Godfrey appeared perplexed and mortified, though he deferred dutifully to his senior.

"Despite the painful and unfortunate incident that took my brother's life, we are grateful for your hospitality and much obliged, Father Abbot," Umberto said with an emphasis on the word "incident." Then he turned to me, his earlier doubts regarding my soothing draft apparently forgotten. "I was much impressed with the infirmary, and your dedication and skill in attending to your patients, Sister. I will report my observations to His Holiness, who is awaiting them eagerly," he added, every inch a diplomat again.

"You are most kind." I inclined my head. "My message to the Holy Father—if I may presume to ask you to deliver one on my behalf—is that these words and images come not from a human being, but from God. I am only a vessel that He fills with insight."

Behind the bishop, I could see the prior making an effort to restrain himself under the abbot's warning gaze.

Bishop Umberto nodded in acknowledgment. "We shall take our leave now."

After the abbey gates had closed behind them, Kuno turned to me and Helenger. "You two will join me for supper tonight. We have much to discuss."

Then, leaning on his stick, he hobbled toward his house.

The events of the past two days had left us all on the brink of exhaustion. Even the prior, normally alert and plotting five steps ahead, was subdued. I brought a pitcher of a strengthening fennel tisane with licorice, sugar, and honey, which I poured instead of wine.

"I think the bishop knows more about his brother's death than he let on," I said when we had finished our meal. "He is hiding something."

"But why?" Kuno was puzzled.

I shook my head. "I don't know. But he was not interested in my findings and insisted that it had been an opportunistic crime, although I am sure he doesn't believe it himself." I paused. "It is unnatural for a man not to want to bring his brother's killer before a judge."

"I had the same impression," Helenger admitted sourly.

"We had no authority to override the bishop's decision to close the case, and justice has not been served," the abbot said bleakly.

"Perhaps not all is lost, Father."

They both gave me a questioning look.

"We know Donato was murdered between here and Sponheim, and that the killer was a man of status. We could send a party to inquire about any recent visitors to the area who might fit that description. It might even be worth visiting the castle." Sponheim was the ancient seat of Jutta's family, and I had ties of friendship with her mother, dowager Countess Sophia.

"Why should we continue to involve ourselves in this?" Helenger asked.

"As Father Abbot has said, justice has not been served. A killer is free, and his motive was far more nefarious than that of high road robbers—it was personal. Besides," I added, "Donato was close to Umberto, who is close to the pope. What if the Holy Father himself is in danger?"

"Let's not exaggerate!" the prior exclaimed. "Even if this was a conspiracy, it was still a local crime. Rome is thousands of miles away."

I shifted impatiently. How could he not understand that although men and news traveled slowly, what happened in one part of the world could eventually impact another? I turned to Kuno. "Father, what is your view? Should we pursue it, or should we let it rest?"

The abbot sighed. "Let's put together a small party and send it toward Sponheim. If we find nothing, let the matter be put to rest, but at least our consciences will be clear."

I saw that he did not relish this plan, but his sense of duty prevailed.

"I want to be a part of it," I offered before Helenger had the chance to volunteer.

"I do too." He gave me a challenging look.

Kuno sighed again, even as a faint twinkle of mischief appeared in his weary eyes. "All right, you will both go. And take Lotulf with you."

Helenger and I eyed each other warily.

"As you wish, Father," I said.

7

Sponheim Castle, June 1145

WE LEFT DISIBODENBERG at dawn on the feast of St. Bonifatius. There were five of us altogether, for I needed someone trustworthy and had obtained the abbot's leave for Volmar to accompany us. Kuno also gave his permission for him to ride a horse, and despite the gravity of our mission, Volmar clearly enjoyed being in the saddle again. He looked as natural as Lotulf, who rode alongside him at the head of the group. Helenger and I traveled in a wagon, an icy silence between us. Closing off the deputation was a former man-at-arms from Disibodenberg, whom we had hired for added protection.

In villages along the way, we asked for news of armed strangers. Peasants shook their heads and opened their arms everywhere, until we came upon a solitary farm in the woods in the early afternoon. It stood in a clearing off the main tract, with a vegetable garden enclosed by a wattle fence in the front, and a pasture with a small byre behind. Craning our necks, we finally spotted two bony cows grazing behind the cottage. When one lowed its greeting, a middle-aged man dressed in a stained, much-mended tunic came out of the shed. He was holding a pitchfork out but lowered it when he saw our Benedictine robes, although a wary expression remained on his weather-beaten face. At first, he denied having seen anybody, but a shifty look in his eyes suggested he knew more than he was letting on. A silver coin quickly improved his memory, and he described a large group of soldiers riding by about a fortnight before. He saw them again two days later, camping half a league north on the banks of the Ellerbach, where he had gone fishing.

We followed in the direction indicated and soon arrived at a trampled meadow. By the size of it, the camp had hosted at least two dozen men with tents and horses. The day was clear, and from where we stood, Castle Sponheim was visible a little over a league upstream. The meadow looked like a good place to search for footprints that might match the wax imprints.

It was not an easy task, but we eventually found several distinguishable marks at the farthest perimeter of the camp. Some of them had fine contours while others were heavier with less graceful outlines.

"These belong to a knight or his squire," Lotulf opined, pointing at the finer ones with an air of authority. "These other ones to a groom or servant."

I studied the footprints one by one and noticed that a particular set stood out. I knelt beside it and placed the wax mold on the ground. Volmar knelt on the other side, and as we leaned over the footprints, our heads touched. For just a moment too long, neither of us drew back.

"Looks like a good match," he said, running a finger from one side of the footprint to the other. "The same shape and pattern of grooves across the sole."

I nodded. "Whoever they were, they were likely visiting Sponheim." I ventured a theory. "Their commander stayed at the castle while the retainers camped here." I stood up and shielded my eyes as I gazed at the castle, its gray stone reflecting the soft amber light of the summer afternoon. It was a beautiful view, but all I felt was disappointment that the men were gone now, and Donato's killer most likely with them.

"I think that is a good guess," Volmar agreed. "Let's pay Count Meinhard a visit to see if he can help us."

"We should not disturb the count now that the murderer is out of reach." Helenger's eyes flicked between me and Volmar with sardonic amusement. "We should return to the abbey."

"Brother Volmar is right," I said. I was disconcerted by the prior's gaze and the way one corner of his mouth curled up. Volmar either did not notice or chose to ignore it as he turned away from us to study the distance to the castle.

"We have an obligation to Donato to ask any questions that might allow us to discover his killer," I added. "And even if we cannot bring him to justice, I am sure his family will want to know where that man came from or whom he served."

The prior shrugged and gave us one last lingering look before he turned on his heel and marched off to the wagon. I followed him, my mind already racing ahead. I wondered what we might learn at the castle, and what it might mean not just to Donato's family, but, possibly, to the pope himself. I shuddered at the thought of the forces that might have been at play in this strange demise of the papal emissary's brother. Climbing in behind Helenger, I prayed that whatever we uncovered, the count von Sponheim was not involved in it.

Countess Sophia was surprised but welcomed us warmly despite the late hour. She had to be in her seventieth year now; she had snow-white hair under her wimple and a lined face, but her eyes and smile still had traces of the old radiance.

"I am afraid you will have to suffer me as your hostess today," she said when her son came out of the keep alone. "My daughter-in-law is still in childbed."

"I am father to a fair son!" Count Meinhard beamed with pride. "After three daughters."

"May God send blessings on the child and your household," Helenger intoned piously.

"Thank you, Brother Prior. To what do we owe this honor?"

"We are come on a most unfortunate mission, Herr Meinhard," he replied. "A guest of our abbey was found dead in the forest five days ago, and clues regarding his killer's identity have led us to this area."

Meinhard was stunned. "Clues as to a murder? Leading to Sponheim?"

"Indirectly, yes."

"You must be tired and in need of refreshment," his mother interjected before he could reply. "I will have the servants lay out supper for you. Then you can tell us your story."

Within an hour, two tables in the hall were covered with platters of cold meats, cheese, bread and honey, and jugs of excellent Rhenish wine that we sipped as the hosts heard a tale of death and deepening mystery. After Helenger had summarized the events, I produced the wax cast of the boot print from my scrip.

"What an astonishing yet simple idea!" Count Meinhard exclaimed, his eyes widening. "It would never have occurred to me to make a mold like that," he added regretfully.

"Can you tell us if it looks familiar at all?" I handed him the cast. I had not revealed the observations we had made at the campsite.

He turned it over in his hands, studied the shape, and began to shake his head, when one of his men rose from the lower table. The count motioned him to approach. The man, wearing a steward uniform, whispered something in his ear. Meinhard's brow furrowed as he listened, then he nodded. The man walked out of the hall in a hurry.

"I recently hosted Wilfred, a knight from Metz, for a few days," the count said slowly, weighing his words. "We had served together as squires at the court of the Count Palatine, but we fell out during the last election when he threw his support behind Duke Heinrich of Bavaria. I myself supported King Konrad's claim. I always believed," he added, "that he should have been crowned already in 1125."

I thought back to the contentious election of the year 1138, thirteen years after the previous one. It had also been fraught with controversy, as was inevitable in the absence of hereditary succession. The last time around, the struggle had pitted the Duke of Bavaria, who was the late Emperor Lothair's son-in-law, against Konrad, the late Emperor Heinrich's nephew, who succeeded in regaining the crown for the House of Hohenstaufen.

"But you have reconciled?" I asked.

"Indeed." The count nodded, smiling lightly. "He came around and is serving in the imperial army now."

I smiled too. Behind it, I wondered about the fluid loyalties of men who found power irresistible. "Do you think Wilfred or any of his men may have been involved in Donato's death?" I asked directly. It was not a far-fetched notion; the count's guest was an imperial servant, while Donato had been part of a papal embassy. The two powers had not seen eye-to-eye in more than half a century.

Meinhard pondered my question before answering. "I am not aware of any connection between them." He glanced at the door through which his steward had vanished, and I could see the muscles of his jaw working under the skin. "Something odd happened on the morning of his departure."

He turned back to us and hesitated a moment longer before continuing, "Wilfred stayed in the castle with his squires and grooms, while his soldiers camped down by the river. That morning he was searching for one of his men, who was nowhere to be found. When the man eventually turned up, I remember noticing that his clothes were splattered with mud as if he had ridden hard. I didn't make much of it—I assumed he'd gone down to the camp. Since it had rained that night, his condition was not surprising. I don't know if that has any significance—"

He was interrupted by his steward returning with a pair of tan leather boots, cleanly scrubbed and oiled. "Jehan here tells me that after they'd gone, a pair of these had been left behind in the grooms' quarters. I sent him to fetch them for comparison."

Deep silence fell as the count turned the boots upside down. Helenger, who sat to his left, brought a candle closer to illuminate the soles and the wax cast.

There were gasps all around as we realized that they matched perfectly.

The count rubbed his forehead. "The wayward squire must have given them to a groom to clean, and the man forgot them when he was packing up."

"Let me guess," I said. "The man to whom the boots belonged was very tall, about six feet?"

He nodded slowly. "Yes, he stood out for his height. How did you know?"

"The distance between his footprints in the forest—his stride—was long, about two-and-half feet, which would correspond to a height of approximately six feet."

The count lifted an eyebrow in grim amusement, but it was clear that he was under a growing strain. He reached for his wine goblet and drained it.

"Do you know the squire's name?" Volmar asked.

Meinhard frowned, raking his memory. "Andreas, I believe." He looked around, at a loss for an explanation. "But why would he—or Wilfred, if Andreas acted on his behalf—want to kill a middling papal servant?"

I was puzzled too. The two knights—one German and one Italian, living on two opposite ends of the empire—were unlikely to have known each other, so it had to have been a political murder. Yet after a flare-up following Konrad's election—the Duke of Bavaria, whose family had supported the papal side in the investiture conflict, had refused to acknowledge his rival's win and was stripped of his territories as a result—a peace agreement had been signed, and it still held.

Nevertheless, it seemed the most likely scenario, and it had to be laid on the table. "One possibility is that it was done on the order of King Konrad or someone close to him." I kept my voice low so that only the count, his mother, and my party could hear. After all, this was a serious accusation to make against a sovereign.

The count looked aghast, but he was an astute man who understood the complexity of the papal-imperial conflict, and so he did not dismiss it out of hand. "The king has his hands full with revolts in Saxony and with his brother-in-law's claims in Poland to bother with the pope's partisans these days," he said instead, sounding like he was trying very hard to believe it.

"He may be busy elsewhere, but the source of the conflict over supremacy has not disappeared." I was convinced, as I had been in 1122, that the Worms concordat had provided no real solution to the desire of kings and popes to rule over both the temporal and the spiritual domains. "Who knows what scheming may still be going on behind the scenes?"

He leaned back in his chair, sighing as he ran a hand through his brown hair, still full and only lightly touched with gray despite his age. "If that is the case, how did someone like Donato become embroiled in all of this—" He paused, the color draining from his face. "Donato and his brother are Milanese, and the city has particularly strong ties to the papacy—" He broke off again, unable to speak the rest out loud, and it was in that moment that I grasped the implication.

I glanced at Volmar and saw understanding dawning on his face too. "I think that is the only sensible conclusion," I said, my chest tightening at the enormity of it.

"What conclusion?" Helenger asked sharply.

The count was still silent, blinking in disbelief.

"The leather purse filled with gold that was left behind was Donato's payment for spying," I explained.

"Spying on whom?" the prior asked, although he and everyone else already knew the answer — the pope.

Countess Sophia's hand went up to her mouth, and a stunned silence fell on us. Yet I reflected that there was nothing surprising about such an insidious game being played for profit. Many more were probably involved in it on both sides, and would be for as long as greed and ambition had such hold over men's souls.

"But if he was a spy for King Konrad, why kill him?" Helenger asked. It was a sensible question.

"Perhaps his conscience had got to him and he'd decided to leave the imperial service," Volmar suggested.

"The night of his death, Donato must have gone to meet Andreas," I said, imaging how those last hours of the knight's life may have passed. "He delivered one last piece of information, took the payment, then told Wilfred's man that he was no longer going to be spying. As to whether his conscience had started to weigh on him, or whether living a double life had become too dangerous, we will never know." In the scheme of things, that hardly mattered.

Meinhard finally recovered his composure and drew a deep breath. "I do not believe Wilfred was involved. He is a good man."

And yet he had no trouble switching his allegiance to the winner, I thought.

The countess laid a comforting hand on her son's shoulder. "He is your friend, and we always find it hard to believe that those close to us could be capable of horrible deeds."

Meinhard shook his head. "But he seemed genuinely puzzled that morning when he couldn't find Andreas."

"He may have acted that way to protect himself should anything come to light later," Lotulf offered with a note of professional self-importance. It was the first time he had sounded competent since the whole affair had begun.

"But why murder at all and risk exposing the fact that the king had a spy in the papal household?" The count was still searching for a way to vindicate his friend.

"That is a good question, but as much as it pains me to say this, it does not matter in the end," I replied. "Neither of them is going to face justice, not in this world."

Heads nodded around the table. Everyone knew there was little chance Andreas and Wilfred—if indeed the latter had been involved—would be brought before a judge for a crime that involved a royal spy.

"But at least we know the truth and can inform Donato's family. Although," Volmar added on reflection, "it might only add to their pain to learn of the treachery their son and brother committed."

"I think Bishop Umberto knew or suspected the truth." I told them of my observations at the funeral. "He was determined to return to Rome without an investigation. The only question is, did he know of his brother's activities all along, or did he put everything together only after his death? Either way, he will be in trouble when the news reaches the pope."

"Do you intend to write to Rome?" the countess asked.

"I assume Abbot Kuno will."

"I will write as well," the count said resignedly, accepting the truth at last. "It is important for His Holiness and his officials to know what is going on so he may be protected."

I recalled that the Sponheim family, like that of the Duke of Bavaria, had been on the papal side in the investiture dispute before the concordat was signed. Clearly, Meinhard was steering a different course now with his support for Konrad, so it was surprising to hear him say that. I wondered if he was playing both sides or trying to remain neutral. The latter would have been more noble — and rare in those days — but it was not my place to ask. Besides, out of regard for Jutta and the countess, I did not want to know.

"What I don't understand is why Andreas did not take the gold back." Lotulf broke the heavy silence as we crossed the courtyard toward our quarters later that night. "He took such pains to stage the killing as a robbery."

I had thought about that. "The staging was probably a force of habit; I doubt this was the first time he had carried out such a commission. But he may also have had orders to leave a clue as to his motive to shame Donato before the world by branding him a traitor." Then something else occurred to me. "He took a jeweled brooch and a silver dagger, which will go a long way toward recovering the cost of that last bribe."

"If the goal was to unmask Donato as a traitor," Volmar mused, "then perhaps his master wanted to destroy Bishop Umberto as well. After all, it was through serving his brother that Donato would have learned about the pope's strategy for dealing with King Konrad." He shook his head ruefully. "I will never understand what makes men so attracted to politics. It is but a game — and a vicious, soul-crushing one at that — played for no better reason than gaining riches and fame."

"And the simple folk never benefit, no matter who prevails in the quarrels between the mighty," Lotulf added in his second sensible remark of the evening.

8

Abbey of St. Disibod, June 1145

BACK AT DISIBODENBERG we found that Abbot Kuno had fallen ill. When I went to his house, he was asleep, looking small and fragile in his bed. Despite our differences, I felt a clutch at my heart at the sight of his shriveled neck, his bony fingers clutching the blanket, and his papery, mottled skin, all of which spoke of a life that had come full circle and arrived at a second, cheerless infancy. I took his pulse. His skin was cool under my touch despite the warm evening.

The abbot opened his eyes, and his breath became raspy with effort. "Have you learned anything?" At least his head was still working properly.

"We have, Father." But he seemed in no condition to hear the story. "Can I get you some water or broth?"

He shook his head and appeared to fall into a slumber again. On the nearby table was a half-eaten dish of roasted hen in a spicy sauce, his favorite. I sighed. I would put him on a diet of bread and boiled vegetables, but there was little else I could do except let him sleep. In his condition, sleep brought more relief than any medicine I could make.

Kuno rallied the next day and immediately complained about the plainness of his food, though he submitted to the restriction. "At least I can still have my wine," he grumbled when I came in with a small jug. I had infused it with powdered oak bark and dried sage to boost its strengthening properties, but he did not seem to notice, another worrying sign given his once discerning palate. "Send for the prior and Brother Volmar. I want to hear about Sponheim."

Helenger arrived with an air of even greater importance than usual. He had just presided over the monks in chapter, and I felt a throb of anxiety at seeing him assume the abbot's duties and privileges. Something similar had happened during another illness many years before, and it had been the strength of Kuno's *viriditas* that had saved me from being shut away back then.

That *viriditas* that was no longer there. I may have enjoyed significant recognition, and the pope's interest in my work provided a powerful shield, but the transition I knew was coming would bring me no benefit at St. Disibod.

Kuno was propped up on two straw-filled pillows as he listened to Helenger recount the discovery at the campsite and what we had learned about Wilfred and Andreas. He was silent for a long while, and when he finally spoke, there was something akin to resentment in his look, but it was mixed with a deep sadness. "To think that I hosted a traitor to the Church under my roof in these last days of my service on earth." He sighed. "God has sent me this last trial, and I intend to face it humbly."

"You could not have known, Father, nor any of us." I sought to comfort him.

Kuno shivered as if a draft of cold air had run over his shoulders, then he looked at each of us. "Do all of you share these suspicions regarding Signor Donato?" he asked, and there was a faint note of hope in his voice.

"They are more than suspicions," I said. "The evidence pointing to him is too strong."

The abbot nodded slowly, whether to signify understanding or resignation, I could not be sure. "Count Meinhard is sending a message to Rome, and so will we." He paused for breath. "We must protect the abbey's reputation. Brother Prior, draft a letter on my behalf."

"Of course." Helenger puffed up.

The abbot's eyelids grew heavy, and saliva was pooling in a corner of his mouth. "We should let you rest," I said, rising. "I ordered boiled chicken with vegetables for your supper, and I will bring you a fennel draft afterwards."

The abbot sighed as we headed for the door. "At least have them send me more wine," he said plaintively.

Kuno's health continued to decline over the summer. He suffered a series of seizures that left him unable to speak, and without the use of the right side of his body. As the news spread, the monks, lay brothers, and eventually also the townspeople began to prepare for the end of his tenure, which, for many of them, was the only one they had ever known.

By then, Helenger was running the abbey in all but name. A formal election would still have to take place, and he was personally unpopular — he was feared more than admired — but he was among the most senior brothers, and no strong contender had emerged from among the middle ranks to challenge him. His succession was a foregone conclusion, and it left me fearing what his first move would be with respect to the infirmary. When he had once banned me from working there, it had caused an uproar among the patients and complaints from some of the monks. He would not do that outright again, but I could not help imagining the different ways in which he could make my life and work difficult.

As it turned out, I did not have to wait long to find out. Shortly before the feast of St. Disibod, the prior paid me an unannounced visit. I received him sitting behind my desk in the surgery as he remained standing, having rejected my offer of a chair with exaggerated politeness. Instead, he swept the chamber with a calculating glance before pausing to survey, with feigned interest, the jars and bottles that lined the shelves.

I felt my apprehension growing. "How can I help you, Brother Prior?"

"I come to inquire after the abbot's health." He rested his gaze on me, which he could make impenetrable whenever he wanted.

"There hasn't been much change lately in either direction," I replied warily.

"What is his chance of recovery?"

"Not high. It is a matter of time."

"How much time?" He tried to appear sympathetic, but his eagerness came through nonetheless.

A rising anger was threatening to choke me, but I restrained myself. Chastising him would not help. I took a steadying breath. "Only God knows that, Brother, and I am not going to speculate on His will."

A flash of irritation crossed his face, but he did not reply. Instead, he planted himself firmly in the middle of the room and regarded me for some moments. "I also want to discuss the future of infirmary care with you, Sister."

I stiffened, and a flicker of malicious mirth appeared in Helenger's eyes. His face remained composed in a look of authority, already assured and arrogant.

"What do you mean?" I asked coolly. "The Rule requires us to maintain an infirmary to cater to the needs of the community."

"To the community, yes. But not to strangers."

"Strangers?"

"Anybody who is not our brethren or a lay worker for the abbey is, by definition, a stranger. And you treat many such people."

I scoffed. "What are you saying? That we should shut our doors to those in need who hail from outside these walls? That we should turn ailing pilgrims away?"

At the mention of pilgrims, the prior hesitated. "You know I am not saying that."

"I am glad to hear that, because refusing aid to the sick, whether they be noblemen or penniless laborers, is unworthy of a Benedictine — or any Christian, for that matter. May I also remind you that The Rule prescribes that we welcome the poor with the greatest care and solicitude because it is especially in them that Christ is received?"

That was a bold tone to take with someone of Helenger's position and temperament, but to my surprise, he did not seem offended. Instead, a wry smile twisted his lips. Confused, I found myself trying to catch up to him in what seemed increasingly like a game of cat and mouse, when he delivered the blow. "I am not going to turn away the poor who come here for free care, but" — his smile broadened as he savored his words — "I will implement fees for the maternity visits that Sister Elfrid makes."

"Fees?" I echoed.

"Five deniers for a peasant, half a silver mark for the wife of a tradesman, and a mark for a merchant's wife."

"On whose authority?"

"Mine. As acting abbot."

I was reeling but took great care not to show it. "May I ask why you are doing this?"

"To help fund the infirmary."

"But we are fine with the donations we receive from our benefactors," I protested. "The abbey has not had to pay for linen, glass, and other necessities for years. We are also able to pay the kitchen to feed our patients."

"And we want to keep it that way."

"Then why not wait with such measures until our finances demand it?" I suggested.

Helenger ignored my question. "The fees will be introduced beginning with the feast of St. Disibod."

That was only a week away.

"Brother Prior, you know that this is going to prevent many women from being able to receive care," I pleaded.

"If they value your care so much, they will find the money," he replied brutally.

I averted my face in disgust. I should have known better than to expect compassion from Helenger. "It will force us to stop the visits," I said. As the words left my mouth, I knew that I had lost—that was exactly what he wanted.

I rose, still unable to look at him. "I must return to work. My patients are waiting." I walked past him and out of the room.

Throughout the afternoon, as I lanced boils, dressed cuts, and administered medicines, I mulled over this new situation. The fee was an excuse to stop Elfrid from leaving the abbey precincts. The scriptorium fee would likely go up next, all in an effort to eventually force us back behind the convent doors. What I had been fearing for years was beginning to come true.

I had been waiting two years for a resolution of the abbot's inquiry with Rome, and now he was dying. I could no longer afford to wait for the announcement of papal support—or risk his ban catching me still at St. Disibod under the unfettered authority of Helenger.

The prior had issued a challenge, and I had to respond.

By the end of the day, I had a plan.

9

July 1145

I SUMMONED RICARDIS to my workshop, where we could speak privately. I had been ill with a strong headache of the kind that would once have put me to bed for days. But I could not do that now. I drank infusions I made from a powdered root of butterbur and rubbed mint and rosemary oils onto my temples, and I kept working all throughout it.

Ricardis arrived after her work at the scriptorium was finished and sat across the table from me, holding a cup of wine between slender fingers stained with gold, red, and green ink. But instead of detracting from her beauty, those shimmering spots of color on her skin only enhanced it. Her smile lifted the veil of gloom that had surrounded me since my meeting with Helenger.

"The prior is moving to curtail our freedom of movement." I poured more wine into our cups, then I told her about the maternity fees.

Ricardis's dark eyes widened. "But most women will not be able to afford that."

I nodded. "I can cover the fees from our funds, but he is bound to find out, and then he will come up with another scheme to prevent us from doing our work."

"He would not do that!" Ricardis protested. "Who would copy and decorate your manuscripts?" I was surprised to hear so much confidence in her voice, although somewhere in the depths of her eyes, there was a flicker of uncertainty.

"Oh yes, he would," I assured her. "Without a second thought. You don't know him like I do. He uses others—takes what he can from them for as long as is expedient. He will not hesitate to give up the advantages if he finds a way to hurt those whom he perceives as enemies. And that"—I pointed a finger from myself to her and back—"is what he considers us to be."

My words had a strange effect on her. The uncertainty I had first seen only in her eyes spread over her features, and they became tense, almost fearful. "So what are you going to do?" she asked, dropping her voice. She was alarmed now.

"It is time for us to leave the abbey," I said with grim determination. "We cannot wait any longer for the pope to issue his proclamation on *Scivias*. It might take years the way things are going in Rome." I laid my hand on hers. "It will be difficult, but we will be together and have one another to offer comfort and encouragement."

She nodded, swallowing. "Where will we go?"

The afternoon was at its hottest, and the air of the workshop was thick from the scent of exotic spices. Earlier that day, Renfred's son, who now ran the shop in town, had delivered my order of ginger root, cinnamon sticks, saffron leaves, and pepper seed. I inhaled deeply, letting the pungent aroma fill my lungs. "That is why I wanted to talk to you."

Light returned to Ricardis's eyes as she lifted them eagerly to my face. "I will do anything in my power for you, Sister."

"The first thing we must do is find a suitable location. That means a grant of land. Among the sisters, only you and Gertrude come from landed families, and I thought—"

"I will write to my uncle!" Ricardis fairly bounced on her bench. "I should have thought of it myself." She made a move as if to run back to the scriptorium that instant.

I held her back, feeling suddenly embarrassed. "The Count von Stade already gave us a large endowment to secure your entry; perhaps I should start with Gertrude's father. If he doesn't—"

"No!" She interrupted, grasping my hand with a gesture that seemed almost desperate. "They do not have as much land as we do. I will write to Stade today, and my uncle will not refuse me. My cousin Hartwig will persuade him."

The image of Hartwig—quiet and dour where this girl had been all lively chatter during our first meeting years ago in Sponheim—flashed through my mind. For a moment, I wondered about the need to involve him in the matter. But I put that thought aside. Our time was running out, and we needed all the help we could get. "I would be grateful," I said instead.

"It will be my greatest pleasure to do this for you," Ricardis said, and a broad smile—part mischief, part mystery—illuminated her face. "I can even think of a place that would be perfect."

I reached for the wine flagon again, and we drank a toast. I was still savoring the sweet elderberry taste on my tongue when the door opened. Griselda entered with a broom, ready to sweep the floor and strew it with the fresh rushes that lay in a neat pile outside.

"Oh." She halted. "I didn't know you were still here. I will come back later—" she made to withdraw.

But I was already rising from the table. "No need. We are done." I smiled at Ricardis as we left the workshop and Griselda behind.

There was one more thing I needed to tell her. As we walked down the path toward the gate, I lowered my voice, casting a reflexive look over my shoulder. "Keep this to yourself for now." Then I added, "I have a feeling that some of the things we discuss among ourselves somehow reach the prior's ears. I hope I am wrong, but I just don't know who to trust anymore, so I need this to remain a secret for as long as possible. Only you and I will know." *Not even Volmar*, I thought with a stab of regret.

"As you wish." Ricardis lowered her eyes, and I saw darker color rising under the pink skin of her cheeks. "But are you certain that we will obtain permission for the move once Prior Helenger becomes abbot?"

I stopped and considered Ricardis. She was quick; perhaps I had underestimated her all along. "I am not certain at all." I shook my head. "He wants to profit from our presence if he can, but what he wants even more is to have us under his control. And," I added, "he intends for us to have no voice." I paused to let it sink in. "But I will not stand for that."

"What are you going to do?"

"I don't know yet, but I *will* find a way to fight him."

That night, I slept fitfully and awoke well before lauds, when the sky was still dark. I lit a candle, found a sheet of parchment, and took comfort from the sound of the goose feather as it scratched softly under my hand.

I was writing to an old friend for advice.

10

November 1145

ABBOT KUNO DIED in the autumn, and I could not stop my mind from imagining the blackest schemes Helenger would conjure for us. Would he turn us out of the infirmary and replace us with two or three monks? Only recently I had consoled myself that he would not dare do that again, but I was no longer sure. Would he ban me from writing letters, so the world would never know the extent of our oppression? I closed my eyes at the brightness of the candles that blazed around the church during the funeral Mass to dispel the gloom of the November day. *Please don't let me be ill again, not now.*

But that same night, on our way back from matins, I heard a soft whisper behind me. "I have a letter from Stade."

My stomach gave a lurch of anxiety and anticipation. Finally. It had been four months.

I turned and Ricardis touched the side of her robe, indicating that she had the letter on her. We stepped aside, and when the sisters disappeared inside the dorter, we returned to the chapel. I unfolded the square of parchment and read the letter as my heart hammered against my ribs. The count was offering a place called Mount St. Rupert as a freehold possession if we wished to establish our own monastery. The location overlooked the Nahe where it flowed into the Rhine near Bingen, two days' journey north of Disibodenberg. The property included the ruins of an old church, several acres of forest, fertile vineyards along both rivers, and fishing rights to a small section of the Rhine. In addition to the defunct church, there were some old farm buildings, currently overseen by a caretaker and his wife.

For the first time in months, I was able to take a deep breath without feeling like an iron band had been fastened around my chest, and the effect was invigorating. The pain in my head was gone. The offer was generous and the location excellent, close to the great cities along the Rhine. Patronage from a nobleman as powerful as Rudolf von Stade would be helpful in the challenges that lay ahead.

Ricardis's face glowed in the soft candlelight, and I embraced her warmly. "I had begun to fear that we might be condemned to a grim fate under Helenger. But this" — I lifted the letter as if it were a container full of treasure — "is going to save us. I am forever grateful to you and your family."

Her cheeks colored with pleasure. "I know that place very well, and we are going to be happy there." A wistful expression crossed her face. "When I was a child, I often traveled with my father, and we would stop at St. Rupert on our way back home. The church was already in ruins, and my brothers would pretend it was a fortress they wanted to conquer. Afterward, we would run down the slopes, stumbling and falling, and rolling all the way down. There was always so much laughter!"

"These are precious memories." I felt a surge of emotion, remembering the Bermersheim forest and the outings with my governess, Uda. Some of my first herbal healing lessons had taken place there. I still missed it, even after all these years. "I am glad you will get to revisit it. Few of us are lucky enough to be able to do that."

In the silence that ensued, we could hear the rain, which had been falling steadily all day, slowly tapering off. A sliver of starry sky broke through the clouds as we came out of the chapel, suggesting a calmer and clearer day to follow. "I will write to your uncle to thank him for the offer," I said. Then I added, steeling myself, "I will also have to speak with Helenger."

In bed that night, my mind would not quiet down, plans and worries banishing all sleep. The count had pledged men to dismantle the old church, clear the overgrowth, and build temporary accommodations for us to use during the construction of the new foundation. That would be enormous help, and I was glad of it, but I also despaired of the fact that no work could begin before next spring, assuming everything else went well.

But would it? Besides the obvious challenge of securing Helenger's permission, various legal aspects of severing ties with St. Disibod would have to be argued. The matter was complicated; although we were nominally under the abbot's jurisdiction, we were a separate house. The old friend to whom I had written for advice in July was Brother Bertolf. He had been a novice at St. Disibod and one-time apprentice to Brother Wigbert before I replaced him. He was then free to return to the scriptorium, for which he was forever grateful to me. Later, he had developed a taste for legal studies and moved to the Abbey of St. Eucharius — now renamed St. Matthias — in Trier, where he had become a scholar and an expert in canon law. According to Bertolf, the Archbishop of Mainz could override the abbot's objection and release us, although he was under no obligation to do so.

Rising with time to spare before lauds, I carefully re-read our charter to prepare my argument. But, once again, I was at the mercy of the men of the Church.

Helenger's reaction was entirely predictable. There would be no amicable parting for us. When I walked into the parlor of the abbot's house two days after his election, he was sitting behind Kuno's old desk with an air of complete ownership that I found unseemly. His predecessor had not been buried a week, and Helenger had not yet been formally installed — that would happen in the presence of the arch-bishop on the feast of St. Cecilia in two weeks' time.

The wall hangings were still in place. The benches along the walls were now covered with sheepskins, and a silver wine goblet stood on the desk, strewn with rolls of parchment. *So much for the pious modesty*, I thought. But subtlety had never been part of Helenger's personality. Since taking the cowl, he had spent every day of his life plotting his way to the top, and only Kuno's long life had kept him in the anteroom for so long. But he was finally here, and he was not going to let troublesome considerations of good taste and propriety prevent him from enjoying it. His eyes flickered with suppressed rapacity that made him resemble the tiger from the library's illuminated *bestiarium* that watched his prey from hiding before launching an attack. I made an effort to shake off that impression; this was hardly the first time he had looked at me like that, though never from a position of such authority.

"My felicitations on your elevation . . . Father." I inclined my head. "May God grant you a blessed tenure that you may do His work in the spirit of sacrifice and service on which our Order was founded."

"Thank you, Sister." He acknowledged me with a slight nod.

"I hear the Archbishop of Mainz is to honor us with his presence at your installment."

"Indeed." His stern mouth relaxed in a prideful smile, but his face darkened again a moment later. "You have asked me for a meeting — surely this is about more than your desire to convey your well wishes." His eyes narrowed suspiciously.

I cleared my throat. Perhaps it was best to get it out right away. "I have given much thought to your decision to introduce fees for maternity care, and I have concluded that your approach to the service we provide to the poor and the sick leaves me no choice but to relocate the convent." I held his gaze.

"You have no right." Helenger was calm and confident. He had been prepared for it. "The convent was established within this abbey, and it remains under its authority."

"With all due respect, Father, there is not a word in our founding charter that says that it is to remain so forever. We are not bound to the Abbey of St. Disibod in perpetuity, and the final word on our location does not belong with you."

"I will declare you in breach of The Rule. You will be shunned by the Order."

"Surely you would not go so far as to vilify the convent that has such a strong reputation in the Rhineland," I said coldly, knowingly full well that it was not beyond Helenger at all.

"We shall see." There was a challenge in his voice.

"I have come here hoping that we could reach an agreement that would leave both our houses on good terms." As Helenger did not respond, I added, "I also hope that by coming to a private understanding, we will avoid involving the archbishop and causing a scandal with such an unseemly quarrel."

"The archbishop?" He feigned surprise. Later, when I found out about Abbot Kuno's early inquires at Fulda, I realized that Helenger was fully aware that the jurisdictional archbishop had the final say in disputes involving monastic arrangements such as ours.

"Yes," I replied. "I will take my case before Archbishop Heinrich if you refuse your permission."

"What makes you think he will back you?" There was an edge of contempt in his voice. He was unable to imagine that, so he remained supremely confident.

"Archbishop Adalbert, his predecessor, was a friend of mine, and my convent is well-respected at the episcopal court. The new archbishop is bound to hear me out, and I have the weight of the law and tradition behind me." I paused to let him register this. "The law because our founding charter does not explicitly prohibit us from moving, and tradition because anchorite enclosures existing within abbeys are an exception and are not formally regulated. In fact, anchorites have been known to pick up and move as they please."

There was a long silence as Helenger's eyes wandered over the tapestries on the walls. One of them depicted David slaying Goliath, and I could not help smiling inwardly. Eventually, his gaze returned to me, and it was full of suppressed fury.

"You are deceived by some vain imagination, Sister Hildegard."

"Am I?"

"Yes." His voice was cold as a blade. "My consent is denied, and we will let the archbishop decide."

So he would fight this to the last. And if I lost, he would make my life hell.

A veil of drizzle drifted across the herb garden and the tops of the trees. After six weeks of early winter storms, a thaw had finally arrived. The ground was still covered with snow, now melting into puddles of grayish water. I contemplated the view for a while, then turned from the window, my gaze resting on Volmar's face. In the soft light from the brazier, he looked almost as youthful as when we had been sneaking out of the abbey and running down the hill to the Glan as children. It made my heart ache because I had just told him of the grant of land that brought me a step closer to leaving the abbey.

"You have no choice," he said. After Kuno's death, Volmar had sought to allay my fears of being banned from the infirmary. It would cost them too much, he had said, and it would bring widespread condemnation. He was right, but only partially, for Helenger had instead evicted me from the scriptorium so my books could no longer be copied and illuminated. I had hoped that the archbishop's visit would stop him from going after me, but after it had been postponed due to the unexpected assault of winter in the middle of November, Helenger's spite had only increased.

"I have been corresponding with Brother Bertolf. You remember him, don't you?"

Volmar nodded. "You and I were still oblates when he left St. Disibod, but I remember rumors about him falling out with Helenger."

"I can easily believe that." I snorted. "In any case, he is learned in canon law and says the archbishop has the power to release us over Helenger's objections. I wrote to Mainz to ask Archbishop Heinrich to adjudicate the dispute when he comes here in the spring."

"Of course you did." Volmar's eyes flickered with amusement, and I could not help smiling.

"If he rules in our favor, we will be gone by the end of next summer," I said.

Silence fell between us. Volmar's face grew somber. I knew he did not want me to move, and the prospect of another separation tore me on the inside. "If you could, would you move with us as our priest?" I asked.

He thought for a moment, but there was no hint of hesitation in his voice when he spoke. "You know I would." He smiled briefly. "But it would also require Helenger's permission."

"I know." I sighed. "And I know he will not give it. But if he did," I added, loathe to let go of hope just yet, "it would make me very happy."

The light was fading outside, and I lit a candle on the table between us.

"Tell me more about that place," Volmar said.

"It is located at the confluence of the Nahe and the Rhine, a bountiful country." I closed my eyes, imagining the breathtaking view of the mighty river from our vineyard-draped hill. "When the temporary accommodations are ready, we will move in and start on the cloister and the church, tall and light, like the ones you saw in France." I had gone over the plan in my head a hundred times. "And, of course, a large infirmary with spacious wards to accommodate all kinds of patients." I could already picture myself and Elfrid free to do our work without anyone's interference. "Ricardis tells me there are good hunting grounds, which means fresh meat will be easy to procure," I added, smiling at how practical it sounded. As if I were the lady of a manor.

"It sounds perfect."

"I want to continue to write, so I will need a scriptorium." I gazed dreamily into the low-burning fire. "Which means there will be much Latin grammar for you to correct." I laughed.

For the space of time it takes to draw a breath, it seemed that Volmar would reach over and take my hand, but then he rose and went to add more wood to the brazier. Vaguely disappointed, I watched his silhouette outlined against the fire, solid in full maturity, then I turned my face to the darkening window. The last night of the year 1145 was fast approaching. The drizzle had changed back to snow, small and fast, like grains of white sand pelting from the sky. It was going to be a long winter, but eventually spring would come, and with it a new life for me.

Or an irrevocable defeat.

11

April 1146

"MY LATEST INFORMATION suggests that Donato Visconti's death exposed a web of conspiracy and treachery that reaches all the way to the imperial court. It also points to the participation of at least some of the rebellious Roman authorities that expelled Pope Eugenius from the city." Archbishop Heinrich of Mainz shook his head with more sadness than outrage. "The Holy Father has now taken up residence at Viterbo."

The archbishop was seated at the refectory's high table before a sumptuous supper of roasted venison and geese, peeled walnuts, cheese, sugared fruits, and spiced wine. He ate sparingly, reminding me of his predecessor. I was relieved to find that he seemed to follow in the footsteps of Archbishop Adalbert with his dignified carriage, modest attire, and sincere piety.

"He ordered an investigation after the letter from Abbot Kuno — may God rest his soul — had reached him." The archbishop nodded toward Helenger, who flanked him on his right. He had officially installed him as abbot earlier that day. "And although it did not prevent his exile, it found evidence that Donato had indeed been an imperial spy while holding various secular appointments at the court of the Archbishop of Milan." Heinrich shook his head again, presumably despairing of man's deceitful ways.

Grief was painted on all faces except Helenger's. His entire frame oozed sanctimonious outrage mixed with self-satisfaction. "The whole affair was suspicious from the beginning!" he exclaimed. I drew in a sharp breath at this blatant obfuscation, for he had been opposed to pursuing an investigation into Donato's murder.

But the archbishop could not know this. He continued, "My envoy brought a message in which the Holy Father says he is deeply grateful for the abbey's persistence in solving that crime."

Again, Helenger's was the only beaming face at the table, and a deepening frown on the archbishop's forehead suggested he had noticed it. "In particular, he declared himself impressed with the skill and determination with which Sister Hildegard had uncovered the clues and reasoned as to their meaning," he added pointedly, leaning forward to acknowledge me.

I reciprocated the gesture from my seat at the far end of the table, feeling a surge of hope. The archbishop's demeanor had been guarded so far, and it was hard to gauge how disposed he would be to grant my petition. Unlike Archbishop Adalbert, who had visited us frequently after his release from the imperial jail, Heinrich was not known for traveling widely, and this was his first visit to the abbey since he had ascended to the see almost four years before.

"What about Bishop Umberto's role in this unfortunate affair?" Helenger asked loudly. He was not going to allow anybody—especially me—to deflect attention from him.

"The bishop is no longer a papal emissary and has been relieved of his functions at Milan. He may well end up stripped of his title and sent to a monastery."

"Was he also a spy?!" Brother Aelred exclaimed, his mouth a perfectly round "o." He sat on the archbishop's other side. He was short, but loud and quick, and had a sycophantic streak that made him one of Helenger's favorites. As the circuitor—responsible for discipline among the monks, a duty he carried out with consummate skill and much enthusiasm—he was the top candidate for the newly vacant post of prior.

"I understand that no evidence has been found, but even if he was not a spy himself, he may still have had knowledge of his brother's activities," the archbishop replied. I recalled Umberto's vehement denial that the death had been anything but an accident—and, of course, his hasty departure. "Whatever the case may be, the Holy Father cannot risk having someone like that among his advisors."

"Naturally," Helenger hurried to agree. "Even the slightest suspicion of disloyalty toward the Church must be dealt with swiftly and without mercy." There was more than a touch of vengefulness in his voice.

"Father Abbot is right," Brother Aelred chimed in with a vigorous nod, which Helenger rewarded with a smile that was probably meant to be gracious but came out wry.

"At least Abbot Kuno had the courage to select for his deputy someone who challenged him," I whispered to Volmar, who was seated next to me.

The archbishop gave Helenger a measured, and—I thought—disapproving look. But it was lost on Helenger, which I noted with some satisfaction because it seemed to increase the archbishop's irritation. Already during the installment ceremony, he had taken a dim view of the new abbot's haughty attitude, for no matter how many times he repeated that abbacy was a post of ultimate service to be accepted with humility and not as a fulfillment of personal ambitions, Helenger's manner exuded a sense of triumph he did not even pretend to hide. As I recalled that uncomfortable ceremony, it pained me to see Helenger as the new face of St. Disibod.

As the conversation turned to other topics, I leaned toward Volmar again. "I fear hard times are in store for the abbey," I said ruefully, realizing that I had grown fond of the place in which I had spent thirty years. "God willing, we will relocate soon."

"I think the archbishop is irritated with Helenger." Volmar's observation struck me with its parallel to my own. "He may be open to your plea."

"That is my hope also," I said. Then I added, voicing a long-standing worry of mine, "but we are only women. Why would he risk antagonizing an abbot, even one like Helenger, to help *us*?"

"Because yours is not just any convent. You have a great deal of influence."

"But will it be enough?"

Volmar lowered his voice. "I have it on good authority that the archbishop has other reasons not to be friendly to Helenger." After Kuno's long-time envoy, Brother Bernardus, had died four years before, Volmar had undertaken missions to Mainz on the abbot's behalf, and he knew many officials at the episcopal court.

I leaned closer, my curiosity pricked.

"Apparently," he continued, "Archbishop Heinrich is at odds with some of the cathedral canons, a faction led by Canon Walter." He gave me a meaningful look.

"Helenger's nephew!"

"That's correct. He has set his sights on the post of provost, which the archbishop is trying to prevent."

"Why is that?"

"A family quarrel. The archbishop is descended from the Counts von Saarbrücken, who have been feuding with the von Schönbergs — Walter and Helenger's kin — for years."

"Over what?"

"That much I don't know," he admitted. "But if I were to guess, it would be land."

I contemplated this intelligence and the possibilities it presented. I was not entirely surprised — Abbot Kuno had often complained about the Mainz canons, calling them a "meddlesome lot," though never in Helenger's presence. I wanted to ask more, but Helenger's voice rose over the murmur of conversations, announcing that the supper was over.

After the archbishop and his attendants had left for the guest quarters, the monks filed out of the refectory with the efficiency and order born of hundreds of years of practice. As they vanished down the arcade, their footfalls on the flagstones fading by degrees, I crossed the garth toward the church.

The sound of a cloak rustling softly over the new grass stopped me. It was a chilly and moonless night, the only light coming from the refectory, where servants were clearing the tables, and from a few small torches in the brackets along the cloister walls. I peered through the shadows, but I was unable to distinguish the rank of the large man in clerical garb who walked toward me.

"I am sorry to startle you, Sister," he said as he came to a stop less than two paces away. "I am Deacon Turpin, sent by the archbishop to invite you to join him and Abbot Helenger at breakfast tomorrow."

My stomach fluttered with nervous excitement. For better or worse, everything would be settled soon. I took a deep breath. "Thank you, Deacon. Tell His Excellency I will be there."

The cleric inclined his head and turned back toward the guest quarters. The light from the refectory was fading as the servants went on extinguishing the candles, and I moved swiftly to the church and the surety of the perpetual altar lamp within, before it became completely dark.

The breakfast table at the abbot's house was set with dishes of thick porridge seasoned with cinnamon, sugar, and raisins; slices of white bread; spicy quince preserves; and pears baked in honey. Clearly, Helenger was determined to impress the archbishop, perhaps hoping that a satisfied palate would result in a more favorable ear for his argument. If so, he had miscalculated, for Heinrich took only a slice of bread and a few spoonfuls of porridge from around the rim of his bowl to avoid the sweet seasonings.

For a while, the conversation revolved around the mundane issues of the ongoing transition at the abbey, to which I listened with only one ear. Just as I started wondering if the archbishop was going to address my request or whether I would have to bring it up myself, Heinrich turned to me.

"Sister Hildegard, you will soon be receiving important news from Rome, or, more specifically, from Viterbo," he said. "His Holiness Pope Eugenius was much impressed by *Scivias*. My envoys tell me that he read it to his closest advisors and declared it sure to become a 'life-enriching perfume for many'." The archbishop smiled indulgently at the Holy Father's famous poetic predilections. "I am told that your name is on everybody's lips these days."

This matter was so far from my mind that I was momentarily at a loss for words. Across the table, Helenger's cheeks paled, giving him a ghostly look.

"I hoped His Holiness would look favorably on it," I managed finally, "but I never expected this kind of recognition. I am honored."

"It is well deserved. I read *Scivias* myself and found it to be a powerful testimony of our faith. Its wisdom will guide many toward God."

"That is what I aspire to, Your Excellency."

"But there is more," the archbishop added with a brief glance at Helenger that told me he enjoyed his reaction. "His Holiness wants to have your writings read at the synod, which will be held at Trier sometime next year. When that happens, your fame will increase manifold. You are already referred to as *Prophetissa Teutonica* around the papal court, according to my envoys' reports."

I was too stunned to answer immediately, which gave Helenger time to regain his wits. "*I* have not heard anything official, so I will refrain from commenting on this for now." I could see him struggle with the urge to lash out against the papal pronouncement, but he checked himself. "I believe that we are meeting here today to discuss a more pressing issue."

"Indeed we are." Archbishop Heinrich switched the topic smoothly, and his face assumed a neutral expression. "I received a letter in which Sister Hildegard asked for my support in her quest to dissolve the convent's ties with the abbey and to establish a new house. What is your view on this, Father Abbot?"

After Helenger repeated his objection, the archbishop turned to me. "Give me a good reason why I should defy the will of the abbot, Sister."

This was the moment for which I had waited so long, and I had rehearsed my speech thoroughly. "As Benedictines," I began, "our main vocation is spiritual, so that through our sacrifice and devotion we may facilitate the salvation of souls. But we also have an earthly duty to heal the sick, in accordance with The Rule set by our Order's founder. The need is great, as Your Excellency well knows, and we could do much more but for our size. Our dwelling is simply too small to accept more sisters, and there is no room to expand within the abbey, which was never intended to house a female community in the first place. A new location, without these constraints, would permit us to accept more novices, train them in the healing arts, and grow a large infirmary, open to all."

"The infirmary is large enough!" Helenger interjected.

"It could be much bigger and still full of patients," I countered. "Besides, you have limited our ability to provide vital medical care through the fees you have imposed for maternity calls."

"I did it because ever since you replaced Sister Jutta at the head of the convent, you stopped ceding your income to the abbey." No sooner had he said it than he realized his mistake.

I turned to the archbishop. "Father Abbot is punishing us for using our income as we see fit, which is our right under the charter. But he is doing this at the expense of women in need, which is against The Rule as well as Christian charity."

Heinrich frowned, but he did not say anything.

"This is only an excuse to break The Rule by disobeying your superior," Helenger tried his favorite defensive tactic, which was to attack. "For years, you have taken advantage of Abbot Kuno's indulgence to leave these precincts whenever you wished, and in doing so you perverted the nature of your establishment, which was anchorite at its inception. And to make matters worse, you allow the anchoresses to grow their hair long, wear robes of fine cloth, and go around bareheaded. It is all highly unseemly and distracts the monks from their holy work!" The veins on his sinewy neck were bulging dangerously, and his face was flushed with anger. "But try as I might to curb these excesses and return you to the state for which you were intended, you constantly dispute my authority!"

I was determined not to let the barrage of accusations unsettle me. "I respect your authority, Father Abbot," I replied calmly, "even if you have used it repeatedly against us. But we advocate for the sick and those least able to care for themselves" — I turned to the archbishop again — "and it is my responsibility to fight for the right to do our work without hindrance and harassment."

"Nobody is harassing you; that is a base aspersion! You want to do things your way, but the monastic hierarchy is strict, and you cannot ignore it. By being disobedient, you are breaking The Rule."

"I have faithfully kept all the vows I took."

"Is that so?" Helenger snickered, and I went cold. I knew exactly what he was alluding to. Since our trip to Sponheim the previous year, whenever Volmar and I found ourselves together in his presence, I would catch Helenger giving us long considering looks. But just as I steeled myself to fight this on an even baser level, the archbishop spoke up, visibly tired of our bickering.

"Would you reconsider your position if the fees were to be revoked?" he asked me.

I shook my head. "The fees were only the beginning. Since then, we have been banned from the library, and the carrel in the scriptorium that Abbot Kuno rented to us for years was taken away. No, Your Excellency, this persecution will not end until we are gone. We need your protection," I appealed, my desperation rising as I realized he wanted to find a compromise that would allow me stay at St. Disibod. "As God is my witness."

"Do not invoke God's name when you seek to vilify me and mislead the archbishop!" Helenger thundered.

But the archbishop had had enough. "You are fond of invoking The Rule" — he glared at him — "so let me remind you that it also exhorts the brethren not to presume to discuss their views heatedly."

Helenger opened his mouth to reply but thought better of it. The archbishop turned to me, his face still stern. "Have you given any thought to the practicalities of your plan? You would need a site on which to build, to begin with."

I told him about the Count von Stade's offer and listed the advantages of the location.

"I am familiar with Mount St. Rupert," the archbishop said, "but if my memory serves me, there is nothing there but a ruined chapel. Do you have sufficient funds to build a foundation from the ground up?"

I nodded confidently. To this, too, I had given much thought. "We have funds to start the construction, and the count has generously offered his men as builders, along with stone from his quarries at a discounted price. Over time, we will obtain new patronage and endowments, and manuscript work will provide additional income. Besides" — I looked straight at Helenger — "some of the lands the abbey currently benefits from were originally bequeathed to the convent, and they should be returned to us."

"Sister Jutta ceded them to the abbey," Helenger said firmly.

"Yet no documents have ever been drafted to formally sign these estates over. The abbey has been collecting rents for years that lawfully belong to us."

That was a blind guess because I did not have access to abbey rolls and had never discussed the matter with Jutta. But a flicker of apprehension in Helenger's eyes told me that I had hit the mark.

Before he could respond, the archbishop waved his hand as if to stress that our financial dealings were of no interest to him. "I have heard enough. I must take some time to consider it," he said. "I will give you my decision tomorrow before I depart."

One more day, then, I thought with a tinge of disappointment. Perhaps it was for the best; thoughtful judgments were always more likely to fall on the side of justice.

I spent another sleepless night, and each time the bell sounded for the nighttime offices, I was grateful for the distraction. By lauds, I was prepared for either outcome. Pope Eugenius's endorsement and the support of Bernard of Clairvaux would make it hard for Helenger to silence me if I were to remain at St. Disibod, miserable though my life would be. So when an abbey servant found me in the workshop reading Aurelius Celsus in the late morning and announced that the archbishop wished to see me, I was calm.

Heinrich's spare silhouette was outlined against the single window of his guest cell as he extended his hand, which I genuflected to kiss. When I rose, his face was grave.

"I decided to overrule Abbot Helenger's objection and allow your move," he said without a preamble. "You also have my leave to travel to the new site if you wish to prepare for the relocation in person."

The relief that flooded me made me so light-headed I had to steady myself against the back of a chair. "I am grateful, Excellency." I moved to kiss his ring again, but he motioned me to remain standing.

"I have already informed the abbot, and he was not happy." The archbishop paused as if considering whether he should say more. Then he added, "I have seen his attitude toward the convent—and your work—and I would be neglectful in my duties if I stood in the way of your freedom from his interference."

"With God's help, you have made the right decision," I assured him fervently. "Abbot Helenger has disliked me since the day I first set foot within these precincts as a young child. I do not know why"—I have always been puzzled by it—"for I have always sought to get along with him."

The archbishop hesitated again, and I feared I had overstepped the boundaries in confiding this to him. "Forgive me—"

He waved his hand. "I had not met Helenger in person before this visit," he said quietly, "but we are distantly related as one of my sisters married a cousin of his mother's." He turned to the window. "I don't know how much you know about his family . . ."

"I know nothing about his life before I arrived here."

"He was born the only son of Baron von Schönenberg, who had a castle in the Hunsrück, not far from the Rhine," Heinrich spoke again. "His father had died when he was still in the cradle, and he and his older sister were raised by his mother. Some said she was a witch, others that she was mad, but what is indisputable is that she stayed in mourning for her husband for the rest of her life, always dressed in black and shunning the society of others. She transferred her entire affection onto her son, and those who—on rare occasions—visited Schönenberg spoke of a boy who was forbidden from playing with his peers, completely under his mother's spell, and lonely after his sister married and moved to the March of Nordgau.

"The baroness was particularly worried that he would fall in love; it was rumored that she had banned women from the castle, so that all servants—even the cooks—were male." I listened, riveted, for his words began to illuminate so many things. "On reaching manhood," Heinrich went on, "Helenger left the castle and took the cowl. Nobody knew if that was against or in accordance with his mother's wishes, but the old woman died soon thereafter. That line of the family is now effectively extinct, as Helenger's sister's only son also entered a consecrated state, and the castle stands empty, falling into ruin."

Through the window of the cell, the archbishop gazed down at the cloister garth, where the first grass of the season was coming up in a lively green blanket. A lay brother was cleaning out the marble fountain at one end of the quadrangle, removing last autumn's leaves from its dry basin. In a few days it would trickle with water again.

I mulled over this strange story and found myself feeling pity for this unfortunate man when I recalled my own childhood, which, although cut short, had been a happy one by comparison. "It is hard to emerge unscathed from such an upbringing," I said at length. "Misuse often begets misuse, and as much as it may seem justified to blame those who suffered ill treatment for injuries they later cause others, is it always entirely their fault?"

"The depths of the human soul are inscrutable," the archbishop said philosophically. "But be that as it may, I cannot allow the convent and its good works to be affected by one man's whim."

I felt a new respect for his principled stance; he was overruling Helenger for a reason better than an old family rivalry. "I will write to the Count von Stade and start planning the transition," I said. "There is much work to be done."

"Keep me apprised of your progress."

I bowed my head. "Thank you again for all you and Archbishop Adalbert have done for me. I will do all I can to ensure that the new foundation is worthy of the province under your authority."

I was already at the door when the archbishop's voice reached me again. "Oh, and one more thing."

I turned around.

"The abbot has refused his permission for Brother Volmar to join you at St. Rupert. He says his skills as a scribe are too valuable to the abbey. I am sorry," he added when he saw my face fall. "I hear you work closely together."

All I could do was nod. There was nothing to say. It had been a quiet hope of mine that Volmar would be able to move with us; instead, we would be parted again, this time for good. Yet another sacrifice I would have to make.

"But rest assured that I will send you an excellent priest from Mainz to see to your community's spiritual well-being," the archbishop said, believing, no doubt, that was enough to comfort me.

12

October 1146

THE CONVOY OF four wagons piled with our pallets, sewing implements, medicine jars, and boxes of dry herbs rolled out of Disibodenberg's gate. The townsfolk had lined the streets to bid us farewell on a day that was emotional for everyone, save the monks, whom Abbot Helenger had barred from coming out of the cloister to see us off. Instead, only the stable grooms and the servants—looking somber, some even wiping their eyes furtively—had come out and stood silently as we rode out of the abbey.

Helenger had refused my request for a private meeting the night before, but he approached me before I climbed onto the wagon and said, softly and with a thin smile to give the impression that he was bidding me goodbye, "Archbishop Heinrich may favor you, but it is the canons who oversee the day-to-day affairs of the archdiocese when he is busy serving as the imperial chancellor." He paused to give me time to absorb his meaning. He added, in a voice that swelled with venom, "My nephew serves as a canon in the cathedral chapter. Know that I have warned him about your excesses. He will keep an eye on you."

If I had any remaining doubts about the move, his words dispelled them. This was the best decision for me and the women who had put their trust in me, although I regretted leaving the infirmary behind. Brother Fabian, who had been appointed physician, was competent enough, but there was a timidity in his nature that all but guaranteed he would be a malleable tool in Helenger's hands. From now on, the dispensation of medical care at St. Disibod would be dictated by its abbot.

I turned for one last look at the place I had called home for most of my life. Disibodenberg had grown substantially since I was a child, with many new dwellings erected outside the town gates. The new section was not walled, and the old wall had never been reinforced or rebuilt in stone. It was doubtful that would happen under Helenger's leadership, and it worried me because I had friends and patients living within those walls — and Volmar, of course. He had promised to write to me every week, but our separation was already a dull ache I knew I must carry with me every day from now on, for I did not expect to ever see him again.

But at least I had my books and manuscripts with me. The wagon in which I rode held a chest with my medical guidebook I intended to use as a training manual at St. Rupert, as well as copies of medical treatises by Dioscorides, Hippocrates, Galen, Aurelius Celsus, and Avicenna. I had also packed Donatus's *Minor Grammar*, Cato's *Moral Sayings*, Boethius's *On the Consolations of Philosophy* and his treatise on music, and, of course, Abbot Bernard's *De gratia*, which Volmar had brought for me from France. It was the only tangible link to him I had left, just as the lump of salt was my sole reminder of my mother. I clutched the box in my hand throughout the journey, and it gave me comfort every time I opened the lid to gaze at the solid, unchanging shape that would stay with me as I embarked on a new life, my own woman at last.

The road ahead was bathed in the soft sunshine of a mild autumn day that smelled pleasantly of ripe earth and dry leaves. Escorted by several men-at-arms sent by the Archbishop of Mainz, we reached the bridge across the Nahe, its waters gleaming silver, and turned first east then north to follow its winding course toward the Rhine. As the spire of the parish church of Disibodenberg vanished behind the bulk of Mount St. Disibod, I contemplated the six women in the wagon ahead. They were a devoted lot and had a strong desire for a life of service, for I had made careful choices when admitting them.

Until perhaps the last time around. In truth, I was a little worried about the novice who had joined us just a few weeks before, a girl named Judith. She was devout and well-born — a daughter of a count, like Jutta had been — and although she was making an honest effort to adjust to the austerity of the convent, it was clear that she missed the comforts of her former life. And who knew what we would find at St. Rupert? The Count von Stade, true to his word, had restored the old farm buildings for our temporary use. I did not doubt they would be sufficient for us, but even so, I needed to keep an eye on Judith.

But the others — the sweet-singing Gertrude, the wise and dependable Elfrid, the quiet Burgundia, the faithful Griselda, and the beautiful Ricardis — were all brimming with excitement, and the chatter of their voices was a welcome accompaniment to the squeaky turning of the wheels. Perhaps, like me, they felt the exhilarating sense of freedom, of spirits — and minds — finally unfettered. So many things were possible now. We may have left the familiar life behind, but a new and better one awaited us at the end of this road.

Despite the archbishop's permission, I had not visited Mount St. Rupert before, but through letters exchanged with him and the count, I knew that a Father Baldwin had already taken up residence there. One of the farm buildings was to be converted into an infirmary, and work on the stone cloister would start next spring. I had cause to hope that our permanent quarters would take no more than two or three years to complete, for when the news had spread that we were moving, generous gifts had poured in. Now I had sufficient funds to build a scriptorium, a large infirmary, and a guesthouse. I also wanted to have my own bakery and brewery within the precinct.

But the crowning glory would be a church, and that would require additional, and substantial, resources. There would be new novices' endowments to cover some of the cost, but I had one more battle left with Helenger, who had kept his promise and refused to relinquish control over the lands Jutta had given to the monks to administer. But I would not give up. As soon as we were settled, I would find a way to recover what was ours, even if I had to appeal to King Konrad himself. It was more than a question of money and fairness; the new foundation would not receive its own charter until all legal disputes were settled. Otherwise, it would remain St. Disibod's daughter house, formally under its authority. That, above all, I wanted to avoid.

Mount St. Rupert, accessible by a path from the village of Weiler, was bisected by a stream that flowed down its slope to merge with one of the Nahe's tributaries. Having been enthusiastically greeted by the locals, who had come out in force from the surrounding villages, we arrived at our destination in the afternoon of the second day to find our accommodations ready for us. The count's men had raised a stone wall around the perimeter, higher on the side of the approach from the village, and lower on the other, where the slope was steeper. As the sisters took possession of our quarters, I surveyed the property in the company of Rego, my new steward. He lived in Weiler and was a son of Egbert, the man I had treated at St. Disibod three years before after he had lost two fingers to a scythe.

"This spring is a source of the purest water, and it eliminates the need to carry it all the way up from the well in the village," Rego said as we crossed the crystalline stream that murmured softly as it moved over its shallow stony bed.

I could see the advantages of the place right away. The stream created a natural demarcation line, dividing the property into a bigger section where the farm buildings stood — and where the cloister and church would be erected one day — and a smaller plot on the eastern side that was a perfect location for a workshop and an herb garden.

At the far end, the wall was only waist high. As we reached it, I was greeted by a breathtaking view of the valley of the Rhine. I had never seen the great river, and I was left speechless by its breadth and the dark coloring that spoke of a depth and power hidden beneath its calm surface. Compared to it, the Glan near St. Disibod was but a brook.

Rego smiled when he saw the effect it had on me. "The count's men have prepared a beautiful and safe place for you, Sister," he said. He was slightly built, but there was a solidity to him that spoke of a natural strength. His long, handsome face was framed by curly dark hair and a neatly trimmed beard. I had liked him immediately for the serious and honest look in his hazel eyes, which reminded me of Volmar's. In fact, he resembled him somewhat, which I found both pleasing and disconcerting. "They built the wall from the stone left over after the old church had been taken down. That is why it is lower here — they ran out of the material. But the steepness of the slope" — he pointed toward the valley below — "makes it impractical as a point of attack."

Impractical or not, I promised myself that I would build the wall up so it provided a solid defense all around our new home. Until then, I would enjoy the view of the Rhine and the Nahe, now gleaming redly below us in the last of the day's sunshine.

———◆◆———

Armed with provisions of food and fuel, we settled in and prepared to wait out the winter. I still loved the season, which I thought of as being just as full of life as spring or summer, only in a different way. Winter's slumber was the restorative part of the cycle of life, nature's well-deserved rest before the blossoming and ripening recommenced. But that year, I was counting the interminable days until its end.

At least Volmar kept his promise to write regularly. Once every week or two, I would withdraw to my private chamber to read a letter in which he would apprise me of Helenger's increasingly tyrannical governorship of St. Disibod or of Brother Fabian's surprisingly deft management of the infirmary. In turn, I would describe the beauty of the landscape I observed from my perch. On some mornings, wrapped tightly in a woolen cloak against the biting gales, I would go to the low wall and gaze over the valley as if I were seeing it for the first time. Only when my fingers began to stiffen with cold would I return inside to warm myself at the fire, then go to my chamber to tell Volmar about the dazzling colors of autumn leaves adorning the Hunsrück; the steely majesty of the Rhine on full display when the trees along its banks stood bare; or the pristine quietude of the valley once snow had covered its slopes.

There was sad news too, when my fears regarding Judith came true. Just after the New Year, her parents wrote to me to inform me that they were moving her to Andernach. They said they had selected the convent of St. Disibod for its connection to Jutta von Sponheim and did not want their daughter's dowry funding a new establishment far from the site of the former *magistra*'s burial. I released her, disappointed but telling myself that I had probably avoided more trouble in the future.

Judith's departure inspired me to compose a hymn in praise of a local saint named Ursula. According to a legend, she had been noblewoman from Cologne who had gone on a pilgrimage to Rome with her handmaidens. During their absence, their native land was overrun by the Magyars, and the women were killed upon their return.

> *Tunc diabolus*
> *Membra sua invasit,*
> *que nobilissimos mores*
> *in corporibus istis*
> *occiderunt*

> Then the devil entered
> The invaders' bodies
> and they slaughtered the maidens.

> *Et hoc in alto voce omnia elementa audierunt*
> *et ante thronum Dei dixerunt:*
> *'Rubicundus sanguis innocentis agni*
> *effuses est.'*

> And the Elements heard their voices on high
> and before the throne of God they said:
> 'The crimson blood of the innocent lamb
> is spilled.'

When I was writing these lines in a letter to Volmar on a February afternoon, the sounds of the sisters practicing the hymn floated in from the chapel on the clear winter air. By a strange turn of events, that piece — or, more precisely, what it led me to compose next — would have profound consequences for the Abbey of St. Disibod only a few years later. But I did not know that yet. As I pondered the contrast between Ursula's sacrifice and Judith's abandonment of our fledgling foundation for the comfort of an established house, an idea dawned on me to write a story to the fortification of all those who struggled with life's difficult choices.

But it needed a new form. The story I wanted to tell was more complex, the message more nuanced than a short hymn could convey because deep down, I sympathized with Judith's decision, as I did with all human weakness. The sisters finished the hymn, the faint echo of their voices still suspended in the air, when I decided to write a play and set it to music. It had been done before; there was the famed *Visitatio Sepulchri* performed during Easter celebrations at the Abbey of St. Gall, and Hrotsvitha's martyr plays, of course.

When my play was done, I mused, we would rehearse it and put it on for the people from the surrounding villages. I hoped it would help smooth the transition for the sisters who had remained with me.

I had no idea that it would do much more than that.

13

May 1147

OUR FIRST SPRING on the Rupertsberg was warm and sunny, with just enough rain to yield an abundance of herbs, but not so much that it would delay the breaking of the ground for the new foundation. The work proceeded apace, with a good number of villagers joining the count's builders whenever they were not working in the fields.

By the end of May, the herb garden was in full bloom, and I spent much of my time weeding, trimming, and watering. During the hottest hour of each day, the kitchen distributed refreshments to the builders. For a while, the men's shouting, the noise of wood planks being hewn and nailed, tools striking stone, the clang of metal and hissing fire from the forge subsided, leaving my garden an oasis of peace and quiet.

Taking a break from gardening, I sat on the bench with my back against the wall of my new workshop, enjoying the timber-scented shade, when a warm, living shape wriggled its way under my hand. I smiled before looking down at the white cat I had received as a gift from a village woman. Gaius Plinius had quickly accepted me as his mistress, and had in turn won my heart by his fascination with my books, which lined the shelf above the workshop table. He spent hours slumbering next to the books, but whenever I appeared, he would wake up, stretch, and extend his right paw to run it gingerly along the spines, as if inviting me to pick a volume. When I did, he would sit still like a statue, staring at me with his mesmerizing green eyes for as long as I remained reading.

I leaned over and whispered as I scratched behind his ears, eliciting a contented purr. The planks of the little bridge over the stream squeaked, and soft footsteps padded along the grass. I looked up to find Ricardis and was flooded with pleasure at the sight of her loose white robe and her unbound hair shining richly in the sun as it cascaded in black coils over her shoulders. Freed from the constraints imposed by the monks, I allowed the women to adorn themselves, and Ricardis chose to wear a thin golden circlet with a cross in the front that rested on her smooth forehead. She was breathtaking to behold, even more radiant than before. Not for the first time, I reflected on what a waste it would have been if Ricardis had married and faded before her time instead of shining as a constant reminder of God's creative energy, the purest *viriditas*.

But Ricardis was not the only one thus transformed; all of the women had cast off their drab habits and wore white or cream-colored robes. They walked with a new spring in their step, entombed no longer.

"This has to be the most peaceful place I have ever seen." Ricardis sat down next to me.

"Wait until the hedgerows grow taller." I indicated the line of short bushes planted along the stream and around the back of the garden. "It will become the refuge I have always wanted."

Ricardis had a small package with her. "This arrived for you," she said mysteriously, "but I will not tell you who sent it. It's a surprise." She could barely suppress her excitement.

I took it, intrigued. It had a telltale rectangular shape. "I think it's a book." I started unwrapping it, my cheeks warm. I was half hoping it was from Volmar.

I lifted the last fold of the oilcloth, opened the soft brown leather cover, and gasped at the beautifully illuminated title page of *Commentary on Hospitals and Treatments*. Both Ricardis and I had seen many finely decorated manuscripts, but the colors of this one were so dazzlingly vivid, so sparkling we had to squint.

"By Anna Komnene, Porphyrogenita of the Byzantine Empire," Ricardis read the author's name under the title.

"She is the aunt of the eastern emperor," I said. I smiled wistfully. "I first heard of her from Brother Wigbert soon after I started working as his assistant. Later, pilgrims who had traveled to the Holy Land told me of her reputation for being deeply learned." I turned the first page and found a letter with the seal of Stade.

"I told my uncle how much you love to read." Ricardis beamed. "He has quite a collection of books and always puts in orders for new copies at Metz and Trier. I hope I did not presume too much in sharing with him the pleasures of our life?"

"Of course not." I broke the seal and read the latter. After the customary greetings, the count wrote:

> The Commentary *was authored by Her Highness Anna Komnene, the eldest daughter of the late Byzantine Emperor Alexios. She is, by all accounts, an extraordinary woman, having been educated in literature, rhetoric, arithmetic, astronomy, and – of perhaps greatest interest to you – medicine. As a well-regarded physician and overseer of a hospital at Constantinople founded by her imperial father, she wrote this volume*

to serve as a manual for medical practitioners. She is said to be an authority on gout, from which her father had suffered, and for which she treated him with great success. This is one of only a handful of Latin translations, and I am offering it to the Convent of St. Rupert so its lessons may find proper application under your guidance.

I folded the letter. "This is an exceptional gift." I turned the pages to where the text began. Anna started her book with a description of the large hospital where she worked, a city hospital unattached to a monastic house, right where the masses of the poor and the needy lived. What I strange idea, I marveled as I read, and yet how practical!

"Sister?" Ricardis's voice reached me.

I looked up. "I am sorry, were you saying something?"

"I asked if women are free to become physicians in the Eastern empire."

"I don't know—Anna is a princess, so she is in a position to bend the rules," I replied distractedly. Normally, I loved talking to Ricardis, but a new book always made me shun the company of others in order to immerse myself in it. "I must learn about her methods as soon as possible," I added apologetically.

Ricardis rose and smiled her glittering smile, full of indulgence. I gazed after her for a moment as she walked back toward our quarters, past the stone foundations of the cloister, then I turned back to the book. Next to me, Gaius Plinius sat motionless on the bench, the tip of his white tail swaying gently. We both knew one thing—there would be no more gardening that day.

The fair weather ended halfway through the month of July, when heavy rains and ferocious winds visited the region. The construction slowed, and there were days, sometimes several in a row, when no work could be done at all. By August, the peasants' faces grew grim at the prospect of a failed harvest, and village churches overflowed with folk entreating God to spare their livelihoods. Up on the hill, we gathered in our little chapel each day to hear Father Baldwin say Mass in that intention, often to the sound of rain lashing at the timber walls and falling in sheets from the roof.

It was during one such service — when everyone was feeling hopeful because it had not rained for two days, although dark clouds were still tumbling across the sky — that there was a burst of commotion outside. We went out and were greeted by the sight of an agitated crowd gathered at the low wall. Some of my infirmary patients were among it, lamenting loudly. A woman was holding her arms out to the sky in desperate supplication, while others were tearing at their clothes and scratching their faces.

"What is happening?" I rushed toward them with Father Baldwin in tow. He was a thin old man with a birdlike face, taciturn by nature but passionately devoted to his vocation. He was always ready to offer spiritual comfort, if not much in the way of practical advice.

"The river has burst its banks and the fields are becoming flooded!" It was Rego who had brought the news, and he was still breathless. His wife, Ermina, and their two little daughters had come with him and stood nearby, wide-eyed, holding small bundles of their belongings. "People are fleeing the low-lying villages, trying to salvage what they can of their possessions. Many beasts have already been lost."

"We have come to the End of Days!" a woman wailed. "It is God's Judgment!"

Another one fainted and had to be carried back inside the infirmary. Anguish was painted on all faces, and everyone looked at me as if I had the power to stem the tide of death and destruction.

"Do not despair," I said. "Such disasters have occurred since time immemorial without the world ending. We will survive and replant our fields, regrow our vineyards, and rebuild our homes."

But my words failed to dispel the look of doom among the crowd.

"I will send word to the archbishop," I added. "He will not leave his people without relief in the face of a calamity like this." I tried to sound convincing, although I had no way of knowing the scale of the flood, whether it also affected Mainz, and whether the diocese had the means to provide succor.

"Yes, the archbishop . . . God bless him . . . he will help us . . . he won't let us die!" Voices rose from all sides, grasping at every shred of hope.

I met Father Baldwin's eyes and saw that despite his habitual trust in Providence, there was a flicker of worry in them. Still, he went on, making the sign of the cross on the foreheads eagerly turned to him. "Remember the words of the prophet, who says *'Lord, you have been a refuge for the poor, a refuge for the needy in their distress, and a shelter from the storm'*."

They crossed themselves repeatedly, kneeling on the muddy ground, and the old priest added, "The apostle tells us of how Christ's disciples went to him in the midst of a fearsome storm and woke him, saying, 'Master, Master, we are going to drown!', and Christ rebuked the waters, and the storm subsided."

Gradually they calmed, desperation giving way to a quiet hope, or perhaps an equally quiet resignation. They began to return to the infirmary or head down to the villages to see what had become of their homes.

I turned to my steward. "How bad is it, Rego?"

"It is bad in the valley. Homes have been carried away by the waters and crops destroyed." He added grimly, "Without help, we will be looking hunger in the face this winter."

"I will write to our patrons. I hear it has not rained as much in the Palatinate."

We walked past the herb garden, whose ruined plants lay soggy and flat on the ground. There would be a shortage of medicine too. "I am glad your family is safe," I said, trying to find a bright spot amid this unfolding cataclysm.

"Our house is high enough on the southern side of St. Rupert that we have been spared the immediate devastation. We will go back as soon as waters stop rising so those who have no place to go can seek refuge here."

When we came to the wall, we were greeted by a change in the landscape that I would scarcely have thought possible the day before. Then, it had been patterned with fields of wheat and rye, large squares of pasture land, and ripening vineyards on its slopes. Now the fields were gone, covered by the turbid waters of the Rhine, so high I thought I could see its grim swirls. The river had swallowed the land and come all the way up to the forest.

I gazed at the desolation for a long while. "No wonder people think it's the end of the world."

Rego scoffed. "The end of the world!" He shook his head fiercely, and there was bitterness in his voice. "Though I am a faithful Christian, I cannot help but notice that some disasters are brought about by forces that are very much of earthly origin."

"What do you think has caused this flood?"

"The cutting of the trees along the river," he replied hotly. "My grandsire was a forester on the diocese lands. He used to say that when he was a young lad, all these fields were covered with oak, beech, and pine. In those days, floods were rare, and when they came they were small. But now" — he swept an arm toward the destruction below, passionate anger rising in his voice — "all that forest is gone to make way for tillage and pasture. There is nothing to hold the river within its banks anymore. And the towns up and down the Rhine are growing too; when I was a boy, all of Rüdesheim fit within its ancient walls, but now it is twice as large. Most of the new buildings are outside the walls, and the forest around it has been cut as far as the eye can see."

He turned to me with an air of defiance, perhaps expecting a reprimand and readying himself to defend his position. But I knew he was right. "Water is a basic element of creation, alongside air, fire, and earth. God designed these elements to exist in harmony with one another. So it cannot be that wild beasts obey God's commandments while we defy them, because it is then that the elements cry their complaints and raise their voices in outrage."

Rego's eyes widened. "I could not have said it better, Sister." Then he added, his tone wondering, "How strange that a Benedictine should understand the order of nature better than the men who live in the world and work the land every day."

I smiled ruefully. I was aware that many people considered monastics as being solely concerned with matters of the afterlife. "Sometimes," I said, "being too close to a problem makes it harder to see its full scope."

14

August 1147

T HE FLOOD WATERS receded to reveal a land destroyed,
and its tenants fled with whatever belongings they had
managed to salvage. Those who stayed were soon visited by
yet another scourge, for after the rains, the summer returned
hot and sunny, causing animal carcasses to putrefy in the
fields, filling the air with foul odors.

People began to come down with painful stomach
cramps and chills, accompanied by watery discharge of
blood and mucus pouring out of their bowels. Many of the
stronger ones recovered, but the death toll was high among
children and the elderly, who weakened quickly under the
strain of the fever and the purging.

The infirmary remained half-empty as most of the suf-
ferers were unable to drag themselves up the hill, so I left
Elfrid in charge and went down to the villages with what

few medicines I had after the rain had destroyed my herbs. I visited the homes of the afflicted, bathed their foreheads, and instructed their caregivers to make them drink beer — or wine if they could afford it — but not well water. Many wells had been flooded, and their contents had turned muddy brown. It was a warning I made sure was carried throughout the countryside, for Hippocrates had written extensively about the dangers of stagnant water and its link to diseases of the stomach.

My steward's family remained healthy, as I noted with relief every evening walking back up the hill. Rego worked from dawn to dusk, carrying water from our spring on the Rupertberg so it could be distributed among the peasants for washing and brewing beer. His two little girls stayed up longer those days, often playing outside as the day was fading; one time I asked them why they were not in bed yet, and they said they were waiting for their papa to return home.

Then came the day when Elfrid sent a message that Rego had not shown up to collect spring water; I knew immediately that something was wrong. As soon as I was I was able to, I went to his house.

His wife opened the door, pale and tired-looking. "The little ones are sick, Sister, and fast getting worse." Anxiety colored her voice.

In a corner of the only room of the house, the children lay on a soiled pallet. "The bloody flux comes so frequently it is becoming impossible to clean it up," Ermina explained, wringing her hands. Rego was sitting on a stool by the bed and acknowledged me with a silent nod. He was hollow-eyed and grim. Having spent much time among the sick lately, he knew the danger in which his daughters had found themselves.

I touched their foreheads. They were both hot, and their lips were parched. I reached for the cup on the nearby table, and before I could ask the obvious question, Rego assured me in a quiet voice, "It is from the spring."

I was puzzled. If they had not been drinking well water, where had the illness come from? Then a thought struck me. "Where is their favorite place to play?" I asked.

"Sometimes they play out front," his wife said, "but they love the backyard best." She pointed toward the window that gave onto it. I looked through it to see a ruined vegetable plot and a well behind it. Half of the yard was covered by knee-deep puddles of what must have been receding flood water.

Evidently, it was not sufficient to just refrain from drinking it; even wading or splashing in that foul water was unhealthy. It was a favorite pastime of many peasant children, which would explain the high mortality among them. "The ill humor from the water must have other ways of getting into the body." I turned back to Rego's girls. Both were awake now, their eyes shining with fever. The younger one appeared sicker; her eyelids were half-closed, she was breathing with difficulty, and seemed scarcely aware of her surroundings. "Perhaps through cuts on their arms and legs." Like most children, the two had limbs covered with them.

"Will they live?" Ermina's lips trembled.

"I don't know," I said honestly. "But it is important that they drink plenty — spring water or watered-down beer. Otherwise, they will weaken quickly."

The elder child was racked with convulsions, and she threw up a small quantity of yellow mucus. I cleaned her up with a cloth and took out a small sack of dried yarrow and the remaining quantity of rue from my scrip. "Pour boiling water over these. Use the yarrow to bathe their foreheads to help reduce the fever, and give them the rue to drink to help expel the noxious humors from their bowels," I instructed Ermina.

She took the herbs, then her face flushed. "It is those wretched lepers, isn't it?" Her voice screeched at the edge of hysteria. "They poisoned our wells after the flood so we would suffer even more."

"No." I put my hand on her arm to calm her as I tried not to sound exasperated. It was a common allegation, and baseless, as far as I could see. "Those poor souls are as much victims of this disease as everyone else—even more, perhaps." The unfortunates, who wandered the countryside in rags that ill-concealed the ravages of their infection, were shunned and often blamed for disasters like this. Yet, poorly fed and homeless as they were, they had less strength to fight off the flux than most, and few were likely to survive it. I had wanted to build a leper house in the woods near St. Rupert before the flood, and I vowed to do it as soon as the situation returned to normal, for the ranks of those touched by leprosy would soon be replenished.

But there was no time to explain that to the stricken woman. "Keep bringing fresh water from the spring," I reminded Rego as she turned to the stove. "Do not let it stay in the bucket for too long, otherwise it, too, will become corrupted. Crops and dead animals are rotting in this heat, and that is what poisons the air and the water," I added loudly, so Ermina could hear me.

Despite our efforts, Rego's younger daughter died two days later. The elder one began to improve soon after that. Over the next few weeks, the plague abated, and we were saved from starvation by shipments of grain from Mainz, and gifts of root vegetables, salted meat, and live chickens our patrons sent us that I shared with the villagers.

At the end of November, the builders covered the foundations with turf to protect the mortar from frost and departed for the season. It was only then I could finish the play, more eager than ever to take the sisters' minds off the events of that terrible summer. I even enlisted the secret help of Gertrude—whom I officially made chantress, in charge of musical training and singing during services—to refine the manuscript.

"A play? Set to music?" Burgundia's eyes widened in amazement when I presented it at a chapter meeting that we held in a small chamber, furnished only with a rough-hewn table and a few chairs.

"Yes. A composition that will help us celebrate a new beginning and the grace of God's redemption."

"What is it about?"

"A battle between the Virtues and the Devil over the Soul that has succumbed to worldly temptations," I explained. "I want us to perform it for our own edification and that of our neighbors in these turbulent times."

There was a silence. "Is it a mystery play?" Burgundia asked uncertainly.

I shook my head. Plays were supposed to commemorate Christ's birth or crucifixion, or tell the lives of saints. But this was not that kind of story. "It is different," I admitted. "New."

"New?" Now there was outright worry not just on Burgundia's face, but also on Griselda's and even Elfrid's.

I sighed inwardly. "It is new, but that doesn't mean it is wrong. Last year, we moved here" — I made a sweeping gesture encompassing our makeshift chapter house as well as the rising foundation — "and we are happier and enjoy more freedom despite the privations." Heads nodded again, this time with more conviction. "We could not have done this if we had been afraid of trying new things. Let us not be afraid now!"

Ricardis beamed at me. "I think this is very exciting. It will be fresh and interesting, people will talk about it far and wide, and you will become even more famous."

"Thank you," I said, more than a little flattered, although fame was not what I was after. It was what we needed right then — a message of hope and a means of distraction from the grim reality of death, the failed harvest, and the coming winter months. "I hope that you will all see the value of doing this for ourselves and the community."

I reached for the psaltery on the table and handed it to Gertrude. She played a passage from the opening chorus as the sisters listened intently. I could sense their interest rising.

"It is titled *Ordo Virtutum*," I said when she had finished. "The Rite of the Virtues."

A gaggle of excited voices rose up, eyes glittering. Their earlier concerns forgotten, they began speaking all at the same time.

"Are we all going to perform in it?"

"Where will the stage be?"

"What about costumes?"

"I can sew the robes!"

Laughing, I raised my hand to restore order. "I will answer your questions, but Sister Gertrude and I will read it out to you first." I passed a copy of the text to them. "If you place yourselves in a semicircle, you will be able to follow along."

They rearranged the chairs, and a moment later they were listening to the opening chorus of Patriarchs and Prophets; the parade of Souls from which the adventurous one splits; and the Virtues praising the attributes they embody as the errant Soul is lured away to enjoy the pleasures of the world. Eventually, the Soul returns penitent to seek the Virtues' help while the Devil taunts them. Encouraged by the Virtues, the Soul resists the Devil, who is then bound with his own chains and rendered helpless by the Virtues' triumph.

"This is marvelous!" Ricardis exclaimed again when we had finished.

"But does it have to be sung?" Elfrid looked worried, for she was not very musical.

"The words inform the mind, but music nourishes the spirit," I said. "The harmony of sound is a sign of the divine." Seeing Elfrid's face fall, I added, "Of course if you prefer not to sing individually, you can be in the chorus of Prophets or be one of the Souls."

"There aren't enough of us to fill all the parts," Griselda pointed out practically.

"I will invite lay people to join us to make up the chorus and the parade," I said. "Some of the village women have beautiful singing voices."

"So who will perform which role?" Ricardis asked, and I knew that she wanted the most prominent one. For a moment, I was tempted to make her the Queen of the Virtues, but Gertrude was more senior and had helped me with the score. I had to be fair.

"Sister Gertrude be will Humility," I said. Ricardis's face darkened, though she quickly recomposed herself. "The role of Chastity will be played by Sister Burgundia, and Obedience by Sister Griselda."

There was one more solo role. "Sister Ricardis will be the Soul."

She smiled graciously. I hoped she was satisfied, for it was a complex and challenging part.

Burgundia exclaimed, "But what about the Devil?! It is a part for a man."

I hesitated. "I have been thinking perhaps Father Baldwin . . ." Even as I said it, I knew it was not a good idea. It was hard to imagine a less convincing Devil than our good-natured priest. Besides, he was so diminutive that the Virtues—which the Devil tries to intimidate—would tower over him. Clearly, I was not the only one who had that image before her eyes, for the sisters were already giggling into their sleeves.

"I suppose Father Baldwin is not going to work," I conceded. "Sister Elfrid, maybe you will take it on? The Devil's part is unsung," I added by way of encouragement.

"Why not?" Elfrid raised her chin in mock defiance. "He has to shout a lot, and heaven knows I had plenty of practice when my husband was alive."

We were still laughing when the door in the back of the room opened with a creak of the wood. I was the first to see the figure that stepped in, and I must have paled because the women fell silent and turned to follow my gaze. For a moment, they were quiet, then cries of surprise and joy filled the room when they recognized the newcomer.

"No doubt Sister Elfrid has powerful lungs, but I am a more convincing man," Volmar said, putting his satchel on the floor. "If you wish, I will take on the role."

I stared at him silently, not trusting myself to speak, but we both knew the answer.

I found what I needed.

15

January 1148

I FOLDED THE parchment sheet and tossed it impatiently to the side of my desk. "Draft a response to this application," I said to Ricardis, who had spent the morning helping me go through my voluminous correspondence. "We are not accepting children as oblates at St. Rupert." It never failed to irritate me when parents or guardians made such petitions, tithe or not.

Across the desk in my little parlor, Volmar narrowed his eyes, which accentuated the creases in their corners. He had grown grayer at the temples in the year and a half since we had last seen each other, but he was as limber and energetic as ever. In fact, although he had left St. Disibod in the proper monkish fashion — that is, riding a mule — he had traded the beast for a horse at the first opportunity. It was now stabled across the courtyard, and he rode it every day for exercise.

"As you wish." Ricardis smiled brightly, collecting a pile of letters, each with an instruction on how to respond. "I will have it ready for your signature tomorrow, so you can take your time responding to Sister Elisabeth." Then she was gone, Volmar's gaze, under furrowed brows, following her to the door. Clearly, the absence had not softened his dislike.

"A young woman from the convent at Schönau has written to me complaining that she has been maligned by some in the Church because she dared to speak about things that God has seen fit to reveal to her," I said. "But although Elisabeth sought only to make people aware of the consequences of their sins, as those whose proper job it is to do so — priests and monks — have long neglected their duties, she now stands accused of presuming to prophesy about the Day of Judgement, which she claims she certainly does not." Then I added, not without a certain pride, "She is asking me for advice on how to handle such unjust treatment."

"She could not have directed her query better."

I was happy to see his mood lifting. "Ricardis is a treasure," I said, hoping that perhaps things would improve between them. "I could not handle so much correspondence without her."

"I can help too," Volmar offered. "She seems to spend more time as your assistant than in attending to her devotions." From his expression, I read what he did not add — *just as she did at St. Disibod.*

I sighed. "I need you for more important things." I lifted another parchment sheet from the desk, bearing a broken seal of the Archbishop of Cologne. "I received a request from Archbishop Arnold for another copy of *Scivias*." I laid a hand on a nearby stack of sheets. "And my medical guidebook needs a new copy. I have added and changed things so many times, it is becoming hard to read."

Volmar inclined his head with amused gallantry. "That is what I came here for." With Father Baldwin in residence, he had taken up the duties of a scribe, not a priest, which suited him better in any case. His lips relaxed into a small smile. "And also so you can reach a settlement with Abbot Helenger."

Now *my* mood darkened. "I cannot believe you accepted that offer."

"I did not think twice about it. As you said" — he nodded toward the manuscript — "I can be more useful here."

I let my irritation subside. Helenger's machinations and his use of the two of us for his gain were galling. Still, despite his dishonorable intentions, he had managed to make me a gift of happiness, although it must have pained him greatly. The essence of his offer was this: he gave Volmar leave to join us at St. Rupert as a goodwill gesture, in exchange for which I would drop my claims to the convent lands that the monks administered. There could be only one explanation for why he would do that: St. Disibod's financial situation must have deteriorated.

Now Volmar was looking at me expectantly. It had been a month since he had arrived and presented me with this proposal.

"But I cannot do that!" I bit my lip in frustration. "That man . . . all he does is scheme!" I rubbed my eyebrows with my thumb and forefinger. "And now he forces me to choose between you and what rightfully belongs to us." I felt the quickening of anger again. "What should I do?"

"It is your decision to make." He said it neutrally, but I saw the challenge in his eyes. If I rejected it, we might never see each other again.

"I will not give up our rights, but I cannot lose you again either," I said quietly.

Volmar's face softened. "You can propose a compromise," he said. "Ask for some of the lands back and leave them the rest."

That was a reasonable solution. "I will think about it, but I will take my time. Let him stew for a few months," I added, reflecting on the cycle of pettiness that Helenger's dealings always engendered.

The previous autumn, shortly before Volmar's arrival, had marked the start of the synod at Trier, where Pope Eugenius was to present *Scivias* to the bishops and prelates. But it was not expected to conclude for several months, and I had to be patient as I awaited news of its reception by that highest Church assembly. As it happened, the first person to bring a report was my old friend Brother Bertolf, now abbot of St. Matthias, who had participated in the early sessions. In late January, while the synod was still under way, he stopped at St. Rupert on his way to Mainz.

During a harsh winter of economizing, I could not treat him to the kind of feast the monks at St. Disibod would have offered, but he did not seem to mind as he sat at my table in the refectory listening to Sister Elfrid read from the Scriptures.

"Your temporary accommodations are excellent," he said when we finally started our meal of fish, bread, and pickled vegetables. "So solid, in fact, that you could spend another winter here if necessary."

"That is true, Father." I smiled as I addressed him with that title. I still remembered Bertolf as a gangly youth breaking anything breakable in Brother Wigbert's infirmary. He was still slender but veinier now, and his mop of black hair had gone mostly white. "But my hope is that we will be able to move into the cloister in the summer. The Count von Stade has been a generous benefactor," I added, my eyes resting on Ricardis's beautiful profile. The sisters' table stood perpendicular to ours, and from that perch I could see all of the women. They sat in two rows facing each other. Their ranks were swelled by two new arrivals — novices Johanna and Hiltrud.

Hiltrud was my niece, my sister Clementia's youngest daughter, and as similar physically to her mother as she was different from her in temperament. After more than thirty years, the details of Clementia's features may have lost their sharpness in my memory, but I still remembered her honey-golden coloring and dark blonde hair, which Hiltrud had inherited. But where the mother had been boisterous, fickle, and much given to gossip, the daughter was quiet and poised, a fact I had discovered with some surprise.

"You will find more patrons now, no doubt." Bertolf's voice reached me. It had a polite, learned quality, just as his face, though marked by lines of premature aging, had preserved its gentle and amiable expression. "I always knew you were destined for better things than that poor enclosure at St. Disibod."

"Did His Holiness present my writings before the synod, then?" I asked, unsure how to feel about Bertolf's characterization of Jutta's convent, however well-intentioned. "The Archbishop of Mainz told me that he would, although I would understand if weighty affairs of the Church prevented him from doing so."

"On the contrary." He shook his head vigorously, and the unruly hair around his tonsure quivered to the movement of his head. "He had his deacon read from *Scivias* on the third day of the proceedings."

I had never imagined that my work would be given such a prominent place, and I was at a loss for how to react. I was still trying to gather my thoughts when the abbot added, "He likened it to 'conversations in heaven', after the Philippians."

"I am indebted to the Holy Father. His support has made it easier for me to serve God in my own way," I said.

"By all accounts you have made splendid work of it. Your house is gaining recognition from the Rhineland to Rome." Bertolf smiled as he helped himself to more wine. His spare frame belied his appetite, for he had eaten his supper with relish. He took two long sips, then sat back. "Pope Eugenius has an admiration for you that he often makes known to those around him. I am told that he likes to quote from *Scivias*, his favorite being the image of the Church — *Ecclesia* — as a woman, large and pregnant, giving birth to the faithful."

I could see the papal acknowledgement impressed him. "I was once going through a difficult time" — I hesitated — "a crisis." I spoke in a low voice, grateful that Volmar was distracted by a conversation with Father Baldwin. The image to which Bertolf had referred was one that stood in my mind in the days after Volmar had come to my workshop at St. Disibod to ask if I had ever contemplated a different kind of life. It had been the hardest choice, harder even than leaving St. Disibod. "It gave me comfort then. It beckoned me back into the fold, if you will," I said, then added, "I believe that God wants me to write about things He allows me to know."

"Indeed, you have exceeded your sex in addressing issues that the rest of us are often afraid to approach," he said. "The conflict between Abelard and the abbot of Clairvaux, though now laid to rest in more ways than one, still has many in the Church unwilling to discuss the Trinitarian dogma for fear of being accused of heresy, yet you managed to avoid that controversy with your interpretation." As if to emphasize the ongoing delicacy of the matter, he changed the subject, his voice taking on a slightly gossipy tone. "And what do your future plans entail? After the cloister is completed?"

"I will build a church unlike any this land has ever seen," I replied without hesitation. "It will have tall windows and be full of light, the way they build them in France now. But it will require considerable funds." I gritted my teeth as I recalled Helenger's offer once again. "I am also finishing another book that I already started at St. Disibod."

"Oh?"

"It is something different this time, more practical," I said. "My struggle to free myself from under Helenger's control, which is not entirely over yet" —I could not help adding—"has taught me the value of paying more attention to matters of everyday life, especially conflicts between people. It is a treatise on the nature of vices that prevent men from living in peace and achieving redemption."

"I look forward to it." Bertolf raised his cup. "We are making a copy of *Scivias* at St. Matthias, and it appears that you will be keeping our scribes busy for a while yet."

"And mine." I touched the rim of my cup to his. Then I smiled to myself, thinking about Volmar working in his chamber. By daylight or candlelight he labored over my notes, his fingers stiffening from the cold. When he wrote, he often forgot to keep the fire up in the brazier. I visited often after compline to bring more charcoal and to discuss the copy. Waiting for the brazier to burn stronger again, we would only have the steam of our breaths to keep us warm, but neither of us ever complained.

"What will be the title of your next book?" my guest asked.

"*Liber vitae meritorum.*" The Book of the Rewards of Life.

The second floor of the newly completed cloister had a large hall, and we set up a wooden stage at one end of it. One summer afternoon, it began filling with peasants from the surrounding villages, none of whom had ever seen music performed, save by a wandering minstrel act. But as several of their women made up the ranks in the procession of the Souls or sang in the choir, their kin were eager to see them. Surveying the crowd through the slit between the drawn curtains behind the stage, I was satisfied with the numbers in attendance but anxious about how the play would be received.

As *Ordo Virtutum* began, I moved to a bench under a window. From that vantage point, I was able observe the audience's reactions even as I kept an eye on the stage. The crowd was captivated by the story from the very first scene.

The performers were in a great form, each transformed entirely into their character, their voices clear and strong, handling the phrases marked by soaring melismas with ease. It was obvious that the colorful robes of the Virtues and their flowing hair under white flower wreaths made an impression when they entered and sang in response to the inquiry from the choir of Patriarchs and Prophets, "O Ancient holy ones, why do you marvel at us so?"

When it was time for Volmar to appear as the Devil, there was a collective gasp. He was dressed in a black and red costume complete with a pair of bull's horns painted black and a tail made from several strings of rope tightly wound and blackened with tar. He took commanding possession of the stage in the first part of the play, when his temptations succeeded in diverting the Soul from the path of goodness; then he relinquished it by degrees as the tide began to turn against him. The role did not involve singing, but it required shouting and snarling, which Volmar did admirably well for one whose intonation was normally so calm.

Toward the end of the fifth scene, when the Virtues bound the Devil with rope — serving as chains — in order to protect the Soul, Sister Burgundia as Chastity sang about the miracle of Christ laying the Devil low and causing the heavens to rejoice. Nearly defeated, the Devil launched his final taunt, mocking Chastity for transgressing the command that God enjoined in lovemaking.

At that point, a chuckle swept through the crowd, and a few of the men broke into laughter before being hushed by their wives. I had worried that the Devil's ribald words might offend; instead, they entertained and lightened the mood, and the audience cheered loudly at Chastity's reminder that she had brought Christ into the world to rally humankind against the Devil.

As the play progressed, my thoughts drifted—as they did many times a day—back to Helenger's offer. Should I give up our lands? Our building costs were great, and our savings were depleted after the cloister had been completed. I also wanted to finish the wall that year as the empire was again in turmoil after a second, disastrous crusade, with remnants of the French and German armies streaming back home to who knew what mischief.

Against those expenses, I had the income from rents, milling fees, river tolls, and fishing rights from our endowments. We also received donations for prayers for the sick and for the souls of the deceased; families, especially the wealthier ones, tended to be generous when facing their mortality. But all of that went to current upkeep—to maintaining the infirmary, buying inks, brushes, and parchment for the manuscripts, and to almsgiving, our Benedictine duty.

No, I reflected as the play approached its conclusion and the audience waited breathlessly to see if the Soul would be saved. I owed it to Jutta's memory, and to the sisters who had entrusted their lot to me, to do everything I could to build a church where they could worship with pride.

I decided that I would offer Helenger the option of continuing to collect rents from half of the lands for the next five years, before they reverted to us. The other half we would take back immediately, so I could start the new construction.

The play came to an end, and the crowd was on their feet, cheering the performers as they bowed, flushed with exertion and excitement. I rose and applauded with them. It was a triumph. In a flash, I decided to have *Ordo* performed at the consecration ceremony for the new church.

I had no idea that it was a decision that would bring disaster and the final solution to my conflict with Helenger.

16

April 1149

I HAD REGRETTED not establishing, during my time at St. Disibod, a refuge where lepers could find shelter from wandering, respite from want, and such medical care as was available for this mysterious and terrifying disease. In my third year at St. Rupert, I finally built a leper house in a clearing of the woods half a league to the west. But the malady was a powerful adversary, and an effective remedy eluded me as much as it had the great physicians of the past. None of my soothing baths and ointments appeared to bring significant improvement in the condition of the four current residents of the cell. Still, I kept trying, my latest effort being a salve that contained quicksilver, known also to bring relief to those afflicted by the burning disease.

I had other expansion plans too. "I will build a separate priory once we have our own charter and are a proper abbey," I told Hiltrud and Elfrid one day as we were walking back from the leper house.

Hiltrud was carrying a clay jar with the remnants of the salve. "An excellent idea," she said, her face lighting up. It had rained earlier that day, and the freshness of the air had brought out the first gentle scents of spring. It made Hiltrud's complexion — honey-golden even after a long winter — shimmer in the sunlight streaming through the canopy of the budding trees. "It could also serve as a medical outpost so we could reach more patients," she suggested.

I felt a surge of pride in her instincts. In the short time since she had joined me, medicine had helped us bond as much as our blood ties had, perhaps even more. She was right; there were many people in need of care who were unable to come all the way to St. Rupert, especially if they lived on the other side of the Nahe. It was, in fact, one of the reasons I wanted us to expand. "Bingen would be a good place," I said, pointing easterly across the river.

"And we will sell more of my remedy there." Elfrid was constantly improving her treatment for men's marital difficulties, which she had been selling for a handsome profit for years. Now she rubbed her hands together at the prospect of a whole new market.

My niece blushed and dropped her gaze to the jar. "I don't know why we are concerning ourselves with such a worldly problem."

Elfrid and I exchanged an amused glance over her head. "It is an obstacle that may prevent wives from conceiving. If that interferes with God's creative plan, we have an obligation to intervene if we can," I said.

"The girl may have a point." Elfrid winked at me in her own effort to put Hiltrud at ease. "From my married days, I remember times when I wished that my husband, God rest his soul, had been similarly afflicted, especially when I came home late from a house call." She roared with laughter, causing even my bashful niece to smile.

"When do you think we will have the charter?" Hiltrud asked when Elfrid's mirth had abated.

"Impossible to tell." I shook my head. "But we have taken the first steps in the right direction since Abbot Helenger finally agreed to my offer." Agreed in a manner of speaking, I did not add. For Helenger, ever a conflict seeker, had taken it upon himself to decide which of the lands he would continue to profit from for the next five years. Of course he had chosen the most fertile and highest income-generating estates. But I had refused to be drawn into another dispute, which I could ill afford with new construction set to begin that summer. "The financial settlement is important," I explained, "but it won't be until the church is consecrated that we can apply to the archbishop for the charter."

More years, then. Impatience gnawed at me, but I knew I could do nothing to speed things up. Instead, I slowed our pace to enjoy the *viriditas* — the busy life energy of the universe — with which the forest was brimming. In truth, my plans were bigger than what I had revealed. I was going to build not just a second infirmary, but a proper hospital like Anna Komnene and her father had established in Constantinople.

More years.

Back at St. Rupert, I went to the scriptorium. A long room with plenty of light streaming through the arched windows, it occupied the southern range of the new cloister. There were already three slanting desks in place, complete with inkhorns, quill holders, and various color dye jars, but there was room for more. Ricardis was working there, along with the novice Johanna, who was training as illuminator, but Volmar was not at his desk.

I crossed to a table in the middle of the room, picked up the top sheet from the recently finished manuscript, and examined it in the amber light of the afternoon. The borders of the page were covered with intricate tracings of green leaves edged in gold leaf, and brilliant blossoms in deep red and sunny yellow, all of them in Ricardis's hand. It framed the title — *The Book of the Secrets of Various Types of Nature* — written in Volmar's elegant script. The next sheet was covered with immaculate text, the ink fresh and sharply black against the creamy whiteness of the sheet. The initial letter D was enlarged and decorated with twining vine. Looking over the next few sheets, I found nothing amiss and put them back in order. By the time the book was bound in calfskin, it would be worth as much as the revenue from the Binger Loch mill after last year's harvest, and the Archbishop of Cologne was willing to pay for it.

"This is a first-rate copy," I said. "Archbishop Arnold will have no cause to complain. Are we going to be on time with the delivery?" I had promised it would be in Cologne in the first week of June, in six weeks' time.

"We should be." Ricardis pointed to the stack. "Brother Volmar will be sending this to Ingelheim tomorrow. The bookbinder already has the measurements and says he will have the cover ready when the copy arrives."

There was a sound of footsteps on the stone flags, and Sister Burgundia appeared in the doorway a moment later. "We have a visitor," she said. "From France."

My heart leaped with excitement. I followed her down to the courtyard and found the newcomer talking with Volmar outside the old farm buildings that had once served as our accommodations but had since been converted to guest quarters. I had been expecting someone from that faraway land of splendid new churches for months now, and there he was — a short man in his mid-thirties, broad-shouldered and powerfully muscled with a heavy-looking traveling satchel slung across his chest with a strap. I noted his strong physique with appreciation as if it were tangible proof of his skill. Hearing my approach, the two men turned.

"May I introduce Master Achard from Saint-Denis?" Volmar indicated our visitor. "Sister Hildegard, the founder of this house."

The man bowed deeply, and I acknowledged him with a nod.

During his time at Cluny, more than twenty years earlier, Volmar had accompanied Abbot Peter on a visit to the famed abbey church outside of Paris and had been greatly impressed by it. It had since been extensively renovated by Abbot Suger, a close adviser to the French king, and its magnificence was the talk of pilgrims on routes from Santiago de Compostela to Prague. Multitudes of visitors had gone to the new Saint-Denis in recent years, including Abbot Peter again. He had written to Volmar, calling it one of the wonders of Christendom.

Volmar had shown me the letter, which included a description and a sketch of the church's façade, so different in its level of detail from the bland fronts of Rhenish churches. It had two tall towers with pointy roofs and rows of tall arched windows flanking the entrance, three large doors, and a rose window above them. I had been so captivated by it that Volmar had written to everyone he knew in France and eventually found Achard, who had honed his craft under the master builders of Saint-Denis and was highly praised for his talents.

"I am honored to meet you, Sister," he said in good German. When he saw my surprise, he added, "We builders work with men from many nations and learn one another's tongues."

"Your reputation precedes you, Master Achard." I smiled. "I look forward to working with you on the project I have in mind."

He opened his satchel and produced a flat round object, similar to a large coin. He extended it to me in the open palm of his broad, callused hand. "This is a pilgrim badge with a miniature of the Abbey of Saint-Denis," he said. "I brought it for you."

I took it and admired it for a long moment. It showed the façade from Abbot Peter's sketch, proving him a skillful drawer. I was again struck by the rose window, which I knew was made of painted glass so that on sunny days the rays of sunlight fell on the floor, the pews, and the altar in a multitude of colors and hues. I closed my eyes, the better to imagine the beauty of that scene. "This is a most thoughtful gift, master builder," I said. "I can call you that because that is what you will become once the construction is underway."

Achard's large chest seemed to swell even more with the pride and anticipation of being in charge of his own project. "I am ready to hear your ideas," he said with a glimmer in his eyes that told me he lived for this work. "Once I know the scope, I will make sketches and start assembling a team of builders."

I was pleased to see his dedication, but I had a duty as a hostess. "Tonight you are a guest of this house, and we would be remiss in our hospitality if we put you to work immediately. You will find a table in the kitchen, where you can fortify yourself after the journey, and a bed in the guesthouse where you can rest. We will start tomorrow morning."

Achard inclined his head, and I noticed that his curly black hair was sprinkled with grayish white. I wondered whether this was a sign of age or a mark of his trade—a fine layer of dust that he carried with him everywhere.

When he was gone, I turned to Volmar. "I am glad to see he is equally anxious to start. This place"—I gestured toward the cloister that exuded the freshness of newly quarried stone—"provides fitting quarters to us, but we still hear Mass in a wooden chapel that barely fits two dozen people, and we store the relics of St. Rupert in a chest."

"It will be a long time before it is finished," he reminded me. "We must steel ourselves for years of tedious work before we can give those bones the place they deserve."

For the second time that day, the feeling of anguished impatience gripped me, but Volmar's calm presence was like a balm for my restless, sharply tuned soul. Without him, it would rarely find respite.

"You are right," I admitted. *As always*.

17

September 1149

I CAME TO the edge of the pit along with Agnes, a kitchen servant, who was pulling a cart filled with flagons, mugs, and trays of honey cakes. Every day at noon, she brought refreshments for some two dozen workers who were digging the foundations for the church in the northwestern section of St. Rupert.

"It is never too early for that." Achard came up, grinning and wiping his brow. Even though the summer was coming to an end, unrelenting white heat was pouring from the sky. "You are in a fine mood today, ladies," he added, noting the smiles we could not quite suppress.

The pit's depth exceeded his height, and Agnes had to kneel at the edge to pass the heavy flagon, pleasantly cool from the cellar, to his outstretched hands. A moment later, the mugs were distributed among the sweaty and sunburned men, quiet as they expected more watered-down monastic wine. But when they started pouring, they erupted in cheers.

"We began brewing our own beer, Master Achard, and this is the first batch," the girl said merrily. "And it is fitting that it should be ready on the hottest day of the summer."

The men drained their cups in long gulps. "This is just what we needed, eh, boys?" the master exclaimed, and they nodded enthusiastically.

"We thought you might like it." Agnes laughed as she passed down another jug and a plate of cakes. Looking around, she asked, "Have you got far to go before the foundations are all dug out?"

The pit lay at our feet like an enormous cross. The top faced east, in the direction of the herb garden and the Nahe, while the foot, where the main doorway would be, pointed west toward the woods along the Rhine.

"Another week for the nave, I reckon," he replied, taking another draught of the beer and wiping his mouth with his sleeve. "Then we will secure it with those granite blocks." He nodded toward the slabs of gray stone ranged along the far wall. They had been delivered from the Count von Stade's quarry a fortnight before. Since then, the stonecutters had been busy cutting and filing them to appropriate sizes and shapes.

"God give you strength to continue your work, Master Achard," Agnes said. She collected the empty cups, then went back to the kitchen while I stayed behind.

"I was wondering when you would come to check on us, Sister," the master said cheerily, climbing a ladder out of the pit. He and I were getting along well. Achard was competent, hard-working, and fair with his men, who evidently looked up to him. But I had also come to respect him for his honesty. He had considered various options for modeling the church after Saint-Denis, and had concluded that while some of the features would be possible to replicate, others would be too costly, or the size of the church would make them infeasible. I was disappointed not to be able to have a decorative tympanum carved with biblical scenes, but his arguments were valid. In the end, I was grateful for his sincerity, for stories of commissioned builders spending lavish sums, risking the solvency of their projects and then being unable to finish them were not uncommon.

"You don't need my supervision," I said. "I am happy to hear you will soon be ready to start lowering the granite blocks."

Achard raised his hands to signify caution. "It depends on how much time the stonecutters need to prepare them. But if there is a delay there, we will start digging the foundations for the apse," he added to reassure me.

We walked east toward the top of the cross, where a semicircular shape had been delineated with wooden sticks connected by a length of rope. Similar but smaller semicircles had been plotted in two places along the nave, like bulbs growing out of a stem. That was where side chapels would be located.

"Do you think you will complete the foundations before the first frost?" I was suddenly anxious. I wanted the walls to start going up as soon as the winter was over.

Achard considered. "We need six to eight more weeks of fair weather, and since it is the middle of September, we might be lucky." He gave a soft chuckle. "But it would not hurt to petition the Lord for a dry autumn."

"We offer prayers in that intention every day."

The sound of a heated discussion erupting from the pit stopped us, and Achard took his leave to see about it. I walked to the end of the apse and stood there for a long while, proud and nervous in equal measure. "You cannot always win," Volmar had once said, after I had complained about my continuing difficulties with Helenger, "but when it comes to this church, your success depends only on you."

Now, looking down the length of the foundations, I saw myself moving through the church, descending from the chancel, down the main nave framed by rows of slender columns, and out through doors flanked by two towers into the courtyard. One day, those doors would be admitting pilgrims, abbots, bishops, and — who knows — maybe even the pope himself.

And not just during my lifetime, but for centuries to come.

18

September 1151

"WHERE IS SHE?" Volmar's voice reached me from the parlor. "Let me see her!"

I had locked myself in my bedchamber. Griselda, who had been sitting guard outside, ran to the door, and the scrape against the wood told me she was barring it with her own body. "She will not see anybody." Despite my distraught state, I imagined her mild eyes rising to his face, blazing with fierce protectiveness. "Not even you."

After a long moment, I heard his footsteps—back and forth, back and forth—as he began to pace the parlor. Abruptly, they fell silent. Did he stop at the window that gave onto the back of the cloister, its northern wall overshadowed by the rising bulk of the church? In the third year of construction, the walls stood as tall as they would ever be, and work was underway to lay the roof on. How many times had I looked through that window, admiring the structure that rose week after week, month after month, filling me with pride and joy? But that day, even that thought could not bring me out of the depths of my despair.

"I always knew she was trouble." I heard his voice again, taut with suppressed anger, so unlike him.

"Best let Hildegard rest until the shock passes. I will send for you as soon as she has calmed down," Griselda said.

Two hours earlier, Ricardis had told me that she would be leaving St. Rupert. In that short span of time, the news had spread through the community — now numbering four-teen sisters — and had evidently also reached Volmar. By the sound of it, the stories were already growing fanciful — he was now asking if it was true that Ricardis was running off to be married, and that her lover was one of the stable boys.

"She is leaving because her cousin has secured for her the post of abbess at Bassum," Griselda explained patiently. "It is in the diocese of Bremen, where Hartwig was recently appointed archbishop."

Before Volmar could respond, I opened the door. I was aware of the state I was in, having hastily wiped my eyes, but he deserved to hear it from me. "Brother Volmar, I want to make a confession."

He hesitated. "Should I send for Father Baldwin?" Vol-mar had never heard my confession, although he had those of the other sisters on the occasions our priest was indisposed.

"No. I would confess to you." I moved aside so he could enter the chamber.

When the door closed, I sat on the edge of my bed. The only other seat was a stool at the little desk by the window, and Volmar placed it in the middle of the room, facing me.

I bent my head and laced my fingers in my lap so tight-ly my knuckles and fingertips went white. "May God forgive me," I began, eyes cast down, my chest heavy as if filled with stones. "I let myself be deceived by a vanity. I elevated Ricardis above the others in my mind because I confused beauty with goodness. I am weak and wicked — " I heard my voice crack.

"Stop." Volmar came to sit beside me. "You are nothing of the sort. You loved her. Do not lose your faith in beauty — fundamentally, it is good." He took my face in his hands, and his gaze swept it like a caress. "That is what you taught me when I was just a hunter boy walking with you through the woods. I have always found it to be true, even when life seemed determined to disprove it."

I pressed my fingers to my eyes, feeling pressure rising under them again. "I loved what was visible and ignored what lurked beneath the surface."

"Surely that is a little harsh," he said mildly, as if speaking to a capricious child.

I was oddly touched by his defense of Ricardis, whom he had never liked and had clearly understood better than I did. It made me feel even guiltier for having once doubted him. "It was she who had been informing Helenger and Kuno about my plans, so when I told them about my decision to leave St. Disibod, they were ready to block me." My words were strained with humiliation. "It must have started when I secured the job for her at the scriptorium — she was passing on everything we discussed at the convent."

Volmar frowned. "Are you sure?"

"At some point I began suspecting that someone was betraying my confidence, even though I didn't want to believe it. But now it is all so painfully clear." My voice caught as I lifted a hand to my mouth to stifle another sob.

"But why would she do that?"

"To gain favor. She was doing that with me, and she was doing that with the monks. She needed to be everyone's favorite so that when the right moment came, she could redeem the credit and advance in the world. She must have hoped that if I died, Helenger would support her candidacy to replace me as *magistra*. What she did not count on" — I laughed bitterly — "was that he played his own game and used her too. That is what people like them do.

"Unfortunately for her, I have gone on living, and she — probably all of them, the ambitious von Stades! — must have been casting around for another opportunity all these years. Then Hartwig became archbishop. Do you know that I met him once? The day he brought Ricardis to Sponheim to meet me . . . there was something weasel-like about him that I disliked right away." I paused, recalling Hartwig's air of triumph that I now belatedly understood. "I saw through him, but I was too in thrall to his cousin to care. Little did I know that she would use me so cruelly and betray my trust in more ways than one!"

I closed my eyes as fresh tears rolled down my cheeks. I was sobbing again. "But the worst thing, the thing that hurts me the most"—I pressed a clenched fist to my chest—"is that I thought it was you. You!" I hung my head. "She let me suspect someone of your character of being capable of allying himself with Helenger." In desperation, I clung to him, burying my face in the folds of his robe. I felt his collarbone against my brow, his hand on the back of my neck. "You have brought nothing but happiness into my life."

Despite everything, I felt a sense of relief. For years, I had wondered how the monks could have known the things I had wanted to keep secret, and the possibility that they could have come from Volmar had crossed my mind more than once. He had not been happy about my decision to leave St. Disibod, and I had reasoned that perhaps that was his way of trying to stop me. At least Ricardis's betrayal proved me wrong on that score.

"I have my own confession to make." I heard his voice close to my ear. "There were times when I thought Ricardis was all you needed, and I felt the sting of envy." He spread his fingers around my head and pressed it more tightly to his chest.

"Nobody has ever been more important to me than you," I said into his heartbeat.

The silence tightened around us. Even the clang of metal from the forge on the construction site seemed to be separate and outside of it. At length I pulled away, wiping the last of my tears with the sleeve of my robe. "She is leaving on the feast of St. Matthias." I went to the window. It, too, gave onto the new church, where work continued as if nothing had happened. But the noise, which had been like music to me before, was now jarring. "In three weeks' time."

I pressed my fingers to my temples. For the first time since my move to St. Rupert, I felt the pain in my head coming on, piercing me, hurting my eyes, closing in and enveloping me. I turned back to Volmar, and he knew with one glance. "I will ask Elfrid to mix you your draft," he said.

When he had gone, I lay down and curled into myself, welcoming the pain's disabling power. I longed to drift away, to move to those higher realms where I would feel light as a feather, and where there would be no other thought.

That same week, Father Baldwin died in his sleep, having reached the age of sixty-five years. Volmar performed the funeral rites and wrote to Mainz for a replacement on my behalf, for I was unable to rise from bed during that time.

But the day of Ricardis's departure came eventually, and I summoned her to my parlor in the morning. I did not know what I wanted to tell her until she arrived. When she did, it was as if someone had put out a fire and left a heap of ashes behind. Her smile was gone, replaced by a look of sorrow, though it was tempered with something else—whether guilt, defiance, or regret, I could not tell. There was still some of the old absorbing, analyzing, calculating look in her eyes—or maybe I was imaging it?

She kneeled, casting her eyes down. "I know I have sinned against you. I made a confession to put my soul at ease, though I have yet to find comfort or relief," she said in a voice that rang hollow in my ears. "I hope you will find a way to forgive me."

"Rise."

"I—" Ricardis started, then faltered. "I hope to have your blessing for my new undertaking."

The wound that had barely begun to heal opened again as if a dagger blade had been plunged into it. "My suffering does not matter," I said, "but you have offended God by taking that appointment not for the sake of serving Him, but to add to your family's distinction."

"That is not—"

I raised my hand to stem further words. "What you do—what you have always done—is to crave worldly honor and advancement. That was the reason you entered St. Disibod, so your reputation would grow with its reputation. You and your family have used me, so do not presume to ask my blessing."

Ricardis lowered her head. In the silence that followed, I realized that there could be no reconciliation between us—not then, anyway—and I bitterly regretted the meeting. "There is nothing more to say. You can leave now."

She hesitated for a moment, then bowed her head and left the parlor, closing the door softly behind her.

I listened to her footsteps fading outside—and shortly afterwards to horses whinnying, grooms talking, and the heavy gate creaking in its hinges—with an odd lack of emotion. In one corner of my desk stood the little box with the lump of salt from my mother, and just then it seemed the only thing that was constant and unsullied in my world.

When everything was quiet again, I went out and made my way across the courtyard. There were narrow wooden stairs just off the gatekeeper's lodge, and I climbed them to the top of the wall. I could see Ricardis riding down the slope on a palfrey accompanied by two men-at-arms sent by Archbishop Hartwig. As they entered the forest—its faded, dusty, late-summer color providing a fitting curtain to hide them from view—a wave of grief swallowed me up again. I leaned my forehead against the stone but could find no comfort in its hard coldness.

19

October 1151

THE NEW PRIEST, sent by Mainz with remarkable haste, made a poor impression on me and proved troublesome from the beginning. A young man of around twenty, Father Nicholas was a dull fellow who performed his duties with a singular lack of enthusiasm and spoke little to anyone outside of church services. He took his meals alone in his room, where he also spent most of his time when not saying Mass, so that we saw little of him overall. Yet the servants remarked that sometimes after compline, when we were asleep, he could be seen wandering the grounds. He may have largely stayed away from us, but that did not prevent conflict from erupting within days.

It was Sister Burgundia who had first come to complain, after having been denied confession when she had wanted it. Father Nicholas apparently did not hear confessions on Mondays, and when she insisted she needed to unburden her soul, he feigned surprise that a Benedictine sister, especially an old one, had opportunities for sinning. I paid him a visit at Father Baldwin's old lodging, which Nicholas had transformed from a neat little cell into a chaotic scene. Parchment sheets were strewn across the desk, and unwashed bowls and cups lined the windowsill.

He invited me to step inside, but I remained where I was, just outside the threshold. "We have a servant who cleans my lodging and the sisters' cells." I pointedly swept the room with my gaze before resting it on the priest.

"I will undoubtedly avail myself of her services when I am fully settled in," he replied in a careless tone that did not bode well for the future cleanliness of the chamber.

Short of patience and not wishing to prolong the meeting unnecessarily, I got to the point. "I have been told you do not hear confessions on Mondays."

"That is correct," he replied languidly.

I considered him, narrowing my eyes, a habit I had developed recently. Could it be that he was simply lazy? I had seen all kinds of priests in my life—saintly, greedy, fanatical—and could well imagine one who broke his vows of chastity, but a lazy one? It had to be a first. "And why is that?"

"I need to rest—"

It was all I could do to stop myself from laughing out loud. "Rest from what?"

"And meditate," he added, ignoring my question. "I must have time to attend to my own spiritual needs and will not make exceptions."

"Father Nicholas," I said with deliberate slowness, the friendly tone I had forced into my speech earlier now slipping away, "here at St. Rupert, you follow *our* rules. And one of them is that whoever needs to make a confession, at any time of day or night, will not be denied it."

Nicholas straightened up, more alert now. "You cannot dictate to an ordained priest how he should perform his duties," he countered in a tone that wavered between defensive and whining.

"I am not telling you how to perform your duties, I am telling you to perform them in the first place. I will do so as long as you remain within these precincts, where I have authority."

The priest scowled, and I could see that his pride had been hurt. Maybe he was vain, I thought. That was common enough among priests, but if he was vain *and* lazy — well, that would have been a particularly unpleasant combination.

"And one more thing," I added, half turning away from him, "the comment you made to Sister Burgundia about nuns not having occasion to sin is unbecoming of the consecrated state that you are supposed to represent."

"I said nothing of the kind," he scoffed dismissively.

The idea that Nicholas might also be a liar was so outrageous it almost choked the words in my throat. "I have no cause to doubt her truthfulness," I said when I could trust myself to speak again. "I consider this matter settled, and I hope I have corrected any misconception you may have had about our rules." In a more conciliatory tone, I added, "Our goal — yours and mine — should be to work together for the benefit of this community. That is all I care about." Nodding curtly, I walked away.

"Sister." I heard him say blandly behind me as he closed his door.

The living quarters were above the scriptorium, and I went down to look for Volmar, only to learn from Johanna that he had gone out to ride his new mare for exercise. Still irritated with Nicholas, I went to the gate and paced back and forth until the sound of hoof beats on the other side announced his return, and the porter came out to open the gate. Volmar, wearing riding clothes, dismounted with a deftness that always amazed me and gave the horse to a groom. I beckoned him to follow me to the construction site.

There, wooden roof beams lay stacked on the ground. Two of Achard's men worked on tying ropes to both ends of each of them before sending them up some thirty feet to where their fellows waited at the top of the scaffold. Volmar and I stood for a while, watching the beams being hoisted up, the men going about it swiftly to finish as much as possible before the first frost.

"We have been lucky with the weather so far," Volmar remarked. Given his flushed air and the scent of wind about him, I wondered if the tight construction schedule was the only thing he had in mind. For all his learning, Volmar had never ceased to be a child of the forest.

"How was your ride?" I asked.

"Invigorating." He smiled with mock guilt.

"You should be careful; that horse is a powerful beast." The mare, though only two years old, was larger than an average palfrey and seemed to have more vigor than a warhorse. When she galloped, the earth shook underneath her hoofs. "You should leave it to the groom to ride her."

Volmar laughed. "Are you saying I am too old?"

"No." I hesitated. "But—"

"You are," he teased, then added lightly, "I may be forty-five, but in the saddle, I feel like a young man."

I sighed inwardly. Now that he was again able to indulge his boyish passion for the outdoors, there was no reasoning with him on that account. "I brought you out here to have a word," I said, turning my mind to business. The din of the work was supposed to ensure that our conversation remained private. "I just spoke with Father Nicholas."

I relayed our exchange, and Volmar shook his head. "What a fool."

"Either that, or he is pretending to be one," I said.

He raised an eyebrow quizzically.

"I do not trust him," I explained. "I want to find out who sent him."

"Why, the archbishop did. You can always write to him and ask for someone else," Volmar suggested pragmatically.

"The archbishop is our friend, which is why it seems odd that he would send someone like Nicholas. Something doesn't seem right about this." I leaned closer and lowered my voice. "Would you go to Mainz and make inquiries—find out who he is truly working *for*?"

"I think you are exaggerating. After what happened with Ric—" He broke off, and I looked away. He added hastily, "I will go if that will set your mind at peace."

"Thank you," I said. "We need to understand what is happening at Mainz if we are to hope for a satisfactory replacement."

Volmar nodded. "I will leave first thing tomorrow."

Despite the sensitive nature of his mission, a glimmer in his eyes told me he was already looking forward to another stint in the saddle.

20

March 1152

T HE AFTERNOON BEFORE the consecration ceremony was overcast but warm for early March. The retinue of deacons, canons, and priests I had met at Bingen made its way up the hill, but my old friend Archbishop Heinrich of Mainz was too ill to attend. Instead, Bishop Osbert led the deputation on his behalf.

I was not entirely surprised. When Volmar had gone to Mainz the previous autumn, he had found the archbishop in decline, and the canons had already taken over many administrative tasks. He had confirmed my fears that it was their new provost—none other than Walter, Helenger's nephew, who had finally maneuvered himself into the post—who had selected Nicholas for service at St. Rupert.

The clouds parted as we approached the gates, and the rays of the afternoon sun gave the new stone a warm glow.

I cast a discreet glance at the bishop and saw his look of approval.

"This is a solid-looking wall," he said. "It would not be out of place anywhere around Mainz."

"Thank you, Your Excellency." I could not suppress a smile. "My goal is to keep us safe. We recently added ten more feet to this side, where we do not have the protection of the steep slope."

"A sensible approach," the bishop observed. "Stone is very expensive these days."

"We were able to procure it at a good price from Count von Stade's quarry," I said with a pang of the grief the mention of Ricardis's family name still gave me.

"And how progresses your work on the church?" Osbert nodded toward the façade. The upper section, crowned with two towers, loomed on the other side of the wall.

"The roof has been laid, although Your Excellency will find that the state of the interior is still quite raw," I replied ruefully, thinking about the incomplete figures of the Apostles stored in a shed out of sight, some with only a head carved, others with an arm or a few folds of robe. "My master builder estimates he needs two more years to finish the chapels, but the sculptures for the portal should be ready by Christmas."

The gate opened, and we rode into a noisy courtyard preceded by two knights of the bishop's guard. Servants weaved around newly arrived guests, and horses whinnied as they were led to the stables. Among a group of barons chatting outside the guesthouse, I spotted Freiherr Giselbert, a wealthy owner of vineyards along the Rhine, and I was seized with a sudden anxiety. Until recently, his relations with the Church had been strained on account of his frequent and loud criticism of the local clergy's greed. He used to make it known — especially during public court days, when, with other landed gentry, he heard petitioners seeking redress for grievances — and it had earned him a brief excommunication by the Archbishop of Mainz.

Giselbert noticed the bishop as we came to a stop in the center of the courtyard, and he gave him a small, slightly mocking bow before offering a deeper one to me. He may have reconciled with the hierarchy, but I doubted his views had changed. "This is Giselbert von Rüdesheim," I explained to my guest, trying to hide my embarrassment.

Bishop Osbert frowned. He knew the name, of course, if not the face.

"As part of his penance, he has been ordered to assume patronage of a monastic foundation, and he chose us," I added, pointing at the church. "His support has helped us finish faster than we would have otherwise."

The bishop turned his attention to the church that rose proudly in the northwestern section of the compound. Built of pale gray stone, it was not large, but it was graceful. Its nave was longer and narrower than that of most churches — which tended to be bulky and compact — and its walls were propped by regularly spaced external supports. They were a recent invention in building that allowed for thinner walls and taller windows.

But it was the façade that was its most distinctive feature; it had two tall, slender towers flanking the main door, yet instead of forming a smooth common surface with the entrance, the towers were separated by vertical protrusions, giving the front a more nuanced, three-part appearance. Above the doors, the colorful glass of the circular window sparkled with blue, red, and golden hues in the sunshine.

"It is true what they say at the court; your church looks like nothing our Rhenish country has ever seen," he said, impressed.

"I had a mind to bring some of the French style of building here and to create a worthy place for the bones of our patron saint."

"A noble sentiment," Osbert commented. "I am a bit of an *artifex* myself," he added in a confidential tone. "Everywhere I travel, I take note of new construction and try to interest the archbishop in replicating it in Mainz. French cathedrals are among my favorite."

I was glad to see a priest passionate about something other than God. It always inspired my trust, for it was my belief that a life of extreme religious devotion that excluded any interest in earthly matters rarely bore fruit. A man of God sensitive to human preoccupations was a better shepherd to his flock in his greater capacity for understanding and compassion.

Volmar came out to greet the bishop, with whom he was already acquainted from his visits to Mainz. "It is an honor to welcome Your Excellency to St. Rupert."

"It will be an honor to perform the rite of consecration in the name of Archbishop Heinrich," Osbert replied, then looked around. "Is the Archbishop of Trier come yet?"

Volmar shook his head. "He is expected tonight with the abbots of St. Maximin and St. Matthias."

"Ah." There was a glint of satisfaction in the bishop's eyes. I exchanged a smiling glance with Volmar; the rivalry between the two episcopal sees was well-known, and it was amusing to see an envoy of the Archbishop of Mainz basking in the glory of being the first to arrive somewhere. "Who else has been invited?" he asked, his tone momentarily gossipy.

"Abbot Anselm of Johannesberg, Adalard of St. Martin in Cologne, and the dean of Frankfort are already here, as are the Counts von Sponheim, Bamberg, and Kirchberg," I replied. "We have yet to welcome the abbots of St. Albans and Jac, and" — the title still seemed unnatural to me — "Abbot Helenger of St. Disibod."

I had only invited Helenger out of respect for Jutta's memory, and had hoped that he would decline. But he was not one to miss the opportunity to be included among Church officials and nobility, no matter how unpleasant my triumph might be to him personally.

"Archbishop Heinrich has apprised me of the" — the bishop cleared his throat — "difficulties there."

"There was indeed a financial dispute after I left St. Disibod, but the abbot and I have come to an agreement," I explained, glad to be addressing the issue so early. "There are no more obstacles to us receiving a charter. I have a petition ready for you to take to Mainz."

"A copy of your settlement with St. Disibod will be necessary too, for the record."

"Of course," I said, but my heart sank. The settlement had taken place through an exchange of many letters with the understanding that an official document would be drawn at the time half the deeds were due to be returned to us. We could have it signed when Helenger was here, of course, but it was not a conversation I was looking forward to having.

I beckoned a servant and bid him show the bishop to his quarters. "His Excellency must be in need of rest and refreshment."

"Indeed." Osbert nodded gratefully. "We have a long day ahead of us tomorrow."

> *O Ierusalem, aurea civitas*
> O Jerusalem, o golden city
> adorned in the Royal purple
> *O aedificatio summae bonitatis*
> O building of the greatest good
> Where light never darkens,
> Adorned with the dawn
> and the warmth of the sun
> *O beata pueritia . . .*

I regarded the crowd that filled the church as the sisters intoned the hymn to St. Rupert. Only three springs and three summers had passed since Master Achard and his men had begun their work, and it would not have been possible to hold the consecration so soon had it not been for a series of strokes of luck along the way. In addition to Giselbert's penance, Count Bernhard von Hildesheim had bequeathed the bulk of his lands in Saxony to us in the year 1150.

At the beginning of the ceremony, Bishop Osbert had symbolically purified the church by sprinkling holy water first on its exterior, then at four points inside — on the threshold, in the apse, and at both ends of the transept. Before entering the church, tradition called for him to tap three times on the door. On the other side, Father Nicholas had asked, also after the ancient custom, "Who is the king of glory?" The bishop had replied, "The Lord of Hosts, He is the king of glory!" Then the door had opened to let the procession into the church. The bishop, abbots, and sisters filed in first, then the lords, followed by pilgrims and the townsfolk from Bingen. The local peasants came in last.

We had composed two hymns and four antiphons for the occasion and opened with the ode to St. Maximin, the patron saint of the great abbey at Trier, as its abbot and its archbishop looked on from their stalls. At the high point of the Mass, the cedar box inlaid with mother of pearl that contained the relics of St. Rupert on a velvet cushion was deposited in a chamber inside the altar.

Our hymn compared the saint to a celestial city gleaming in the sun. I was keenly aware of the admiration the church provoked in the congregation, even in its unfinished state. It was spacious and full of light from the tall widows of the side aisles and the clerestory. Rows of slender columns that ran along both sides of the nave enhanced the sense of height.

Throughout the service, people kept lifting their eyes to the vaulted ceiling to take in that sensation of space. The faces of the peasants, who had never seen anything like this, expressed both wonder and fear, but it was also evident that many of the more worldly visitors were not used to praying in a church that did not crush them with the darkness and weight of thick walls and low ceilings.

The ceremony was followed by refreshments while the sisters changed into their costumes for the performance of *Ordo Virtutum*. The staging was sumptuous this time; the chorus of Patriarchs and Prophets was clad in majestic white robes, and the Virtues wore colorful gowns and golden circlets on their heads consisting of three intertwined bands to signify the Holy Trinity.

As the spectacle began, I saw that Bishop Osbert was moved when Chastity, in blue and gold like a heavenly vision, stepped forward and sang her praise of maidenhood. He was also affected by the Devil's derisive growls that accompanied the song, and it seemed for a moment that all these men who ruled over lands or souls — and often both — paused from their responsibilities and ambitions to ponder the mysteries of faith.

The play concluded with an invitation for the audience to receive God's blessing:

Bend your knees to the Father,
And He will reach out his hand to you.

It was my favorite part because the score called for the sisters to perform the difficult but beautiful feat of singing out the word "reach" over several notes. When their voices came together in a triumphant finale and then subsided, there was a brief silence as everyone savored the sound echoing off the walls. Then the hall erupted in applause.

It was still underway when a dark-robed figure in the second row rose, turned away from the stage, and faced the gathering. The applause faded until only a few claps could be heard here and there before they, too, ceased. The figure was that of a monk, and even before he pulled back his cowl, I knew it was Helenger. The face that emerged from under the hood was pale and set, but the gray eyes flashed with indignation.

165

"How can you applaud such an abomination in a holy place?" His voice boomed through the hall like a clap of thunder. "This . . . play" — he made a grimace of disgust — "tells no biblical story and relates no tale of a saint's life or miracles. It is but a string of songs that wandering minstrels might sing at a tavern to the merriment of a drunken mob. And you" — he pivoted in the direction of the rows occupied by the clergy, and a long finger emerged from the sleeve of his robe, jabbing at them — "how can *you* sit here and stomach this idle entertainment, this ungodly spectacle of women who professed vows of modesty but prance around in dresses, jewels, and with uncovered heads like harlots, making a mockery of The Rule?"

The silence that greeted his words was so deep that it seemed nobody was breathing. Somewhere near me an early spring fly was buzzing, the high-pitched sound oddly interrogative.

"So why did you not leave earlier, Father?" a young nobleman, the son of the Count von Nidda, asked finally. "We stayed, for we liked what we saw." He pointed to his companions, who nodded, laughing.

Mortified, I could not decide what was worse — Helenger's accusation or the youngster's coarse joke. I glanced over the stunned audience. The clerics looked uncomfortable, the older nobles were shaking their heads, and the younger ones grinned. Behind me, I heard a low voice, which I recognized as belonging to Herr Giselbert, murmuring in disdain, "In public those monks are all high and mighty, but they are given to greed and vice behind closed doors, every last one of them." I ran a hand over my forehead, feeling overwhelmed.

"I suffered through it so I might know the full extent of it and report it faithfully to Church authorities," Helenger barked in response to the young von Nidda.

"Church authorities are here, and they enjoyed it too," someone else from the younger ranks proffered, causing another outburst of laughter among them.

But Helenger paid it no heed. "If the Archbishop of Mainz will not discipline Sister Hildegard"—he glared at Bishop Osbert and straightened his spine, which made him look more like a beanpole than ever—"I will write to His Holiness the Pope, and he will curb these heathen practices!"

"There is nothing heathen about the story of virtues overcoming evil, Father Abbot." A soft voice from the stage made everyone turn in that direction. "It shows a path to redemption and gives us hope, and if there is anyone who knows how to do it, it is Sister Hildegard." It was Griselda, dressed as Obedience. Hers was not a powerful voice; in fact, there was a slight tremor in it, but it carried to all the corners of the hall in the renewed silence. "Hope is what she gave us when she removed us from under your authority. Here, we are free to live our vocation as we see fit—yes, even through song and play. Here, we feel closer to God than we ever did at St. Disibod—" She broke off, shaking.

Sister Burgundia put an arm around her shoulder, and heads turned back toward Helenger, whose cheeks overspread with color. "Whoever heard of a mere nun talking to an abbot with so much insolence?" he demanded. "This is yet another example of the lack of respect for The Rule and of disorder running rampant here. I hope the archbishop will keep this in mind when she comes asking for a charter!" He addressed those last words to Bishop Osbert.

Before I could react, the bishop rose to his feet. "Abbot Helenger," he said with dignity, "I will gladly speak with you about your concerns, but this is neither the time nor the place. I suggest you go back to your quarters and calm yourself. We can talk privately afterward."

"I *will* go to my quarters," Helenger shot back peevishly, "but only to retrieve my traveling bag, for I will not spend another night here." With that, he made his way demonstratively to the exit. Two other monks who had arrived with him followed, young men I did not remember from my time, and they kept their cowls on.

When the doors closed behind them, the hall erupted in a cacophony of voices. The sisters were still on the stage, looking crestfallen. A few paces away, Volmar had taken the bull horns off and held them under his arm. He was his usual composed self, and he sent me a look of sympathy.

I walked over to the bishop as the hall began to empty. "I am sorry this has happened, Your Excellency." All at once it flooded me — the humiliation, the anger, and the fear that Helenger might follow through on his threat and write to the pope.

"Abbot Helenger is a troubled man," Osbert sighed. "Our vocation sometimes attracts those who see the Church as a refuge from a world they consider inadequate." He paused, considering. "Which is why it is dangerous to have adorned women put in front of them."

I opened my mouth to protest that I did nothing more than represent the basic tenets of our faith, then decided not to. I had spent most of my life pushing back against resistance, and I knew that the best way to overcome it was to be pragmatic about it.

"Do you think he will write to the pope?" I asked instead.

"I don't know."

"You seemed affected by the play. I saw strong emotions in your face," I said in a low voice, as if in confidence. "Your verdict is bound to carry more weight than that of Abbot Helenger's."

The bishop's chin went up. "Of course." Then he added, "I found no theological fault with it. This way of extolling the virtuous life and the victory over the devil is a worthy occupation for cloistered women. In some cases, it may speak more directly to the layperson than a thundering sermon from the pulpit."

"Thank you."

"You have achieved a rare feat here, Sister," he said earnestly. "Few women who are not queens or royal daughters have been able to establish monastic foundations. Let the recognition you enjoy be a comfort to you."

I looked after him as he followed the others out, then walked to the screen that separated the back of the stage. Low voices mixed with sobs were coming from there. I had my own comforting to do.

The feast was held in the same hall where the performance had taken place just a few hours earlier. It was a subdued affair despite an abundance of unwatered wine, roasted stag, and choice sweets like candied figs and almond-honey cakes. It was beginning to darken outside when Rego approached me and whispered that a messenger from Mainz had arrived.

In my parlor, I found a young man with wet hair, a soggy cape, and leather boots splattered with mud, which testified to rainy conditions on the road. I offered him wine. He took the goblet, but before he drank from it, he said, "I bring a message from the archbishop's court. His Majesty King Konrad has died at Bamberg."

"May God receive his soul."

The man inclined his head. "And we have a new king."

"Oh?" I was surprised at the speed of the succession.

"The electors chose Duke Frederick of Swabia two days ago at Frankfort. Archbishop Heinrich requests that Bishop Osbert return to Mainz immediately."

Distant thunder rumbled over the forest. The storm — rare for that time of year — that the messenger had encountered on the road was approaching St. Rupert.

"I think perhaps it is best to wait until morning," I suggested.

A shadow of anxiety crossed the young man's face, but he knew the danger of traveling with a large party in deteriorating conditions. "Then we will leave at first light," he conceded.

I returned to the hall to make the announcement. Short-ly thereafter, under the first drops of rain, the guests made their way to the church, where the servants hurriedly lighted candles for one more service.

"*Requiem aeternam dona eis, Domine,*" the sisters intoned from the chancel, the candles flickering around the altar.

"*Et lux perpetua luceat eis,*" the congregation replied from the near darkness of the nave.

I closed my eyes, suddenly swept by a wave of exhaus-tion. The last two days—the demands of hospitality, the cer-emony, Helenger's outburst, and now this news that had brought renewed uncertainty to the empire—had drained me of all energy.

But trouble was never far from home either, I remind-ed myself as I listened to Father Nicholas's voice leading the service. He was the canons' eyes and ears among us. I had decided that it was better to let him stay so I could keep an eye on him in turn. Any replacement would just be another of their men. Change would have to wait for a new archbish-op who would wrest control back from the canons, for the rivalry there was long-standing and practically part of that ecclesiastical see. In the meantime, making sure that Nicho-las was not privy to any information beyond that necessary to performing his duties was an effort in itself, and it was taking its toll on me.

The storm had brought a change in the weather. The following morning was chilly, more March-like with rem-nants of fog still clinging to the church's towers as Bishop Osbert's servants loaded saddlebags onto their horses. The beasts pawed the ground restlessly, sensing the nervous at-mosphere, while the bishop and I stood apart.

"Abbot Helenger's hasty departure yesterday prevent-ed us from putting our agreement in writing, but I drafted a formal petition for the charter nonetheless." I produced a rolled up parchment from the folds of my habit. "Perhaps this will allow us to start the process while I send Brother Volmar to St. Disibod to obtain that document."

Osbert took the scroll. "I will present it to the archbishop, but keep in mind, Sister, that his is only one of the signatures that will be required for your charter. It may take a while, given the current situation." He sighed. "This succession could not have come at a worse time."

He looked tired, as if he had not slept last night. I guessed that, in addition to the archbishop's flagging health, he was also preoccupied with the new political reality.

"Who *is* Duke Frederick?" I asked. The name was familiar—he was almost certainly royal kin—but his politics eluded me.

"King Konrad's nephew."

"Ah. Do we know how he will conduct his relations with Rome?"

The bishop shook his head slowly, the downturned corners of his mouth conveying deep uncertainty. "This is what we must try to gauge now. His late uncle was a devout man who had led crusaders to the Holy Land and cultivated good relations with Pope Eugenius and his predecessors. But Frederick is known to be ambitious, iron-willed, and quarrelsome."

Not a good sign, I thought wearily. In this unending struggle for power over men and their souls, hot temperaments and pride were never helpful.

"What happens now?"

"He will be crowned in Aachen before long." The bishop mounted his horse, then turned to me once again. "All *we* can do is pray for a peaceful reign."

But something in his face told me there was little hope for that at Mainz.

171

21

April 1152

I T WOULD BE some weeks before I learned the full extent of what had happened the night Helenger had left St. Rupert in such haste.

It had been a stormy and unsettled night, unusual for that time of year, with rain and thunder from compline until after matins. Helenger had left when it was still light and dry, and stopped to procure provisions for the road at an inn about a league from Weiler. As he and his companions awaited their order, they overheard a merchant traveling to Bingen saying that the Abbey of St. Disibod had been attacked and burned. Instead of hurrying to be with his stricken brethren, Helenger — apparently over the objections of the monks accompanying him — decided to turn around and head for Mainz to seek shelter with the canons there.

The subsequent events were described to me in a letter by Brother Peter, based on what Reinmar, Helenger's servant, had related to him.

The other two monks not only advised against going to Mainz, but were concerned about the approaching dusk and the rising wind. But Helenger was insistent, claiming they would find another inn before nightfall. They set off and continued toward the bridge on the Nahe as the rain began falling, slowly and sparsely at first.

It was not until a thunderclap broke above their heads and the spring shower turned into a downpour that they began to look for human habitations. Finding none, they were forced to move off the road to seek shelter inside the forest, where the canopy of branches — still bare of leaf — was thicker. For the next few hours, as the night fell around them, everyone except Helenger stood quaking in fear for their lives until the storm passed and moonlight filtered through a thin fog. With such scant illumination and amid the soggy landscape, they were no longer sure of the way back to the main road — there were several paths radiating from where they stood — and they chose the widest in hopes that it would lead them there.

Some time later they arrived at a stream, swollen by the sound of the waters tumbling with brisk urgency over the rocky bottom. Nobody knew its name.

"Are we lost, Father?" Reinmar asked.

Helenger considered the position of the veiled moon, then looked down at the stream, barely visible in the shadows below. "It is flowing east — it must be a tributary of the Nahe," he said authoritatively. "We should follow its course and cross at the first opportunity."

Reinmar was not convinced. "How do you know?"

"I do!" Helenger turned to him angrily. "Where else can it lead?"

A skeptical silence fell on the group as they continued on, the abbot making a show of looking out for a crossing and murmuring under his breath until a footbridge material-ized when they were almost upon it.

"Father Abbot, it is too dangerous to make the crossing right now," the servant warned as Helenger headed for it.

"The stream is not so wide, and the footbridge looks solid."

"We cannot know that. There isn't enough light."

"Reinmar is right," one of the monks interjected. "We should wait until daybreak."

"Nonsense." Helenger waved his hand. "By daybreak we will be drying our habits by a hearth somewhere."

He dismounted and approached the bridge as the moon broke more clearly through the mist and clouds. The water glittered momentarily.

"Let me go first," Reinmar offered. "I will see how solid the planks are."

Helenger shook his head. "I will go first." He put a ten-tative foot on the bridge, and they could hear the soft tapping of his sandal against the wood. "It's firm," he announced with his usual confidence.

He took a few slow steps, pulling his horse behind him. When the hollow sound of the animal's front hoofs on the planks echoed in the dripping silence, a night bird shrieked in the nearby underbrush. The horse spooked, rearing up. Helenger must have been holding the reins tightly, for when the horse's head went up, his arm went with it, and he was lifted off his feet before he released the reins. As he tried to steady himself, the soles of his sandals slipped on the wet planks, and before any of his companions had a chance to re-act, Helenger fell into the water with an awful kind of grace, his berobed arms outstretched like the wings of a dark angel descending into the abyss.

The current took him swiftly, and his cries soon turned into increasingly desperate gagging and choking. A moment later, the outline of his thrashing figure vanished downstream as the silvery water swallowed the man and the sound, leaving only an eerie silence behind.

They remained by the bridge until first light, then continued along the stream, hoping to find their abbot. There was no sign of him when they arrived at the first settlement they encountered, a village named Dorsheim. A party of men was dispatched to look for Helenger. They found his body later that day, badly smashed and stuck between rocks downstream from the village.

Dorsheim was farther south than they had thought, and it took some time for the news to reach Mainz and St. Disibod. The latter, in the final twist of irony, had not been burned down at all. It was one of those rumors occasionally spread by travelers anxious about reports of marauders or mercenaries, for our realm remained full of simmering local conflicts that threatened to boil over at any moment. But such bands tended to stay away from towns, preferring to pillage villages and hamlets for supplies.

Despite its poor defenses, St. Disibod was safe, even as its abbot had died in an icy stream while in the act of abandoning his duty.

The night the news reached us, I sat gazing into the flame of the lone candle that burned on Volmar's desk. Helenger's death had shaken me in a way I never would have expected.

For a long time we were both lost in our private thoughts. "As a Christian," Volmar said finally, "I grieve for his demise, and in such terrible circumstances. But he brought this onto himself through his rash actions and a lifetime of ill-will toward everyone."

I walked to the darkening window. It faced the direction of the road to Disibodenberg, buried now under the black outline of the forest, patches of mist floating above it. It would be another damp and chilly night, not unlike the one during which Helenger had met his end.

"Everything has an outward and inward way of being," I reflected. "What is obvious, and what is concealed. With our eyes, we can see only faint shadows, and not the mighty driving force behind all things."

22

September 1152

FOR MONTHS, THE eyes of Christendom had been turned to Aachen. For the first time in fifteen years, the Holy Roman Empire had a new ruler. His predecessor had left it fragmented, although he had managed to maintain an uneasy peace — underpinned by the imperfect concordat of 1122 — with the papacy and the German Church.

When the details of the succession had emerged, it became clear why the Duke of Swabia had ended up victorious. For one thing, King Konrad's son was a child of six years. Frederick, on the other hand, was a seasoned soldier, who had fought alongside his uncle in Bavaria against the Duke of Zähringen, then accompanied the king on a crusade, where his exploits became legendary. On his deathbed, the king had handed over his insignia to Frederick, indicating the duke as his chosen successor. Although there were only two witnesses to that — Frederick himself and the Archbishop of Bamberg — it seemed enough for the electors, and Frederick duly ascended the throne less than three weeks later.

The initial signs had pointed to a more optimistic future under King Frederick. He was a descendant of the two most prominent — and rival — families of the realm; on his father's side, he was a Hohenstaufen like Konrad, and a Welf on his mother's. As such, he offered a greater hope than anybody before him for mediating feuds among the dukes, many of whom aligned along clan lines.

His policy toward Rome was more difficult to anticipate. Despite the long truce, the papacy and the monarchy still vied for control of temporal affairs as well as matters of faith across the empire's vast territory, which stretched from the middle of the Italian peninsula up to Denmark and the Northern Sea, spilling its middle bulk out toward the borders of France in the west and the kingdoms of Poland and Hungary to the east.

But if an overture on the part of the new king toward Pope Eugenius was yet to come in the first half of 1152, rumors of his strained relations with the Archbishop of Mainz reached us by the summer. Archbishop Heinrich had supported the succession of Konrad's young son, and he was now refusing to acknowledge Frederick's legitimacy. Bishop Osbert must have known — or at least suspected — that development, and his anxiety on the morning of his departure from St. Rupert made even more sense now. The news only added to my concerns about the charter. As dark clouds gathered over the ailing archbishop's head, my foundation would be the last thing on his mind.

From my lookout spot above the gate, I watched Abbot Peter and another monk make their way up the hill one afternoon in early September. The forest behind them was just beginning to change colors. The trees were still mostly green, but the greenness was of a dull, sun-scorched quality, the tops of their crowns already browning as if they had been dusted with cinnamon powder.

The election of Peter—and the snubbing of Prior Aelred—for the post of abbot of St. Disibod had been a welcome news. I knew that Peter would be easier to deal with than Helenger's pompous deputy. In addition to being a sycophant, Prior Aelred was one of those men who, when given authority over others, are prone to misuse it in depraved ways. Peter, on the other hand, was a principled man of courage and goodwill. St. Disibod would be in good hands under his stewardship.

I regarded his familiar figure, trim and straight despite his more than fifty years, as he approached the gate, then I made my way down the steps.

Peter greeted me, and I saw that he was as handsome as ever. The aging process had spared him any substantial hair loss, and the subtle lines on his forehead and cheeks only enhanced the look of honest intelligence for which I remembered him. "I have heard much about your church from the few pilgrims who still visit St. Disibod," he said. His tone was frank and without jealousy, but with some bitterness.

I was aware that since my departure, the abbey had suffered a decline in the number of candidates for novitiate, and therefore in endowments, but the dwindling pilgrim numbers must have been due to Helenger's overall mismanagement. How many arguments had I had with him about his efforts to restrict access to the infirmary for those from outside of Disibodenberg or for those who could not afford to leave a donation? A clear violation of The Rule, it must only have gotten worse since then. Peter had his work cut out for him to undo the damage and restore Abbot Kuno's legacy.

When we sat down in my lodging later that evening to discuss the settlement, I offered to improve on the deal I had made with Helenger. "The original agreement from four years ago stipulated that at the end of five years, half of the estates we legally own would revert to us, while St. Disibod would gain formal ownership of the remaining half."

Peter nodded.

"I wish to amend those terms." I raised an open palm in a reassuring gesture when I saw alarm in his face. "I will add more estates to my gift to St. Disibod."

Volmar passed me a piece of parchment with the list I had dictated earlier. I moved it closer to the light of my desk candle, for my eyesight was beginning to grow weaker. "I am ceding the following additional properties to St. Disibod: five of the ten houses we own along the Nahe, another two half-shares, the vineyards at Bergen and Budesheim, and a tithe in Roxheim." I looked up at Peter, who seemed stunned. "This will take effect immediately, so you can start collecting the non-farm rents as soon as possible."

"I do not know what to say. I am deeply grateful."

I waved a hand, momentarily too moved to speak. I had not realized how much St. Disibod still meant to me. "It is my pleasure," I said, my voice thick with emotion. "We have received generous endowments here that earn us a good income, and now that the bulk of the church construction is over, our expenses are not as great." I added, "The abbey and the town walls needed repairs thirty years ago when they were first threatened. If you keep putting it off, one day the kind of news that sent Helenger to his death may not be a mere rumor."

"Our safety is my priority."

"Let it symbolize the final reconciliation between our two houses," I said, pouring wine into three cups and raising mine. "It is what I have always wanted."

When we concluded our business, Volmar went to the scriptorium to draft the final agreement for our signatures. Later, the three of us reassembled for a private supper.

"When I was departing from St. Disibod, Abbot Helenger accused mé of being ungrateful," I said, suddenly indignant as I poured the last of the elderberry wine from a flagon into our cups. Our plates were wiped clean, and we had fallen to reminiscing about old times. "But I still have deep affection for the abbey. It nurtured me from a young child and made me who I am today. And I care deeply about the people of Disibodenberg and their well-being." Tears stung my eyes as I was swept by a wave of nostalgia.

"The brothers have always known that," Peter assured me with great zeal, his face flushed. "There is a great deal of pride among them in what you have achieved."

I raised my eyebrows in exaggerated surprise. My vision was becoming blurry. "I thought that so many years of Helenger had destroyed any goodwill they may have had toward me."

"Not so." He smiled beatifically, a combination of wine and the memory of his own recent triumph. "Already in the first round of voting, it was clear that Aelred would not have enough backers to prevail. Only four monks out of the twenty-five supported him against me. It was"—he raised an index finger high for emphasis—"a total repudiation of Helenger."

I blinked. "I had no idea Helenger was so unpopular."

"He was feared, for as well you know, he had a vindictive streak and could make life miserable for those who crossed him. When he died, it felt like we could talk without looking over our shoulders for the first time." Peter accompanied every word of that statement with a nod.

"And Aelred didn't have the same strength and charisma on which to build his base and get everyone in line." Volmar laughed and took a last swig of the wine.

Peter thought for a moment, then nodded again. "Compared to Helenger, Aelred is a weakling, but such men must not be underestimated. He has a penchant for cruelty and that, too, made the monks reluctant to elevate him to the abbacy."

Despite my fogginess, I remembered with a shudder Aelred's delight in inflicting corporal punishment on misbehaving novices. The monks of St. Disibod deserved credit for stopping him. "How did he take the defeat?"

"Not well. He moped around the abbey for some time, then asked me to release him from my authority last month so he could move to Mainz to take a post at the cathedral there."

A sudden chill cleared my head. The alarm I saw in Volmar's eyes must have mirrored my own. "And you agreed?"

"I was only too happy to oblige." He gave us a quizzical look. "Why?"

Somewhat haltingly, I told him about Helenger's threat to have Canon Walter—now Provost Walter—"keep an eye on me" and about Father Nicholas's connection to the canons. "They first installed their man as a priest here, and now Aelred is in Mainz, bitter about having been passed over for the abbacy. This is not going to help our cause." I rubbed my temples, feeling an oncoming headache. I hoped it was the wine and not my old illness, which had lessened as I entered my middle age.

Our earlier lightness evaporated. "If I can be of any help, let me know," Peter said, sounding guilty. "I will write to the archbishop to confirm that I am not raising any objections to your petition for a charter."

"Archbishop Heinrich is well-disposed toward us, but it is a race against time. We have had news from Mainz about King Frederick's attempts to depose him."

The abbot looked aghast. "I have heard there was a discord there, but I had no idea it was that serious."

"It appears so," Volmar confirmed. "The king cannot do it himself—he needs a papal judgment for that—but Pope Eugenius is said to be listening."

"This is not the kind of cooperation we had been hoping for." I shook my head despondently.

"No."

"The concordat gives the king the right to weigh in on episcopal elections, and if this is any indication, he is likely to enforce it to the letter to ensure a friendly successor at Mainz," I said. The Archbishop of Mainz was also, *ex officio*, the Imperial Chancellor and Primate of the German Church. "So if the signatures are not collected soon, there is no telling when, or even if, we will have a charter."

23

May 1153

I N THE SPRING of the year 1153, the king signed a treaty with Pope Eugenius at Konstanz that was seen by many as a goodwill gesture. Frederick promised to defend the honor of the papacy; refrain from making peace with the troublesome King Roger, leader of the Normans of Sicily; and to force the rebellious Romans to submit again to the authority of the pope. In exchange, Eugenius declared himself ready to bestow the imperial crown on Frederick and acknowledge the rights of the empire on the Italian peninsula. On a separate and more personal note, the pope also granted the annulment of Frederick's childless marriage to Adela von Vohburg. Thus the year had started in an atmosphere of hope for the empire and the Christian world, if not for Frederick's unfortunate queen.

To the Magistra of the Convent of St. Rupert,

I write to inform you that our cousin, Ricardis, has most untimely departed this life. During her last days, and in front of many witnesses, she expressed a heartfelt love and longing for your community, which I know she would have visited soon had death not prevented it.

I therefore ask you that you keep her in your prayers, and may God reward you for the benevolence and kindness you showed her during the years she spent with you.

May He also bring you and your sisters consolation in this sad hour.

Hartwig, Archbishop of Bremen

"Ricardis has died." I folded the letter, surprised at the evenness of my voice even as I felt blood draining from my face and pooling painfully somewhere in my chest.

Griselda looked up from the correspondence she was sorting at a table near the window. There was a moment of sorrowful silence, then she said, "Tell me what I can do for you."

"I would like to be left alone for a little while."

Griselda rose, but before she left, she brought me another letter and placed it on my desk without a word. I saw that it bore the seal of the Archbishop of Mainz. I remained in my chair, drained of all strength, my mind blank, watching the sunlight that fell through the window travel across the opposite wall. It softened, mellowed, and grew more amber, then orange as the day progressed toward evening, measured by the regular sounds of the bell ringing for services.

So Ricardis had regretted her decision. There was some comfort in that thought, even if she was never coming back. The delightful flower once so in harmony with the world was in harmony with the celestial spheres now; why, then, did it feel like punishment? A punishment for both of us — Ricardis for having allowed herself to be tempted by worldly advancement, and me for not having been able to forgive when she had asked for forgiveness on that last day. That was the hardest thing: we had parted without reconciliation, with angry words forever left between us.

When my chamber grew dark, I rose and stepped out into the purple dusk of the courtyard. It, too, was mournfully quiet. The first person I found inside the cloister was Burgundia. "We are going to say the Office of the Dead," I told her. "And take turns keeping a vigil through the night."

I returned to my parlor. I would have to carry the burden of my grief for the rest of my days, but there was consolation in my work and in my mission. I picked up the letter from Mainz — either the archbishop had been deposed, or I had my charter.

Four days later, on the first day of June, fifteen months after the consecration, I set off for Mainz accompanied by Volmar and Rego. As I put distance between myself and St. Rupert, I recalled my first journey to Sponheim years earlier, after Jutta had died. It had helped me in my mourning then, and I hoped it would happen again this time. I felt lighter with each passing league, as if a heavy cloak were being lifted off my shoulders, anticipation pushing out the despondency into which I had fallen. After a full day of riding, we stopped overnight at the ancient Abbey of St. Albans, two leagues outside the city.

"Brother Volmar spent time at Cluny and tells me that your church is not much smaller than that grand French sanctuary," I complimented Abbot Gottfried at supper. Earlier, we had attended Mass with the monks. The church was twice the size of the one at St. Rupert, although it was built in the old style.

"In the Rhineland, it is second only to the cathedral at Mainz." Gottfried's tone was boastful before he remembered his duty as a host. "You do us a great honor by visiting St. Albans, Sister, or" — he dropped his voice in feigned confidentiality — "should I say abbess?"

"Not yet." I strove to make my voice even so as not to betray my excitement. "Not until I put *my* signature to the charter."

"God willing that will happen tomorrow."

"Indeed, it is all in His hands."

The cautionary note was not lost on Gottfried. "The uncertainty surrounding the future of Archbishop Heinrich is unfortunate," he sighed. "And with the heresy of those who deny our holy sacraments spreading again, we need a sure hand at the helm to counter such blasphemies."

I had been so wrapped up with church-building, the consecration, and the implications of Helenger's demise that I had neglected to keep abreast of the phenomenon that had once been deemed suppressed. "Are you talking about the sect that claims the world was created by Satan, and the body is so sinful they reject procreation entirely?"

The abbot nodded grimly. "The same. And they are more zealous than ever." He eyed the generous chunk of roast suckling pig on his plate. "They won't even *eat* anything that stems from coupling."

"Such preaching cannot be popular, surely!"

"Apparently it is. Their ideas are taking hold in the minds of the high- and lowborn alike, who leave their homes to live in poverty and self-denial. They roam the land in bands, seeking more converts."

I squirmed. It was that kind of asceticism, though differently expressed, that had destroyed Jutta. "Then we must do all we can to cast them from our midst."

Abbot Gottfried nodded with satisfaction. "I am glad you see it so, Sister. There are those who think them harmless and easily contained, but these Cathars are unholy people, and very dangerous. They go around accusing men of the Church of worldliness and greed, and they proclaim themselves to be the true successors to the Apostles."

"It is wrong to attempt to undermine the established Church," I said. "But it is the behavior of the clerics who fail to serve it properly and who chase vanities instead that makes it easier for such ideas to take root."

The abbot looked uncomfortable, but I did not take back my words. I would always oppose those who denied the essential goodness of all creation, yet in the Cathars' charges against the hierarchy, I saw more than a grain of truth.

The next morning I rose before lauds to welcome the day I had been awaiting for so many years. The abbey was still quiet when I came out into the courtyard and sat on a stone bench against the cloister wall. From somewhere nearby came the intermittent twittering of the birds waking up to a new day as the eastern sky began to pale. St. Albans stood on a hill overlooking Mainz, and although I could not see it from my bench, I imagined the shutters in the windows of the city's buildings being thrown open to let the rays of the new sun banish the lingering shadows of the night.

A sound of footsteps broke the stillness of the hour, and their cadence was so familiar I did not have to turn my head. "I remember another morning like this just before I took the veil," I said as the footsteps stopped. "I feared that if I went through with it, I would never be able to welcome a new day with you."

He sat down next to me. "Thankfully, you were wrong."

The bell rang out for lauds. A short time later the sound of many sandaled feet, shuffling with a practiced rhythm, announced the monks filing into the church.

But the two of us did not move from our secluded bench for a while.

We arrived at the gates of Mainz shortly before midday. The bustling city, the economic and religious heart of the Rhineland, impressed me immediately with its size and evident wealth. Its status was visible in the imposing stone residences of nobility and the fine timber-framed houses of prosperous merchants lining its main streets. But the side alleys and back lanes told a different story. Dirty faces of hungry children lurked out of them, and sore-covered limbs of cripples and beggars extended in hopes of alms and scraps from the passersby. The cool shadows—for even the sun seemed to strain to penetrate the narrow passageways crowded with crumbling hovels—sent forth a stench that in many places overpowered the savory smells of meat pies sold at stalls along the thoroughfare that led to the cathedral. I had distributed all the coins I had in my purse even before we were halfway there.

At the crossroads of two streets, we came upon a pit being prepared for a bear-baiting spectacle. I had heard much about it, though I had never seen it with my own eyes. Curious, I dismounted my mule, leaving Volmar and Rego behind, and walked up to the man who was collecting money from an eager crowd of mainly loud young men and ragged boys, but also a few women. Behind him, chained by the neck in the corner of the pit and bearing numerous scars of previous fights, was the bear.

I was shaken by a sense of profound wrong. "Master keeper," I said, pointing to the animal. "We are all God's creatures, humans and beasts alike, and have no right to cause pain to another being for sport."

The man turned bloodshot eyes set in a small stubbly face to me as the crowd's noise abated. But his angry look softened into a cynical smile at the sight of my Benedictine habit. "I have eight mouths to feed at home, so I will do my job and you do yours, Sister." His words were accompanied by a gust of a sour beery breath as he jabbed his finger toward the cathedral. He turned back to resume his transactions.

I was about to argue further when I felt a hand grasping my arm. A moment later Volmar was steering me out of the crowd, which promptly closed behind us and returned to whistling expectantly. "It's no use. This is a time-honored tradition and a steady source of income for the animal's owner," he said, though there was sympathy in his voice. "And we are expected at the archbishop's."

We continued onward, winding slowly through the busy throng, and I found myself brooding over the scene at the pit. I had written much about nature and how we humans treat it, and this to me was the purest example of a failure. The relationship between the creation should be like that of one lover to another; when it is not, when a rupture occurs, it is a grave injustice.

I was pulled out of those ruminations only when we arrived at the square in front of the cathedral. It too was crowded.

"Must be a feast day," Rego observed as we made our way through it. "It is St. Erasmus's Day, isn't it?"

But there was something odd about the crowd, and from Volmar's face I could see that he had noticed it too. We were not looking at a bustle of daily commercial activity — no stalls here, no sellers hawking their wares, no mouth-watering cooking smells. Instead, groups of people stood talking animatedly, shaking their heads, and pointing toward the cathedral.

". . . who is going to be the new archbishop?" I caught these words out of the buzz, and my heart dropped. We were too late. Heinrich had died.

Volmar made inquiries with a group of townswomen.

"The archbishop has been deposed," one of them explained, wiping tears from her eyes. It was clear that he had been popular with the people, whom he had ruled fairly for eleven years. Now the uncertainty that had gripped the highest echelons of power for more than a year was casting its dark pall over ordinary folk as well.

"It was Pope Eugenius who made the decision," I explained to the astonished Rego as we hurried toward the cathedral, "but the king was behind it."

As if to confirm my words, we found two guards wearing the Hohenstaufen coat of arms—a black lion on a golden shield—standing sentinel at the great door. I approached one of them and produced the letter from Heinrich.

The guard glanced at the seal and shook his head. "You are too late, Sister. The archbishop is no longer in Mainz."

24

Mainz, June 1153

"WE HAVE COME from the Convent of St. Rupert near Bingen to receive our charter from the archbishop." I was not going to be turned away so easily.

"He is not here."

I exchanged a look of consternation with Volmar. "What about his advisors?"

The guard shrugged. His orders were to stand at the door, not to provide information.

It was beginning to look like we would indeed be leaving empty-handed, when a cleric in a white chasuble appeared in the doorway. I recognized him immediately as one of Bishop Osbert's deacons.

"Sister, welcome," he said. Strain was visible on his drawn face. "Bishop Osbert has sent me to look out for your arrival. He is expecting you."

Leaving the mules in Rego's care, we followed the priest inside. The cathedral was more than a century and a half old, but with a nave almost ninety feet long, it impressed with its size, despite the thick walls, low columns, and small windows. Without stopping to genuflect, the priest led us through a small side door, and we stepped into the cloister, where the archbishop's private apartments were located. We walked down a long corridor, then ascended a narrow staircase, at the top of which our guide knocked on large studded doors that opened promptly.

We found ourselves inside a large chamber. Its walls were hung with fine tapestries, and a massive oak desk stood in the center. Its chair, with an intricately carved back and a soft cushion of red velvet embroidered in gold thread, was empty. Little of the midday sunshine penetrated the narrow windows.

Bishop Osbert stood by the cold hearth—which only enhanced the chamber's forlorn atmosphere—alone, save for a young priest who had admitted us. "Sister Hildegard. Brother Volmar." His voice was somber. He had an air of mourning about him too. "It is a pleasure to see you again, and a consolation on such a sad day."

"We have only just learned the news in the square," I said. "Archbishop Heinrich is well-loved by his people, and they are flocking here as if for a vigil."

"The papal decree arrived last night, and he was forced to leave at first light. He is on his way to Einbeck now, escorted by an imperial guard," the bishop explained, after he had motioned the two clerics to leave us alone. "I fear a true vigil may be in order soon."

"Perhaps God will see fit to restore his strength once again," Volmar said.

Osbert sighed. "I pray for that every day." His tone suggested he did not have much hope for divine intervention this time.

"Do you know who is going to succeed Archbishop Heinrich?"

The bishop glanced at the door and dropped his voice. "I do, but"—he hesitated—"you must keep it a secret for now. Only a handful of people here know."

We both nodded. "Of course."

"Arnold von Selenhofen, the Chief Chancellor. He is still at Ingelheim, but I am told he will be here before the week's end. The official announcement will be made upon his arrival."

I considered this development. The new archbishop was a well-known figure around both the episcopal and the imperial courts, having been appointed Chief Chancellor by King Konrad. Prior to that, he had been provost of the Mainz cathedral, the post Walter had assumed after Arnold's appointment to the royal service. That alone was bad news, but there were other uncertainties as well. "Has he good knowledge of monastic affairs?" I asked.

The bishop shook his head doubtfully. "He has spent most of his career here"—he gestured toward the cathedral—"serving as treasurer of the diocese, then provost after he returned from his studies in Paris."

It was as I had feared. A matter of a small foundation like St. Rupert would take a long time to bring to Arnold's attention. And that was assuming goodwill on his part, which I could hardly take for granted given his association with Provost Walter.

"Obtaining a charter from him will be much harder," I said, any hopes I had entertained even a moment before fading fast.

"Ah!" The mention of the charter seemed to shake Bishop Osbert from his gloom. He moved briskly to the desk, where he picked up one of several sheets of vellum. It had a fresh seal affixed at the bottom, crimson red and shining. "Archbishop Heinrich had signed and sealed your charter before he left this morning, although his strength was abandoning him. In fact, it was the last thing he did . . ." the bishop's voice trailed off, and he was momentarily overcome. When he regained his composure, he pointed to an inkpot and quill.

"He left space for your signature below his own. Nobody will know that the customary order had not been followed."

Close to being overcome myself, I took the sheet and read through the neat black script, then reviewed the signatures of Church officials from around the Rhineland. That of Archbishop Heinrich was larger than the others but also shakier, proof that his *viriditas* was indeed ebbing away.

I placed the sheet back down on the desk, dipped the quill, waited for my own hand to steady itself, then signed it. As the three of us watched the ink dry, I reflected on the bittersweet moment, the culmination of my life's work marred by injustice done to a dear friend. With a heavy heart, I rolled up the sheet and handed it to Volmar. I recognized the same mix of emotions in his eyes.

"I am deeply grateful to Your Excellency." I turned to Bishop Osbert. "I know how difficult it was to gather all the signatures during these last months. May God reward you for championing our cause."

"The honor is mine," he said. Then he added, with vehemence, "The success of your foundation is one of the few bright spots in the Church these days."

I inclined my head. We were about to take our leave when Bishop Osbert added, a small smile softening his face, "There is one more thing."

"Your Excellency?"

"The king's men, the same ones who came to escort the archbishop to Einbeck, also brought a message for you."

I gazed at him, stunned. *A royal message? For me?*

"King Frederick will hold court at Ingelheim this autumn, and he summons you to an audience. He is eager for your advice."

25

Ingelheim, May 1154

Pope Eugenius died shortly after I brought the charter
back to St. Rupert, and Archbishop Heinrich succumbed
to old age in exile two months later. The court never came to
Ingelheim that autumn as King Frederick had fallen ill himself, and his doctors advised against leaving Aachen until he
had made a full recovery.

Yet that did not prevent him from planning a campaign
to bring his Italian vassals to heel, a project to which he turned
his sights after having restored a semblance of peace among
the feuding German nobles. To that end, the king had implemented new taxes, which Archbishop Arnold proved quite
zealous in collecting on his behalf, causing the popular mood
in Mainz to sour and turn against him by the next spring.

It was in that atmosphere that I finally made my way
to the old imperial town for the audience. All through the
journey, I contemplated Frederick's territorial ambitions and

how they were likely to put him on a collision course with Rome. Some said the campaign was about more than just a desire to assert his authority over the peninsula's northern cities and that he wished to claim sovereignty over Rome itself. That would be sacrilegious, of course, and I did not give such rumors much credence; still, the new pope was not likely to tolerate an imperial presence on his doorstep any more than the old one would have. And an expedition across the Alps would result in death and destruction among ordinary people who cared naught for the power struggles of the mighty.

"Nevertheless, it is an honor to be asked for spiritual guidance by a king," Volmar said when I shared these concerns with him. When I did not respond, he asked, "What do you hope to convey to him?"

My answer was ready; I had thought about it for months now. "That he must deal fairly and do his best to find a permanent understanding with the Holy Father for the benefit of his people," I replied as the white walls of the imperial castle came into our view in the distance, outlined against the steely-gray waters of the Rhine. "For that is his Christian duty."

Ingelheim made a worse impression on me than Mainz had the previous summer. A provincial town coming to life only on the occasion of a royal visit, it seemed to have fouler air, more beggars, fewer stalls selling pies, and more arenas for cockfighting and bear-baiting. Taught by experience, I brought more silver coins to distribute among the poor, but it was not nearly enough to relieve the need.

It was a different thing altogether when we left the town behind and approached the castle, which stood on a hill overlooking the mighty river's southern bank. It was a military fortress surrounded by a moat and fortified walls, with only small lookout windows around the perimeter and a large semicircular structure in the northeastern corner.

There were six round towers along the semicircle, and men-at-arms surveying the land could be seen through some of the arched windows.

The castle had been built by Emperor Karolus Magnus more than three hundred years before, but the stone of its walls was still dazzlingly white. It had been one of his favorite residences, but had lost its stature when the administrative center of Rhenish Franconia had shifted to Mainz. King Frederick made only rare appearances here, preferring the palace at Aachen and Kaiserlautern, his new hunting lodge in the south. Still, despite its minor status, the Ingelheim castle remained a formidable structure.

Volmar presented the letter of invitation stamped with the royal seal to a guard. We were ushered through an arched tunnel into the inner courtyard, where brightly-dressed courtiers and clerics in dark lawyers' robes came and went between the buildings ranged along the perimeter. I noted signs of both greatness and decay as we followed another soldier past the castle church, with an arched dome roof and a row of small windows. To one side, I glimpsed a hall stretching the length of the wall, likely the royal residence, with a colonnaded façade that looked elegant but worn, the stone of the capitals chipping in many places. Crossing the courtyard, we arrived at a large rectangular building, whose longer far side formed a part of the rear wall of the compound. It easily towered over all the other structures but bore the same marks of age as the hall. It was the *aula regia*, where the king held his court.

The presence chamber occupied the entirety of the building and resembled an enormous single-nave church lined with clerestory windows on both sides. It had to be over thirty feet high, and a buzz of conversation rose to the coffered ceiling, creating an echo. I had imagined a royal audience would be held in reverent silence, much like the moment of transubstantiation during Mass. Instead, the chamber was full of knights and ladies in sumptuous dress, laughing and chatting; senior officials with gold chains of office discussing business while their attendants held scrolls of documents; and prelates in their finest robes carrying on conversations in small groups. Above the heads of the crowd, military banners and flags of the different imperial territories lined the length of the walls. Among them, I recognized the silver wheel of the archbishopric of Mainz and the golden lions of the Palatinate of the Rhine.

Our escort whispered something to yet another guard, who disappeared into the crowd. He returned some moments later with a richly dressed courtier, who motioned us to follow him down the central aisle. As we walked along the checkered marble floor, people stepped aside, some with curious looks or pausing mid-sentence at the sight of our Benedictine habits, others barely noticing as they carried on their talk.

When we finally cleared the crowd, we found ourselves in an open area at the far end of the hall that ended in an apse framed by a wide and graceful arch. It was there that the throne stood on a three-step elevation, the imperial banner depicting a black eagle against a golden background draped on the wall above it.

The King of Germany and soon-to-be-crowned Holy Roman Emperor was seated on a high-backed chair of carved dark oak, with courtiers in attendance on both sides. He was conversing with the nobleman closest to him, leaning slightly to one side while his beringed hand was casually draped over the opposite armrest. Our guide bid us stop some distance away and wait. When Frederick had finished with the courtier, he turned to us and made a beckoning gesture, and the guide prompted me to step forward to the foot of the throne.

Frederick was a man of medium build, and his large throne only enhanced that impression. But, true to his reputation for physical strength and vigor, he was muscular and broad shouldered, and his erect posture gave him a commanding presence. Earlier, Volmar had calculated that the king was around thirty years old, but his handsome face, framed by a small reddish beard, looked youthful and unscarred, even though he had already led men to battle in the Holy Land. Only the brownish tint of what once must have been a fair complexion betrayed a life of adventure. His dark blue eyes had the keen, intelligent look of a man of broad learning and deep curiosity. I contemplated him until he spoke. A fervent crusader, he had a serenity about him that spoke of piety, but also of a sense of mission and confidence in his divine mandate.

"Abbess Hildegard, your fame had reached us even before our election," he addressed me in a surprisingly warm voice that carried well despite the chatter behind us continuing unabated. "*Scivias* is a soothing reminder of God's power and mercy."

I moved to kiss his ring. "I am humbled by Your Majesty's interest in my writings and the praise you choose to bestow on them," I said, straightening up. "However, these words are not my own; I am but a sounding trumpet, providing a voice for that which is divine so that it can be heard more clearly," I added, laying the ground for what I knew I must say to him.

"That is why we have long wished to invite you to our presence," Frederick replied. "Holding the court at Ingelheim was a great opportunity, as it is not far from your abbey."

"I appreciate Your Majesty's consideration." I smiled. "But I am not yet so old as that. I would gladly have made a far longer journey to have the honor."

Frederick laughed, notes of genuine mirth echoing off the rounded wall of the apse. His attendants followed, more modestly. "You are anything but old, Abbess, judging by the reports of your works." He switched to a more confidential tone, his eyes twinkling with amusement. "In my experience, a sense of humor is uncommon among people of the consecrated state. I enjoy it very much."

Then he grew more serious, again the monarch. "You may have heard that we will soon be embarking on a journey to Rome to assert our rights. We would therefore ask for your view on how to secure the Almighty God's favor in our endeavor."

I made an effort to hide my surprise. I had expected a question of a more personal nature, something that showed that he had struggled with the possibility of going to war with other Christians and perhaps with the Church itself. But this man was already convinced that whatever he was planning to do was the right thing.

"It is my belief," I said, after a moment's consideration, "that if Your Majesty's cause is just and intentions noble — if you act righteously and beware ill advisors — God will bless your effort."

Frederick seemed satisfied. "That is our goal," he assured me.

"But God also says" — I lifted my head and raised my voice slightly for emphasis — "'I will crush those who scorn and spurn me, and my sword will smite them'."

The courtiers' expressions froze as they awaited the royal reaction. Frederick narrowed his eyes, and a calculating expression played on his features for some moments. Then his lips broke into an appreciative smile, true to his reputation for demanding honesty from his advisors. The faces around him relaxed.

"We are going to assert our sovereignty over our unruly Italian subjects, then head to Rome to claim the imperial crown. Surely that is just, for both belong to us by reason of our electors' choice and our anointment by the Archbishop of Mainz."

"A just cause is one that has the peace and prosperity of the land for its guiding principles."

Again, the courtiers tensed.

The king considered me again, and when he responded, his tone was calmly deliberate. "We go in peace and will strive with all our effort to maintain the honor of the empire. However, the reception we receive, either by the Lombards or by Pope Anastasius, remains to be seen."

He does not trust anybody, especially not the new pope, I thought. "Certainly, peace cannot be one-sided," I agreed. "This is why I pray that His Holiness has the same intentions."

"We shall find out soon enough. We leave this summer, and if all goes well, we will be in Rome before the year's end." He paused, a frown creasing his forehead. "Abbess Hildegard, I sense that the relations between the empire and the Roman Church worry you." I inclined my head slightly in acknowledgment of his perceptiveness. "But I would have you know that I do not deny the spiritual authority of the occupant of the throne of St. Peter, for I am fully aware of the obligations my faith imposes on me."

He leaned forward, his crown — a golden band adorned with trefoils around its circumference — glinting in the light of the torches on both sides of the throne, despite the bright day outside. "In this kingdom, I have put the Church's property under my protection. On the peninsula, we have a mutual interest in ensuring that the Normans in Sicily are kept in check. So," he concluded, leaning back in his chair, "there is no reason why the pope should not welcome us with open arms."

"I hope Your Majesty is right," I said, my hopes that the sovereignty of Rome would be respected strengthening. "If that is so, then may the Holy Spirit protect you and guide you in your undertaking."

The king signaled to an attendant, who moved forward and placed a purse in the royal hands, bowing.

"I have always valued monasteries as centers of devotion and learning," Frederick said. "Which is why I wish to present this donation to the Abbey of St. Rupert to support its holy work."

Walking back toward the gate of the castle where Rego waited for us, I felt buoyed with a sense of optimism. "Perhaps King Frederick will be the one who will put an end to this mutual distrust once and for all."

"He will need cooperation on the other side," Volmar reminded me of my own words.

I weighed the purse in my hands. "And I hope he will have it, for he seems a wise and generous man."

There must have been at least a hundred silver marks in it. Enough to build a priory.

26

Bingen, October 1159

A STRONG GUST of wind caused the barge to pitch to one side, and I gripped my seat to stop from tumbling.

"Are you all right, Abbess? Father Nicholas?" Udalric turned toward us. He was Rego's younger brother who operated a service across the Nahe ferrying goods and people to and from Bingen.

I nodded in response, but the priest would have none of it. "I said it was a bad idea to make a crossing on such a windy day." His face was white and his features twisted in an exaggerated grimace. "The bridge is the way to go at this time of year." He set his lips in an offended pout as his knuckles gripped the bench fiercely.

"And I said we don't have the time," I replied curtly. The crossing was rough, but Udalric and his partner Alard were doing a good job keeping the boat on course. "Herr

Giselbert has taken a turn for the worse, and we would lose valuable hours traveling upriver to take the bridge."

"All will be well, Father," Udalric tried to reassure him. "We have worked in much worse conditions—through downpours and hailstorms—and kept our skins, haven't we, Alard?"

"Aye," Alard grunted from the other end of the boat without looking up from his oar.

"Any parish priest from Bingen could have given him the sacraments," Nicholas mumbled.

"He is a friend of the abbey, and it befits you as our priest to do it." I turned my face expectantly to the opposite shore, hoping to forestall further discussion. He was in his thirties, twenty years younger than I. If I could make the trip, so could he.

Needless to say, I did not trust Father Nicholas any more now than I had when he had first arrived at St. Rupert. But I kept him on because Archbishop Arnold, being much friendlier with the canons than his predecessor, would likely have sent another cleric of his ilk as replacement. Fortunately, Nicholas was lazy and fond of comforts—like sleeping late—and I obliged him by never complaining of his missing the morning services. I also frequently sent him undiluted wine—another one of his weaknesses—in the evenings to help him sleep even better. That way I managed to keep him out of my way most of the time.

But today I needed him for once. The patient in the hospital I was building next to the priory was not only a current patron, he had also made it known that he intended to leave a large bequest to St. Rupert. Like many wealthy men, Giselbert was sensitive about how he was being treated and demanded the best of everything, which was why I had made this crossing twice a week for the last two months to check on him. Then last night, Elfrid had sent word that he was ready to make his peace with God.

"How are you faring?" Despite my lingering irritation with the priest, I greeted my old companion warmly when we arrived at the hospital. Elfrid, in her sixties now, seemed to have shrunk with age, her moon face becoming thinner and her once ruddy complexion earthy and wrinkled. But she was still a competent physician and had energy to spare. "And how is Herr Giselbert?"

"I am well, praise God, but he is so weak I sent for a local priest this morning in case you would be delayed." She nodded toward Father Nicholas, who could not resist a snort under his breath. "He is already confessed, but I am sure he will be content to see you," she added, ignoring his reaction, and turned to lead us down the corridor toward a private cell on the ground floor.

Giselbert was propped up on three pillows. "I have been worried you would be too late," he greeted me with a tremble in his voice, a sign that his *viriditas* was departing his body. "Who knew that after all I have done in life, a broken leg would be my undoing?"

I could not help smiling, for there was indeed irony in this self-deprecating remark. For years, Giselbert had been a thorn in the Church's side, haranguing audiences on court days about clerical appetites for property. At local taverns after the day's proceedings, he would also throw in allegations of appointments to holy offices being fought over like bones among dogs or traded like barrels of beer at the market. But after his excommunication — and the death of his wife, who had made him promise on her deathbed that he would not imperil his immortal soul with dangerous talk anymore — he had relented and made peace with Mainz.

I lifted his blanket and palpated the injured extremity, causing Giselbert to groan in pain. I had set the bone properly and immobilized it with specially hewn lengths of wood for six weeks, but it had refused to mend. The bandages were off now, but the leg was too weak to stand on, and the muscle had begun to waste. It was not an unusual outcome in a person of Giselbert's age, and it was not a good sign. I reached for a cup of wine mixed with an extract of poppy on the bedside table and helped him drink a measure.

"This will help you sleep, which is sometimes a better medicine than any draft or infusion." I helped him ease back onto the pillows. "Who knows, perhaps God will see fit to restore you to health yet."

"I think not. Though why He should want the aggravation of my eternal presence is a mystery to me." He lifted his pale blue eyes heavenward before closing them wearily.

When the poppy had done its work and Giselbert fell into a slumber, I turned to Nicholas. "Come, Father, let him rest," I said in a low voice. "I would visit the priory before we head back."

Nicholas cleared his throat. "With your permission, Abbess," he said with uncharacteristic eagerness, "I would rather stay here and pray for Herr Giselbert for a while, especially as I was not able to render him the priestly service before."

I was surprised at this surge of Christian compassion where I did not expect it. It was not like Father Nicholas to volunteer for additional duty, but if that would spare me his company for a while, I would not raise any objections. "Very well. I will see Sister Burgundia and come back to collect you on my way back to the ferry."

Before I walked through the door that connected the hospital to the priory, I stopped by a window that gave onto the inner courtyard. The hospital was the fruit of my study of the writings of Princess Anna Komnene of Byzantium, who had founded one in her native Constantinople, and it was unlike anything ever built for this purpose in the Rhineland. A two-story stone structure, it contained six spacious wards in addition to private cells, exam rooms, a medicine workshop, as well as dormitories for the staff that Sister Elfrid supervised.

I stood watching two maids carry freshly laundered linens and a tray of candles until they disappeared through the doors of one of the wards. Then Sister Beatrix, Elfrid's deputy, came out, supporting a man on a crutch, his cloak thrown loosely over his long tunic. My healing philosophy was fully on display here, encouraging patients who were able to do so to move and take fresh air regularly. The nurse and patient walked slowly around the arcaded perimeter, then Beatrix led him back inside. Despite the continuing wind, the air was unusually warm for autumn, and the sky was overcast. A few stray drops fell on to the dry leaves with a soft rustling sound, but rain seemed to be holding off.

As silence enveloped the place again, I became keenly aware of the space outside the walls invisible to me. My mind's eye rose above the rectangle of the building and moved like a bird along the path to the town, where it circled over the streets grown less crowded as the winter season approached. It crossed the river, its dark waters churning, and flew up the hill toward the abbey, where soft chant was coming from the church. Sister Juliana's words—among the last ones she had ever spoken to me—about a mission I had the obligation to fulfill rang in my ears again.

So it was *this*, and I had seen it through no matter the obstacles in my path. Juliana would be proud. I was convinced that Jutta would be too. Before turning away, I took it in one more time and felt a surge of great satisfaction.

But it still competed with regret in my heart, especially in quiet moments like that, even after all these years.

Father Nicholas did not lose his newfound perkiness on the way back to St. Rupert.

The wind had grown stronger, shaking the ferry and sending occasional sprays of water across the deck, but instead of complaining, he wanted to talk about Giselbert. Why exactly had he been in trouble with the Church? How long had it gone on? It seemed that he was reconciled now?

I answered as circumspectly as possible. I tried to keep my tone neutral. "He had been estranged for complaining that some clerics were more interested in worldly trappings than pastoral work, but he returned to the fold these last ten years."

"Such claims might have exposed him to charges of being in league with the Catharist heresy." Nicholas's tone was matter-of-fact, but his eyes watched me intently.

I held his gaze, but I felt uneasy. He was coming close to guessing Giselbert's past, including the excommunication.

"He was never a Cathar," I replied, trying not to sound defensive. Giselbert had, in fact, been accused of such sympathies, but he had never admitted to them. And his acceptance of the last rites earlier that day meant that he would die in a state of grace.

"No, of course not," Nicholas hastened to agree. "When he passes, do you wish me to go back to Bingen to preside over his funeral?"

I shook my head. "His body will be brought to St. Rupert. It is his wish to be buried in the abbey cemetery."

I thought I saw a shadow of surprise pass over Father Nicholas's face, but he offered no further comment, and I hoped to pass the rest of the journey in silence.

But then Udalric spoke. "Have you heard of the disputed papal election, Abbess?" He was a gossip, and the taciturn nature of his partner, Alard, meant that he often turned to his passengers for news and entertainment.

I nodded. I had known for a week now, ever since Volmar had returned from his latest trip to Mainz. The details of the September conclave following the death of Pope Hadrian were not clear yet, but it seemed that Emperor Frederick had come down on the side of a Roman cardinal known for his imperial loyalties who had broken into St. Peter's with a group of men-at-arms and declared himself pope, taking the name of Victor.

The emperor was across the Alps again on a new campaign, after the first one—which had culminated with his coronation in Rome in the year 1155—had failed to bring him the unanimous submission of the Northern Italian nobles. In hindsight, that had been the high point of Frederick's relations with the papacy, because Pope Hadrian had ended his days calling him "an enemy of the Church." To me, that turn of events was a bitter disappointment after I had personally pleaded with Frederick to work for peace and he had promised to act justly. But that had been in the year 1154, when the gentle Anastasius had occupied the throne of St. Peter. For the following six years, it had been Hadrian, the English pope, who had decided to make an alliance with the King of Sicily in violation of the spirit of the Treaty of Konstanz.

"Pope Hadrian and the emperor did not end on good terms," I said. It was an understatement, as the pope had been rumored to be considering the excommunication of Frederick at the time of his death. "The emperor will want to see someone more tractable on the Holy See this time."

Udalric's eyes widened. "Does he have a say in electing the pope, then?"

"He has a great deal of influence."

"Do you mean bribes?"

I laughed in spite of myself, liking the man's straightforward way of speaking. He was not far off. "It is too late for that. The votes have been cast, and Pope Alexander won under canon law." Victor, on the other hand, had secured only five votes in the Sacred College according to Volmar's information. "The emperor will likely throw military support behind Victor, and both cardinals will go on claiming the right to the title." I sighed. "The struggle will last for months, perhaps even years."

The ferryman furrowed his brow. "There cannot be two popes at the same time."

I smiled sardonically. "No, but there can be an antipope." It had happened before.

The barge approached the landing on the Rupertsberg side, and I recalled how optimistic I had been after the audience with Frederick five years before. The man who had reaffirmed the concordat, signed the treaty with Pope Eugenius at Konstanz, and confirmed the German Church's ancient rights had once seemed like the kind of ruler the empire needed. One it had not had in nearly a century. But that hope had faded as his policies had gradually taken the shape of familiar antagonisms, and now a major conflict was looming, threatening to plunge Christendom into the biggest crisis in twenty years.

As I stepped onto the brownish spare grass of the riverbank, ominous dark clouds began gathering along the western sky, and the rumble of distant thunder announced the approach of a rare October storm.

27

February 1160

I T WAS THE kind of thing I would have thought scarcely possible, yet when it happened, it came as almost no surprise. After I fought down the urge to crumple the letter and throw it into the fire, I folded it back and went to look for Volmar.

He was working on a copy of *Liber vita meritorum*. Three other desks were occupied that morning by sisters who decorated the finished sheets with patterns of green vines edged in gold leaf. They were working in quiet concentration under the supervision of Sister Johanna, now the chief illuminator, Ricardis's old post. I was momentarily comforted by the light of the many candles blazing to dispel the late winter gloom and by the warmth of the brazier burning steadily in a corner of the chamber. Then I remembered the news.

"I must speak with you," I said, approaching Volmar's desk.

He laid down his quill. "Now?"

I took a deep breath, trying to steady my rattled nerves. "That would be best." I had always admired Volmar's composure no matter the circumstances. It was something I had tried to imitate, with varying degrees of success, since the day I'd met him.

As we left the scriptorium, I thought how good it would be to have Elfrid with me now, with her wisdom and practical sense, but she was at Bingen. But when we stepped onto the cloister's inner walkway, Griselda rounded the corner with a stack of clean sheets in her arms, headed for the dorter. Even though we had lay servants, Griselda still liked to perform menial tasks, saying she felt more useful that way.

"Come with us." I beckoned her. "There is a matter I would discuss with both of you."

When we arrived at my lodgings, I motioned to them to take seats around my desk. "It's about Herr Giselbert."

Volmar raised his eyebrows. "But he has been dead these four months."

I nodded. "Dead and buried in our cemetery, but now I am being told" — I tapped the letter with my forefinger — "that the burial was illegal, and he must be moved elsewhere."

Griselda gasped. "How is that possible?"

"It has to do with his excommunication." I rubbed my forehead, still trying to disentangle the argument. "But it had been lifted long before he died. He took his sacraments, so there is no reason for him not to lie in consecrated ground."

"Then why are we being told to disinter him?" Volmar asked impatiently. "And who is ordering it? Surely not Archbishop Arnold all the way from Rome?"

Normally, this kind of decision would be made by the archbishop, but he was away south with Emperor Frederick and other German and Burgundian bishops to attend an imperial council, ostensibly to reexamine the papal election.

"No." I shook my head. "The order came from the canons in charge during his absence."

It took a while for them to absorb the information. "How do they know Giselbert is buried here, anyway? We bury people regularly without notifying Mainz—" Volmar broke off as realization dawned on him. His eyes flicked toward the door of my parlor.

I nodded again, my own suspicion confirmed.

"What are you going to do?"

I only had one choice. "What I should have done years ago." I rose with so much angry energy that the chair's legs screeched loudly across the floor. "Enough is enough."

"Wait!" Volmar called as I crossed the chamber and opened the door. "Let's talk this through before you make a . . ."

A rush of blood to my head cut off the rest of his words. Up until that moment, I had tried to keep my emotions in check, but that was no longer possible. The betrayal was too great. That poor excuse for a priest I had fed and sheltered under my roof had outwitted me. I had assumed that Nicholas's task had been to turn the locals against the abbey, or perhaps sow seeds of conflict among the sisters, and I had let the fact that there was no evidence of that lull me into complacency. Meanwhile, he had been biding his time and waiting for an opportunity to strike.

The courtyard seemed to have shrunk, for I was inside the cloister almost before I could feel my feet touch the ground. A small staircase to the right of the main entrance led to the cells that Volmar and Nicholas occupied on the upper floor. I fought the urge to push the priest's door open without knocking; instead, I pounded on the wood with an open palm, each strike like a slap echoing down the corridor.

"Open up!" I brought my face to the iron hinges that framed the oak planks. "Open the door right now!" I repeated when no sound came from the other side. Where was he?

It was still an hour to Mass. Was he in the church, begging God's forgiveness?

I was about to turn away when I heard a shuffling sound. A moment later, the door opened just enough to show Nicholas's face, looking more like a ferret than ever, wary but not particularly alarmed. "How can I be of help, Abbess?"

Indignation rose up in my chest again. "You—" The word stuck in my throat. "I want you to pack your things and leave the abbey before the end of the day."

"Is that wise?" At least he had the decency not to feign surprise.

"Be out of here today."

"I was posted by the archbishop—"

"You were posted by Canon Walter." I gave him a disdainful look from head to toe. "And to him you shall return."

"The sisters need a priest."

"We have a priest—" I began, then my eyes followed those of Nicholas, whose gaze shifted over my shoulder. Volmar stood at the top of the stairs, a hard look on his face. I had a feeling that were he not a cleric himself, he would have grabbed Nicholas by the collar of his robe and thrown him out right then, an image that delighted me even amid my anger. "So as you can see, we will do very well without you."

"Mainz will not be happy about this."

"Mainz is not happy about many things," I said. "I care absolutely naught for that."

I started for the stairs. "Do not let me find you here after vespers," I added as I passed Volmar, not looking back at Nicholas. "There is an inn in Weiler where you can find lodging overnight."

Griselda was still in my parlor when we returned. She showed no concern over Nicholas's departure, and if the priest had no friend in Griselda, then he had no friends at all. Save for the canons, of course.

"What about Giselbert?" she asked. "You are not going to let his body be ripped out of its grave?" There was a rare note of vehemence in her voice. "God will judge him justly no matter where he lies."

"No, of course not." I wanted to avoid it at all costs, but I knew it would not be easy.

"You may be in the right and the man was buried legally, but is it not better to comply and not risk repercussions?" Volmar asked, resuming his seat. "The canons apparently have little else to do than be a constant irritation." Seeing my surprise, he added, "Giselbert may have openly disavowed his earlier stance, but that doesn't mean that he had a complete change of heart."

"He will answer as to the sincerity of his beliefs before God," I said sourly. "I am sorry," I added, softening my voice. "I know you are trying to protect the abbey."

Griselda spoke again. "Perhaps this order has no real power in the archbishop's absence."

"How do you mean?"

"What if the canons take over his authority only in the most important matters, not all of them?"

I shook my head. "They have complete authority."

"They can defend the formal validity of the order if necessary," Volmar confirmed.

"Formal validity," I repeated as I steepled my fingers under my chin, an idea forming in my head. I looked down my nose at Volmar. "You know this because you are a learned man, Brother, but I am a woman and *indocta*, and therefore not obliged to be familiar with the nuances of canon law."

Our eyes met, and we smiled. We were still accomplices. "I will take your response to Mainz," he offered, amused.

"Thank you. I will inform Canon Walter that Giselbert is staying where he is, and also that you are our priest from now on, and he need not bother send anyone else."

"What if the canons don't know that the excommunication had been lifted?" Griselda asked again. She still struggled to believe that they would have done this out of nothing more than ill will or spite.

"I am sure they checked the episcopal archives. In fact" — I pointed to the letter again — "they refer to him as a 'former heretic' — which is incorrect even so, because he was never found guilty of heresy. It is more likely that fool Nicholas didn't know the whole story when he informed them about Giselbert's burial here. But be that as it may" — I waved my hand dismissively — "they are hoping that with the archbishop so far away, I will not have anywhere to appeal this order, and that I will not risk not being in compliance until he returns. But I will not be intimidated by their momentary authority, especially when it is being misused so egregiously."

Later that day, I wrote a determined refusal, but even as I did so, I was under no illusion that the canons would back down without a fight.

It was a late afternoon in June, a few days before midsummer, the time of day when the scents of flowering herbs are strongest and the busy activity of insects begins to subside. The long shadows of the fruit trees in the back of the garden and the hawthorn hedges separating it from the rest of the abbey enhanced the sense of peace in my private sanctum. I stood outside the workshop, my head uncovered, holding two cups of cool water from the spring and gazing over the neat beds of sweet bay, myrtle, sage, and fennel we had just finished weeding. Until last year, I had done this work alone — it gave me a chance to think undisturbed — but I would soon be fifty-six, and immaculate maintenance of the herb garden was becoming increasingly difficult for me. Fortunately, I enjoyed working with my niece, who was a capable herbalist.

"Village women say the summer will be dry and sunny, aunt," Hiltrud said when she returned from depositing the gardening tools in the shed, her golden complexion flushed from the work. She often used the familiar appellation when we were alone, much like Volmar, who called me by my name when there was nobody else around. I liked it because it reminded me of my life at Bermersheim with my family, even as the details of their faces—now turned to dust, every one of them—were but a blur in my mind after more than forty years.

"That would be excellent." I handed her one of the cups and took a sip from the other, relishing the water's crystalline freshness. "We need a good harvest, especially as I may be gone for a while this autumn."

Hiltrud gave me a surprised and slightly alarmed look. The longest I had ever been away from St. Rupert was four days when I had gone to Mainz to claim the charter. "Where are you going, and for what purpose?" she asked.

I narrowed my eyes as I spotted something between the sage shrubs that did not belong there. I picked up a weeding knife from its hook and went to remove the offending growth. When I was done I straightened, grimacing at a stab of pain in my right hip. "At least my eyes are still good." I laughed as Hiltrud, who had followed me down the path, extended an arm to help me up.

"You said something about a journey?"

"Ah." I smiled, a little guiltily. I had been worried about what she and the others would think about it. Volmar, I was almost sure, would advise against it. "I am thinking about visiting religious communities along the Rhine to speak about the state of the Church." I moved toward a bench at the back of the garden.

My niece was silent for some moments. To cover her uneasiness, she began to brush off the white petals that were falling around us like perfumed snowflakes.

I sighed. "I sense that you think it is a bad idea. But I feel a great need to do it, for I am deeply worried about what is happening."

"But what exactly do you have in mind?"

"I am concerned about the unchristian behavior of the churchmen who use their offices for enrichment, to satisfy ambitions, benefit families, or to hurt those they consider to be their enemies." I felt heat rising to my cheeks.

Hiltrud laid a gentle hand on my arm. "Aunt . . ."

"Yes?"

"Are you sure you are not trying to give voice to a private grievance, however justified?" She paused. "There are many righteous clerics who serve with great devotion and piety."

"'Many' is not enough. Everyone called to the consecrated state has the duty to renounce temporal ambitions, greed, and pettiness. Even if it were only one priest—which it certainly is not—that would one too many. I had embraced Giselbert as our friend in large measure because I agreed with him on the allegations he used to level at the clergy."

"But that does not mean that everyone is—"

I cut her off impatiently. "Why are you against it? Faithful servants of God have nothing to worry about, and the vile ones may be persuaded to change their ways."

"Because the Church is in turmoil as it is, racked with this schism," Hiltrud said honestly. She had little interest in matters of politics, but by now everyone was aware of the growing rift and Emperor Frederick's contribution to it through his continued support for Antipope Victor, despite his protestations of neutrality. It had made his relations with the German bishops worse of late—though not, apparently, with Archbishop Arnold. "This may not be a good time to stir things up even further. And besides, women are not allowed to preach," she added.

It was the same argument Helenger had used when the emissaries of Pope Eugenius had visited St. Disibod fifteen years before. I bristled at hearing it again but swallowed the words that had formed on my tongue; my niece had meant no harm and only voiced a view she had been raised to believe and never question. As a practical matter, she was right; despite my reputation, I would be unlikely to obtain a dispensation from the archbishop.

"That is not what I mean to do. I would talk privately with abbots, deacons, and ordinary priests, and maybe that would spur them to start a debate in their communities. All I want" — I threw my arms up in a gesture of exasperation — "is to save the Church from this self-inflicted wound of corruption that is infecting its body."

The garden gate squeaked and Gertrude stepped through, a square of white parchment in her hand. Spotting us under the apple trees, she walked over hurriedly. "There is an urgent message for you." The letter was from Mainz. I noticed dark smudges, as if from soot, under my hastily written name.

I tore the seal with a bad premonition and scanned the lines as my heart sank. "It's about Archbishop Arnold." I looked up at the two sisters, bewildered. "He has been murdered."

28

September 1164

NEEDLESS TO SAY, I had to abandon my plans for the journey. I had hoped it would be postponed by only a few weeks, but those weeks turned into months and then into years. The world continued as if engulfed by a madness that nobody seemed to know how to extinguish. The city of Mainz suffered years of upheaval following the archbishop's murder in June of the year 1160. Volmar had been in Mainz on that very day with copies of *Liber vita meritorum*, and he had witnessed the hysteria that had swept the populace and culminated in the gruesome tragedy. It had happened shortly after the archbishop's return from the Italian campaign, as the anger over high taxation and his strict administration of justice had reached a boiling point.

As the city rebelled, the archbishop was forced to seek refuge at the monastery of St. Jakob, but it was stormed by the rioting mob. Arnold was hacked to death on the steps of the monastery church, which was then set on fire. After that, Mainz descended into chaos; the citizens elected Rudolf von Zähringen as their next archbishop, but the choice was opposed by the city's nobility and most of its clergy — including Provost Walter — who fled for the safety of Frankfort. From there, they elected Christian von Buch, precipitating a local schism of our own.

It was not until the summer of 1161 that Emperor Frederick returned north and put things in order. When he did so, it was with the goal of teaching Mainz a lesson in respect for his authority. He revoked the city's ancient privileges, razed its walls, and filled its ditches. Then he installed Konrad von Wittelsbach in the archbishop's seat, bypassing an ecclesiastical election altogether in violation of the concordat of Worms.

I had despaired of the bloodshed, even though it had diverted the canons' attention away from the issue of Giselbert's burial. And so, despite its dubious legality, I welcomed the arrival of Archbishop Konrad and wrote him a letter exhorting him to work for a swift reconciliation. A regular correspondence ensued between us, for Konrad had a deep respect for the medical profession, having befriended many students of medicine during his studies at Paris and Salzburg. He wanted to know about the hospital at Bingen, and I obliged him with as much information as I deemed safe. I refrained, for instance, from mentioning the Byzantine inspiration, for Anna's nephew, Emperor Manuel Komnenos, was an ally of Pope Alexander with ambitions to forge an anti-German alliance and unite the Greek and Latin Churches.

Konrad had even sent me a donation of twenty silver marks, and we came to regard each other as friends over time, brought together by a shared love of medicine. But it was an uneasy friendship, for Konrad maintained his loyalty to Victor, the antipope supported by the emperor. The latter was increasingly isolated — the kings of England and France had backed Pope Alexander, who, for his part, had excommunicated Frederick. Then several German bishops switched their allegiance to Alexander. The smoke might have been clearing over Mainz, but the empire still had a long way to go before it saw peace.

Hiltrud waited for me at the landing as the boat came in to dock. Udalric threw the rope to his assistant on the bank, then helped me out of the ferry that had brought me back from my weekly visit to Bingen. I had to lean on his shoulder and grab the wooden railing with my other hand as I teetered on the brink of losing my balance for a moment. There was no escaping the fact that I was beginning to feel the weight of my years, and it was why the idea of going on the journey had come back to me recently, more strongly than ever.

"Old Burchard has brought his son to the infirmary again," Hiltrud informed me when I found my footing on the solid ground. "He is much weakened."

We started up the hill, my niece slowing down to match my pace as she filled me in. Ruthard—a young peasant from Weiler whose puzzling case had been dragging on since the spring—was faring worse. When he had first shown up, he complained of fatigue and headaches, and was prescribed a tonic of oak bark and dried sage. But the symptoms persisted, and Hiltrud asked me for a consultation. I added a strengthening fennel infusion and the mint rub for the headaches, but this was clearly more serious.

"I will have another look at him," I said.

"There is something else . . ." A note of caution entered Hiltrud's voice.

I gave her an inquiring look.

"A prelate from Mainz has arrived to see you. He is wearing canonical garb."

I halted in place. The expression on Hiltrud's face conveyed what I had sensed myself—there was trouble afoot. "Is he come to relitigate Giselbert's case?"

"He wouldn't say."

"Well, he will have to wait until I have seen to Ruthard," I said as we resumed our ascent, twigs cracking under our feet and birds twittering above our heads. The news could not possibly be good, but a part of me wondered with an odd sense of anticipation if Provost Walter had finally had the courage to deliver it in person.

In the exam room Ruthard was resting on a bench under the care of Sister Arnalda, a novice. As I entered, his father, a work-worn laborer with worry sharpening the lines of his face, made a move to help him up, but I motioned to let him be. The younger man—he was not yet thirty—was thinner than when I'd seen him last, his eyes sunken and rimmed with dark circles, and his skin pale and dry to touch. I wondered if it was a case of the wasting disease.

I bid him undress and examined him from head to toe for evidence of a tumor. "I do not see anything that would explain the wasting away," I said after having thoroughly palpated his frame. I remembered him as a big lad at last year's harvest, but now half of him was gone.

"And yet he is, before our very eyes, though he has a wolfish appetite." The old man struck a lamenting tone. "All he wants to do is eat and drink, but where is it all going?"

I frowned. *That* certainly did not sound like the wasting illness.

"I feel tired from the moment I wake up in the morning," Ruthard added. "And I pass water often . . . too often . . . ten times a day or more." He paused from the effort of speaking, licking his cracked lips. "Soon as I'm back from the privy, I have to run again."

"That would explain the thirst," I said, an idea forming in my head. "I will do a urine exam; from what you are saying, you should have no trouble providing a sample?"

"I asked for it before you arrived." Arnalda reached for a bell-shaped glass on a side table. "Oh!" she gasped, bringing the vessel closer to her face and looking inside.

"What is it?"

"Ants have crept inside." She looked at me apologetically. "I'm sorry, I should have covered it."

"I can provide more," Ruthard offered. "I have to go again."

"No need," I said, trying not to sound too excited. My suspicion was strengthening. "I will use this one." I took the glass from the puzzled novice's hand and lifted it to the light. I swirled it, dipped in a finger, and tasted it as everyone looked on in astonishment.

"I thought so." I held the glass toward them. "The urine is brighter than normal and has a sweet taste to it. Master Ruthard, I must ask you this — have you noticed any changes in your carnal desire?"

"How do you mean?" The young man looked uncertain.

"Your fleshly appetite — has it waned? Or perhaps increased immoderately?"

"Increased?" Old Burchard's eyes almost popped out of his head. "My son is a married man!"

Ruthard's pale cheeks bloomed with a blush. "It is *not* what it used to be," he confessed ruefully, avoiding his father's gaze.

"You have a rare condition. Greek physicians already wrote about it, but I have only seen it once in all my years of doctoring. The sweetening of the urine, in your case of the cold type, brought about by an excess of phlegm."

"Is there a cure?"

"The books prescribe no cure, though with a special diet and an herbal mixture, the symptoms might lessen. But," I added, anticipating the next question, "your strength will not return to what it once was, and I doubt you will be able to work the fields anymore."

The men's faces showed relief and worry in equal measure, and I went to the shelf to select one of my medical books. I located the passage in a translation of Aretaeus of

Cappadocia that dealt with this condition of the kidneys and bladder which—and this I omitted to mention so as not to take away their hope—often led to an early death.

"The diet used for the illness," I said, "aims to strengthen the stomach in order to combat the thirst. Aretaeus recommends a juice of raw quinces with oil of spikenard and mastic—of which I have only a small amount, but I will order more in Bingen from a merchant who recently came back from the region of the Middle Sea," I added. "For drink, you will take water boiled with autumn fruit and astringent wine to clear away other humors from the stomach. Tell your wife that your food should consist of milk, cereals, starch, spelt, gruel, and onions, and avoid salty meats because they increase thirst."

Both men, being illiterate, committed the recommendations to memory, and I reassured them that I would procure the exotic ingredients at my own cost. "I have a matter to attend to," I told them, "but afterward, I will prepare a mix of cumin, fennel, thyme, and fenugreek, and send it to your house. You will drink a glass of the infusion after each meal."

The men offered a silver penny in payment, but I refused it. With this mysterious and incurable illness, the family's situation was likely going to get worse soon.

In my parlor, a tall wiry man wearing an ill-disguised look of impatience awaited me, but he rose and inclined his head when I entered. I ignored his offended expression and bid him resume his seat. "I had an unexpected case to deal with at the infirmary, Father—"

"Ulrich," he smiled mirthlessly. "I come to speak with you on behalf of Provost Walter."

I considered him for a few moments. Now that he was about to deliver his message, the impatience had gone out of Father Ulrich's face—his thistly eyebrows were rendered more prominent by his thinness, making him look like an aging hawk—and assumed a diplomatically impassive look. But his crafty gray eyes studied me keenly, another hawk-like feature. This was the first time any of the canons had met me in person, and no doubt he was committing my image to memory so as to give his brethren a better idea of the person against whom they had been so doggedly struggling all these years.

I composed my face into an expression of polite but reserved attention. "I am honored to make your acquaintance after having dealt with the cathedral chapter via letters and messengers for so long. It is my sincere hope that this will help us avoid the kinds of misunderstandings that have overshadowed our relations in the past."

Ulrich inclined his head slightly, his steely eyes never leaving my face. "The state of our relations depends entirely upon you, Abbess," he said. "We do not seek conflict or confrontation."

I cleared my throat so as not to laugh. "What is it you seek, then?"

"To honor and protect our Christian traditions," he replied with a note of sanctimony creeping into his voice, which made him sound eerily like Helenger. I wondered if he too was kin, like Provost Walter. "And we will always speak out against any threat to those traditions."

"Then you and I share the same mission."

"Would that that were true." Ulrich's face assumed a look of studied sadness. "Alas, Provost Walter believes that certain practices of yours are a threat to the uniformity of the Latin liturgy."

I blinked. "I don't understand."

"For centuries the Mass and the Divine Office have consisted of immutable parts, with set antiphons, responsories, and hymns passed down through generations of the faithful," the canon explained obligingly. "Then you, Abbess Hildegard"—his face grew sterner—"began composing your own music and including it in your practices, which in itself is highly presumptuous. And if that were not enough, some of your chants—and we know this, for they are unfortunately sung in churches across the archdiocese, a practice we are trying to curb—eschew religious themes altogether. Instead, they praise flowers and animals and the earth, like something a shepherdess might hum as she watches her flock and swats away the flies." He paused to draw a sharp breath. "It is unworthy of a holy community like yours."

It was as if an invisible hand had choked the breath out of me. I squeezed the armrests of my chair until my knuckles turned white. "Father Ulrich, the late Abbot Helenger of St. Disibod had already tried to lodge a complaint on that account against me and was unsuccessful." I paused to let it sink in. "Our music does not offend God; it praises His creation."

"And the old liturgy is not sufficient for that purpose—is that what you contend?" he asked with a sly grin.

"That is not at all what I contend."

The canon shrugged. "If my memory serves me, Abbot Helenger's complaint was about a play you staged. This is not what I am talking about. I am referring to the celebration of Mass and the Divine Office, a far more serious matter."

"I am sorry, Father, but I still fail to follow your reasoning. What harm do our chants do to the integrity of the Latin liturgy?"

"No direct harm," he replied smoothly, "but today it is more important than ever to defend the Latin Mass, seeing as some in the East are working stealthily to join together the Latin and Greek rites, with Cardinal Roland's complicity."

The reference to Pope Alexander by his pre-accession name and title was a reminder that in the struggle within the Church, the canons had thrown their lot behind the schismatic pope.

"It is a rumor that has been widely discredited." I lifted a finger. "*Pope Alexander* would never support a proposal that would diminish the power of the Holy See."

"That is not how we see it at Mainz."

"I assure you that the music we select for our services is strictly of a religious nature. We sing *canticum laudum*, divine praise, and I will gladly provide Provost Walter with the texts."

"That will not be necessary," Ulrich replied curtly. "In fact, I am here to inform you that you are to cease performing all music in the church and limit yourself to *reading* the horarium."

I stared at him. I had expected a lengthy and tiresome sermon, and the suddenness of this announcement — and the sweeping nature of the ban — left me reeling. "You cannot do that!"

"We can because Archbishop Konrad is away, and we are confident he will uphold our decision when he comes back."

He was right about the first part, but there was nothing certain about the second claim. I met his gaze defiantly. "You had sought to force an order upon us once before that had no legal basis, and we refused to obey. What if we do that again?"

Ulrich's answer came readily enough. "You will be barred from participating in Mass altogether and from receiving communion."

"Is this payback for our refusal to disinter Giselbert?"

"Not at all. The two issues are unrelated."

It was likely a lie, but I had no proof. Besides, it was irrelevant. I was facing, if not the greatest challenge of my life, certainly the biggest heartbreak; I could not imagine a life without music and the abbey without its uplifting sounds. I had to make a quick decision so this loathsome prelate might be out of my sight and I free to deal with the aftermath.

Disregarding the ban was one option, but it would not be as easy to defend as the refusal to exhume Giselbert's body because the man had died in a state of grace and taken the sacraments. This time around, the canons had crafted their argument cleverly, using as the excuse the integrity of Mass, which might open me to charges of heresy if I persisted in the banned practice. Resistance, at least for the moment, was not an option.

"I will comply with the order," I said slowly and deliberately. "But I want you to take this message to the provost. By issuing this interdict, you are interfering with much more than the performance of music in a church. You are defying the words of the Scriptures, where David says in a psalm, 'Praise the Lord with the sound of the trumpet, praise him with the harp and lyre,' and where, in another, we are exhorted to sing joyfully to the Lord."

I lifted my palm to stop him from interrupting me, and my voice rose in emphasis. "You are, moreover, defying the prophets who, inspired by the Spirit, composed canticles that would inflame the hearts of the faithful. Their mission was to arouse souls and remind them of the divine melody of praise that Adam and the angels sang in Paradise. You will remind your fellow canons, Father Ulrich, that the devil that drove Adam from Paradise is tormented by earthly song that imitates the harmony of the music of heaven. He is therefore constantly looking for ways to confound our expression of praise by sowing distraction to eradicate it from our hearts and our mouths."

I sat back, my chest heaving. I saw, with satisfaction, that my words had an effect on my visitor. He asked sourly, "Are you suggesting that we are moved by the devil?"

"I am suggesting that you must be guided by zeal for God's justice and not a desire for revenge, for harsh judgment will fall upon those who rule unless they do so with the purest intentions."

"My impression is that you are threatening us, Abbess," Father Ulrich pronounced in an offended tone. "I will inform Provost Walter of this."

"You can inform him of whatever you wish. He has already silenced our voices; what can he do to us that is worse than that?" I rose, letting my chair screech across the stone floor. "You can leave now and hurry back to Mainz, where I hope you will report our conversation faithfully."

The canon took his leave with a curt nod. As he swept out of the parlor, nearly colliding with Volmar at the door, I called after him. "I will fight this—mark my words! We live in times in which the dispensation of justice is weak, but I will battle against this interdict to my last breath, and it will be defeated!"

In the silence that followed the door closing behind Canon Ulrich, Volmar's brows knitted in a deep frown.

I rounded on him, still livid. "Where have *you* been?" I narrowed my eyes to examine his outfit. He was wearing riding clothes, his boots muddy from the road. His cloak, still clasped at the neck, was blown off his shoulders and hanging down his back.

"I went to the mill at Binger Loch to check on the repairs there. You know how busy Rego is at harvest time," he added, trying to make it sound like a chore.

"You went for the thrill of the ride!"

"Maybe a little."

I let out a breath. "I don't like it." I had been saying this for years, yet he still rode his horse hard, a spirited chestnut that was only too happy to indulge his master's love for the open fields. "You are not a young man anymore." I considered his wind-blown hair, a faded echo of his formerly golden-brown mane, no longer thick or curly. He was also getting thicker around the waist. "At least get a more placid horse," I grumbled.

He said nothing—he loved that beast—and I changed the subject, not wanting another argument on the heels of Ulrich's departure. "How is the work going at the mill?"

"There has been a delay, and the carpenter in charge says his men will start next week. He promises to be done by the time the first batch of grain arrives."

"Let's hope so."

Volmar pointed his thumb over his shoulder. "I came in when he was still with you and couldn't help overhearing."

I winced.

"A warrior for justice in the Church? Is it really so bad?"

"I feel like I have been that for a long time, mostly unsuccessfully." I tried to keep bitterness out of my voice. Then I told him about the ban.

"It is best to obey it," he said.

"Yes. But I will appeal it."

"Archbishop Konrad is on his way to Rome to prepare for Paschal's installment."

Another antipope, another mission. Victor had died a few weeks ago, and now the emperor was backing Guido di Crema, who had chosen the name of Paschal, as his successor and challenger to Pope Alexander.

"I will wait. The archbishop is the only person who can reverse it," I said. "But I will not let the canons deprive us of our dignity and rights."

Volmar took his usual seat across from me. As always, his presence calmed me and allowed me to think more clearly. We sat in silence for a while as I considered our new situation. "This is exactly why I must travel and speak out," I said at length. "Worldly ambitions and petty squabbles are corrupting the Church, and the higher up the hierarchy you look, the more rampant they are. I had wanted to do it before Archbishop Arnold was murdered, and with this new outrage, I can be silent no longer."

I braced myself for his attempt to dissuade me, but it did not happen. Instead, he said, "If that is what you want to do, you will have my support."

"Thank you." I felt a surge of gratitude. "I know it is risky, and that some may use it against me. But I believe that my friendship with Archbishop Konrad will protect me."

He nodded, but I saw that he was not entirely convinced. Neither was I. But we both knew that inaction was not an option. Inaction was no guarantee that we would not be harassed again.

"My advice is to go about this in a subtle way," Volmar said. "As a woman, you will be denied a preaching license, and if you go without one, you will encounter resistance and find your message blunted."

He was right. I could not just ride into an abbey or walk into a church and claim a place at the pulpit, although I was better known than most of the men who roamed the land, preaching to whomever would listen. But rules were rules, and I could not flout them openly. I needed a plan.

"I have a nephew who is a priest in Cologne," I said after some deliberation. "My brother Roric's youngest son." I raised an eyebrow meaningfully. "I think I will pay him a visit."

Volmar nodded appreciatively.

"In the meantime" — I sifted through a stack of parchments on my desk — "I have a letter from Abbot Bertolf informing me that he will be moving to Rome soon."

"I heard a rumor about it last time I was in Mainz. Is it official now?"

"Yes. He has been appointed a secretary in the papal household and will be leaving before the winter. He wants to take a copy of *Liber vita meritorum* to present to the pope."

"We have a spare one that Sister Johanna can illuminate, but it will take at least two months, and she is the fastest."

I shook my head. "We don't have the time, and I prefer to keep it plain in any case." I rested my head against the high back of my chair and gazed into the distance, suddenly nostalgic. "Remember how Bernard of Clairvaux would not even touch an illustrated manuscript?"

We smiled at each other, sharing a memory and an understanding. My plan was so bold that a show of humility was called for. I might need a powerful ally to defend me yet again.

29

June 1165

I STOOD AT the prow of the barge conveying me down the Rhine toward the ancient city of Cologne. Every now and then I would close my eyes and let the gentle rise and dip of the deck and the splash of water against the wood soothe me, but it was not working all that well.

We had started out with a strong southern breeze that aided the barge that would otherwise be dependent on the slow current of the great river. But a few miles down from Bingen, the Rhine turned northward, and the current became more brisk. The course became more meandering, and thickly forested hills, just attaining their peak early summer greenness, emerged into view around each bend. They rose and seemed to hug the river that made its way through the valley in a kind of primordial embrace. Some of the hills were so tall they seemed like mountains. Now and then a rocky cliff rose sharply hundreds of feet over the deceptively placid waters, which on closer examination revealed numerous vortices that seemed small on the surface but concealed powerful forces beneath. Those dizzying heights were often crowned with castles of various sizes—from ones barely visible through the trees to imposing structures elaborate in style, built for the most prominent families in the land.

"The one with the tall white tower in the center of the keep is the Marksburg." Gertrude pointed to a large defensive complex looming on the right bank. "It belongs to the Eppstein family, who are distant cousins to the emperor." Gertrude was my companion on this journey, familiar with the river as a result of having traveled on it with her father as a girl. She was sure-footed on board, unlike the two abbey servants who had never been on a boat before. Terrified of the unstable ground and the expanse of water on both sides, they refused to come out of the cabin in the back. Gertrude, standing beside me without holding the handrail, anticipated every bend, knew every castle's ownership and its history, and delighted in pointing them out.

I studied the Eppstein castle, then my gaze slid down the slope and over the green canopy of the forest, and I sighed heavily.

Gertrude turned to me. "The prospect of seeing your nephew is moving you already," she said softly, touching my hand. "I am sure Father Richart will feel the same."

"I have never met my nephew, nor have I seen my brother since we were both young children," I replied, though that was not the reason for my brooding mood. "But I do hope our ties of blood will facilitate this long-overdue reunion. How long until we disembark for the night?"

Gertrude looked up at the sky, but it had grown overcast and it was hard to discern the time. "I will go and ask the captain."

When she was gone, I turned back to the river, relieved to be alone again. I had been trying to shake my gloom since the morning, since Volmar and Griselda had seen us off at Bingen. It was amid the commotion of good wishes and the crew's final preparations that Volmar had come up to me, and I was seized by a sudden dread that I was doing a wrong thing by going away.

"I should have asked you to come with me," I said. "You would have agreed, wouldn't you?" I clutched his hand in mine, enfolding both in the sleeves of our habits.

Volmar smiled as if I were a child seeking a parent's reassurance. "Of course I would, but you are in good hands. Gertrude will be a useful companion. She knows the world."

"Not as well as you."

"You will be fine. You can hardly get lost on a river," he added lightly.

But I pressed his fingers harder. "That is not what I am worried about."

"What is it, then?"

I searched his face, still handsome and lean, though lined and darker than that of most monks for the many hours he had spent outdoors. But his hazel eyes seemed not to have changed at all, and I still read in them everything that had sustained me all these years. "I don't know," I said helplessly, letting go of his hand. Then I needed reassurance again, urgently. "Will you be all right?"

"Of course."

Anxiety rose up within me again, so strong I could hardly breathe. "But who will take care of you?"

Volmar's eyes flickered with amusement like in the old days. Then he nodded to where Griselda was standing near the embarkation plank. "*She* is here, and always has been. Our truest and most loyal friend."

His words had given me the comfort I needed then, but now the fear reared its head again. Of the last forty-seven years, I had only spent a handful of them apart from Volmar. Now the prospect of a few weeks' separation made me feel — although I was standing securely several feet above the steely waters — as if I were drowning.

The walls of Cologne appeared at last in the hazy distance of the left bank, quickly growing larger and more distinct. It seemed double the size of Mainz, and with its imposing skyline dominated by towers and church spires glinting in the sun, it did justice to its reputation as one the greatest cities of the Holy Roman Empire.

The port was far busier than that at Bingen, roiling with men dressed in a variety of styles and colors, shouting in a multitude of languages as they unloaded the dozen or so ships. More ships waited their turn, anchored at a distance. From the docks, trains of carts creaked under the burden of goods being hauled toward the main city gate, and we made our way among them.

Inside the walls, the stone foundations of which were said to date back to the time of the Romans, the tumult was even greater. Almost immediately, I was welcomed by the familiar spectacle of bear-baiting. I turned my head away from the sight only to witness, some distance away, another disturbing scene. A young woman, slight in stature and almost naked save for a dirty-looking shift, was shouting at a small crowd gathered around a makeshift dais. From there, two men in long clerical robes were trying to haul her off. One gripped her by the waist, and she put up a fierce resistance, while also trying to shed whatever was left of her clothes to cheers from the crowd. She could not fight the men off for long, however, and when the other cleric grabbed her arms and twisted them behind her back, she doubled over, loose hair falling wildly over her face. In that position, she was carried to a wooden cart enclosed by crisscrossed beams like a cage.

I took it all in without stopping, and although the distance and the noise had prevented me from hearing the woman's words, I guessed she must have been one of the Catharist *perfecti*, which is what they called their leaders, there to preach their doctrine.

Moving down Lintgasse, we arrived at Great St. Martin Church and the Benedictine abbey where we were to lodge. The church was new—rebuilt after a fire fifteen years before—with four slender turrets around a soaring central tower hugged by apses still under construction on each side. I was welcomed by Abbot Edmund, who was joined by my nephew Richart. At the age of twenty-eight, Richart was the parish priest at the small Church of the Holy Apostles outside the walls, on the road to Aachen. Over a meal in the refectory, I found Roric's son to be a cultured man. Just as with his cousin Hiltrud, I vainly searched his face for something that would help restore the images of my parents or siblings to my memory. Still, I was delighted to find that Richart was familiar with my writings and eager to discuss them.

"My mind struggles with the idea that humanity may not be above all other nature and destined to master it," he confessed, referring to a passage from *Liber vita meritorum.* "For we are the only creatures that have a notion of the Godhead."

I smiled, welcoming the challenge. "It is a question that has intrigued me since I was very young," I said. "I have always sought to understand our placement in the machinery of the universe, and I have come to believe that we are intertwined with nature, rather than standing apart from it. We are animated by the same greening breath as beasts of the land, birds of the air, and fish of the water, although by virtue of our superior faculties, we are able to use them to our own ends."

"So God has set us above the rest, after all?"

"Yes, but only to give us the ability to understand the requirements of the earth and discern divinity in them, as if in a mirror."

"It is a very humbling view of our race," Richart suggested.

I wondered whether this questioning stemmed from curiosity or a desire to defend orthodoxy. "That may be so if you think of a man who lives in communion with nature as stooping to its level," I replied. "But nature's order reflects divine harmony, and therefore has profound value in itself. It is a gift to be used responsibly and reverently, and which — besides furnishing us with sustenance and livelihood — is a source of great joy and wonder."

My nephew raised his eyebrows. "So you elevate the body to the place occupied by the soul on its earthly journey?"

That was an insightful observation. "I see no reason to ignore the body, as without it the soul would have no dwelling place. If the soul strives to reach perfection, it can only do so in union with the body, acting as its inner framework. In fact," I added, referring to another part of my book, "this unity is mirrored by that of the Creator and the creation — just as the body loses its vigor and withers without the soul, so the universe cannot be sustained without its Maker."

Richart considered this for some moments. "That is not what the Church Fathers emphasize, but when you lay it out this way, it is difficult to argue against it."

"Look at humankind," I urged him, "and tell me that it does not possess heaven and earth within itself. The human form conceals the whole universe inside."

He pursed his lips, but in his eyes I saw the same spark of excitement at a fresh idea that had often gripped me when I was a young woman. It had lit a fire that had set me on my path, a fire that still burned with a dimmer, but also steadier, flame. Suddenly, I felt an urge to tell him more.

"It is something I understood one day during a bout of a bodily illness. I was facing a sore trial after a sister of my community, whom I dearly loved, had left me." I paused to swallow a knot that had formed in my throat. "I spent much time in contemplation, and it was then that I imagined the universe as a great circular structure, and the interdependence of the earthly and the divine became obvious to me. God enfolds that circle in an embrace, and at its center is the human figure surrounded by the four elements, by planets and stars, and by animals and plants. Into all of this He breathes a breath that forces the world into motion." I paused again. "What this means is that a human being is the most powerful creation, but also that we are never alone, but in a mutually dependent relationship with everything else."

"You have not written about this before," Richart observed.

"I had started just before I left for Cologne," I said. *Because it was long overdue.* My mind traveled back to that distant day when, after the fair of St. Disibod, I sat with Volmar at the edge of the woods outside the town and talked about the stars. "It will be a book of my reflections on the universe and our place in it."

"*Liber divinorum operum,*" he murmured.

With a rustle of robes and a scrape of benches, the monks rose from their supper. As we followed them, I mulled over my nephew's words, liking how they succinctly described my idea.

"*The Book of Divine Works,*" I said as we parted ways outside the refectory. "Indeed. And now I must rest, for I plan to be very busy soon."

30

Cologne, June 1165

THE NEXT MORNING news swept the city that the emperor had deposed Konrad von Wittelsbach. It took everyone by surprise, though it should not have. The Archbishop of Mainz had condoned much of Frederick's scheming, even traveling to Rome the year before to help install Paschal to the Holy See. Yet when the time had come to swear an oath of loyalty to Paschal, he had refused and switched allegiance to Pope Alexander. His replacement was Christian von Buch, an inveterate imperial loyalist.

"An ambitious man," Abbot Edmund opined as we left the Basilica of St. Ursula, where two shrines behind the altar were filled with the bones and sculls of the maidens who had perished with the martyr. "Hungry for power, so the emperor will find him more malleable to his will." Edmund was a small and ancient man, well past seventy, but still sharp, busy, and up-to-date on the affairs of the realm. "Also one of those clerics who feel more comfortable in the saddle, brandishing a sword, than clad in priestly vestments and leaning on a crozier."

I twisted my mouth in distaste. The news of the deposition had left me doubtful that I would see peace in my lifetime. There was so much uncertainty at the highest levels of power, where men were appointed then gone before relationships could develop and plans implemented. I could not count on anybody to take up the cause that was so dear to me, which was why this visit to Cologne had all of a sudden become all the more important. I straightened my back. "It sounds like this folly of constant campaigning on the peninsula will not end anytime soon."

"Unlikely." The abbot shook his head. "In fact, it is already rumored that the new archbishop will be leaving for Rome this autumn."

It was, by now, a familiar refrain.

I thought back on the intelligence Volmar had brought from Mainz earlier in the spring. "From what I have heard, the imperial plans are falling apart. Pope Alexander is gaining increasing support among the clergy not just in the south, but also here and in Burgundy. Archbishop Konrad's ousting has proven that to be true."

Edmund nodded.

"I don't understand this strategy." I sighed in frustration. "Campaign after campaign is proving disastrous because the emperor's intentions are not just. I told him once directly, when he had asked for my advice, that God will not bless an effort driven by ambition and vainglory. I later wrote him a letter warning him not to act in such a way that he would lose the grace of God, because the powers of this world receive their name from God alone and must rule by showing the ways of justice and truth."

The abbot studied me for a moment, and I knew what he was thinking—what woman would admonish the Holy

Roman Emperor in such terms? I smiled inwardly. I had never feared temporal authority. "And what was his response?" he asked.

"He repeated the pledge he had given me at Ingelheim that he would strive for the honor of the empire. Then he asked for my prayers, which" — I added pointedly — "I have been offering daily, though they are yet to be heard, seeing as he is setting out yet again to subjugate the Holy See to his will."

"Three campaigns and he has not learned his lesson." Edmund shook his head as if to banish the thoughts of upheaval in the wider world, then motioned with his chin to the road ahead of us, crowded with townsfolk, their carts, and their animals. "But we have enough to worry about here in Cologne with heretics trying to stir up trouble."

He was right. Since yesterday I had seen more signs of the unrest that threatened to spill into violence, and tensions in the streets were palpable. "Why do you think these Cathars are more difficult to bring under control now than they were when they first emerged twenty years ago?"

The abbot considered my question just as a pair of stern-looking clerics in black robes turned a corner from a side alley. I recognized them immediately as part of the corps of officials charged with patrolling the streets against unorthodox preaching. "Perhaps because their members are now claiming that they alone embody the Church," he said.

Now it was my turn to study Edmund. His small head, surrounded by a tonsure of bristly gray hair and set atop a wrinkled and sinewy neck, gave him the look of a chick. But there was wisdom and experience in his faded eyes, and the message they wordlessly conveyed was unmistakable. *It is that claim that is making them more popular than ever.*

The opportunity I had been hoping for presented itself on the second Sunday after my arrival, when Archbishop Rainald invited me to High Mass at the cathedral. I rode north from St. Martin through the main city market, which stretched for over half a mile, bustling with craftsmen and merchants from all over the world — exotic-smelling, louder, and more colorful than anything I had seen in Mainz.

The cathedral — built three and a half centuries earlier, just after the death of Karolus Magnus — was spacious but low, with two short towers at each end of the nave, and rows of narrow arched windows. It hosted the relics of The Three Kings, gifted by the emperor after his recent conquest of Milan. They had been attracting scores of pilgrims, but the cathedral's days might have been numbered; according to Abbot Edmund, there were plans afoot to tear it down and rebuild it in the new style.

I had a private meeting with the archbishop in the sacristy, then one of his deacons led me to the chancel, where I was seated with the other prelates. From there I watched Archbishop Rainald, tall and surprisingly youthful-looking, celebrate the Mass. He was a friend and close advisor to the emperor, and I could not help thinking that he likely welcomed the sudden change at Mainz, even though he had expressed his regret when I had talked with him earlier. Discreetly, I studied the faces of his priests, all locked in the same expression of reverent concentration. I wondered who among them shared that sentiment and who was dismayed at the turn of events, for the Church was badly divided between the two camps.

On a few occasions my eyes strayed from the altar toward the small windows of the apse, through which I could glimpse the clear summer sky, the domain of birds whose shapes flitted across, light and free. For a moment I envied their existence in the airy realms, without the strife and disappointments that marked the life below.

The Mass came to an end and the smoky incense dissolved in the cool air of the cathedral. "Brothers and sisters," Archbishop Rainald addressed his congregation. "We have with us today a special guest. Abbess Hildegard of the Benedictine house of St. Rupert has done us the honor of visiting our cathedral. Abbess" — he nodded in my direction — "your fame runs deep in these parts. We invite you to say a few words of wisdom for our fortification."

I had asked him for it, and he had agreed to grant me that courtesy. My plan on arriving in Cologne had been more modest; I would talk with the monks at the city's abbeys and with priests at the local churches — like my nephew's, which I was to visit later in the week. But to have a chance to speak in the grandest church in Cologne, with the most important prelates in attendance, had been beyond my expectation, and it might not happen again.

Yet my situation had changed since the news of Archbishop Konrad's ousting; I had lost a possible ally and now, more than ever, needed to tread carefully. Pope Alexander had publicly praised *Liber vita meritorum,* but with imperial supporters now at the helm not just in Cologne but also in Mainz, Alexander's backing would count for less.

Those thoughts clashed in my head as I approached the lectern to the side of the altar. But when I saw the eyes turned up to me — gleaming with youthful energy, dimmed by life's cares, devoid of luster by age, or extinguished by the milky film of blindness — I was reminded of what my duty was, and that I must follow through no matter the consequences.

"Excellency," I acknowledged the archbishop, who graciously reciprocated. "Fathers." I bowed toward the clergy in the stalls. "Brothers and sisters." I faced the congregation. The crowd gazed back with curiosity and expectation.

I took a breath and began with what I knew everyone expected. "I have, since my arrival in your fair city — and indeed, for years before — heard many words condemnatory of the Catharist heresy and urging its elimination. I declare my support of the effort against those who deny the humanity of the Son of God and the sanctity of His body and blood." A murmur of approval from the officials coursed through the chancel. "They are blinded with false belief and therefore cannot know the true God. Just like their seducer, they seek to destroy by rejecting the commandment to multiply, and by restraining their bodies with fasting that threatens their undoing."

I paused for a moment as the image of Jutta's wasted body rose before my eyes. Blinking it away, I caught sight of several clerics to my left, and their flashing eyes brought me back to the heretics' transgression. "Stem their influence among the faithful, but do not cause them harm, for like you, they bear the image of God," I exhorted, remembering the charged atmosphere of the streets and the woman carted away by the religious patrol. "In this, as in other things, let the Holy Spirit guide you in compassion."

I let my message resonate in the silence that followed, and the audience began to stir, evidently assuming I had come to the end of my remarks.

But I was not done yet.

"There is, *however*, another evil that has befallen the Church."

The murmurs died down.

I raised my voice to ensure it carried to all corners. "I stand before you not as one who brims with knowledge or scholarship, but as one who relies on God's help for insight. And it tells me that a disease is weakening the Church's foundations and allowing unseemly attitudes to flourish like weeds among poorly tended flowerbeds."

Wariness and consternation had entered the priests' expressions. I faltered momentarily, but then Juliana's words echoed in my mind. *You are doing God's work. They only pretend to do it to satisfy their lust for power over human souls.* "I see the Church as a beautiful woman," I resumed. "Her face shines, and she is clad in a robe of white silk adorned with pearls and sapphires. But" —I lifted a warning finger— "her cheeks are smeared with dirt, her garment is torn, and her shoes are soiled."

By now the clerics were looking at one another with ill-disguised discomfort, casting dismayed glances at me as if I were speaking in some barbarian tongue. "And I hear her weep that those who are supposed to nurture her, make her glow and gleam, have instead blackened her face and ripped her dress." I could see a pallor rise to the archbishop's face, though, unlike some of his deacons, he remained in a pose of polite attention. "They have done so through their corrupted morals and the rapacious buying and selling of offices and privileges.

"Having strayed from the path of reform that originated at the great monastery at Cluny, they no longer walk in the light but in the dark, and thus they are not capable of guiding anybody. They are supposed to be like pillars holding up the universe, but instead they are weak and soft and support nothing."

"Wake up!" I cried into a complete silence, my hands gripping the lectern. I had waited for this moment for half a century, since the day I had overheard Bishop Otto direct Abbot Kuno to sell novitiates to the wealthiest candidates. "Save your garden by cutting away the withered branches that sap *viriditas* from the rest. Pay heed to the whispers of the Holy Spirit and drive the godless from their offices so the Church may cease weeping from their injustice. That is my message to you!"

My challenge reverberated off the walls as the congregation stood spellbound. I could feel a nerve that connected with my own as heads began to nod, lips pursing, brows drawing together. In the chancel the silence was absolute, and not just for a lack of speech, but also any movement or breath. I released the grip on the lectern and walked back to my stall. As I did so, I heard a hollow sound from the nave, as if a walking stick had fallen to the floor. Almost immediately, it was followed by another and another, and swiftly they merged into an applause that was like water bursting through a dam. It thundered and thundered through the church, magnified by the walls and the vault, as the clerics sat there like so many stone statues.

The archbishop was gracious, but it was obvious that he did not appreciate the direction in which I had taken my remarks. For days, Richart reported breathlessly on the shocked reaction reverberating through the ecclesiastical circles of Cologne.

"Catharist sympathies run high in this city, and some people like nothing better than for priests to be denounced as errant like any other mortal. That is what the hierarchy fears the most," he said one day.

"They cannot honestly accuse me of heresy," I scoffed. "That would expose them to ridicule. My allegiance has always been to the Church and its dogmas; I said as much the other day, and there is ample evidence of it in my writing, of which I have done more than the lot of them."

"I would not presume to criticize someone who has had the ear of popes and the emperor," he hastened to assure me. "My only point is that this may make you unpopular in some quarters."

I understood his concern. "I do not wish to jeopardize your relations with the hierarchy here in Cologne, nephew. I will gladly swear to anyone who might attack you for my words that you knew nothing of my intentions and had nothing to do with the content of what I said."

But for every detractor, there was a supporter who would pay a visit to St. Martin to thank me. Privately and in a low voice, he would praise me for having said aloud—and with a manly spirit, he would often add—what he had been afraid to do. Invitations began to arrive from parishes and abbeys, where in addition to holding debates, I also did some doctoring.

By the time I returned to St. Rupert, the summer was nearly over, and the community was in a state of agitation for my notoriety. The first chapter meeting was a noisy affair, with the sisters unable to agree whether it would help or hinder our quest for the lifting of the music interdict. Archbishop Christian—who by now would have learned about the ban and the speech—continued to remain silent on both counts.

"You have not offered your opinion," I said to Volmar as we left the chapter house together. "Is it because you think that with the archbishop's imminent departure, our appeal will be stuck in the limbo of Provost Walter's office?"

"I don't know which way the archbishop is going to rule when he finally gets to it," he answered earnestly, "but whatever happens, Walter will have no part in it."

I halted abruptly. "Is he dead?"

"Worse than that—at least for the likes of him. He has fallen out of favor."

Just days after his appointment, Archbishop Christian had deposed Provost Walter and sent him to a retirement at the imperial Abbey of Fulda, Volmar explained. It was not clear what had precipitated the move—the whole thing had been done with as little noise as possible, and with no official announcement—but it was no secret that Walter had few friends around Mainz who would defend him against the ruling.

"Serves him right." With uncharitable satisfaction, I imagined my old foe submitting to the rigors of monastic discipline at long last. "This will allow him to do some spiritual work for a change." Then a dreadful thought occurred to me. "And Canon Ulrich?"

Volmar read my mind immediately. "He is still there but has not been elevated," he said. "The new provost's name is Engelard. I have met him a few times, though I cannot say

I know him well. What I do know is that he was not part of Walter's circle."

I let out a breath of relief. Christian von Buch's stance on the interdict might still be anybody's guess, but his first decisions were promising indeed.

31

Abbey of St. Rupert, September 1167

E VER SINCE I stayed at St. Albans on my way to claim
the charter, Abbot Gottfried and I had been friends and
regular correspondents. He had proven a steady and reliable
source of news and gossip from Mainz; he was also, as it happened, well-acquainted with Provost Engelard.

Gottfried had written to me on his behalf some months
after my return from Cologne to let me know that the provost
was unwilling to annul his predecessor's interdict without
consulting Archbishop Christian first. Since his appointment,
the new archbishop had been spending most of his time trying to install the imperial antipope, leaving the running of
his see to the canons. But — Abbot Gottfried also informed
me — Provost Engelard would not enforce the interdict, nor
would he seek to defend it when the archbishop returned to
Mainz. That meant that we could resume the singing of services, provided we did so in private.

But in the autumn of 1167, as I was nearing the completion of *Liber divinorum operum*, the news that shook Mainz was of such magnitude that, instead of writing a letter, Gottfried came to St. Rupert to deliver it in person.

"The imperial host was forced to make a most ignominious retreat from Rome. The Italian project is in ruins," he announced, covered in the dust from the road as I arrived to greet him.

That was a shocking development, for just a few weeks earlier, those few who had still clung to the schismatic side had celebrated Emperor Frederick's triumph as he had finally managed to put Paschal on the papal throne and chase Pope Alexander from the Holy City.

"But how is that possible?" I asked as I led him straight to my parlor after sending Agnes to fetch Volmar and a flagon of unwatered wine. "The siege was supposed to be a resounding success."

"This undoing was not of military making. It was the wrath of God."

"Ha!" I could not help exclaiming, even before I knew which instrument God had chosen. "As I warned him long ago."

"I do remember reports of your audience with the emperor," Abbot Gottfried said. "Your warnings were much repeated."

"Clearly, others took them more seriously than he did. What caused the retreat?"

"A plague," he announced, just as Volmar entered the parlor. "The contagion killed most of the army, a great many generals, and sickened the emperor himself. He is on his way back as we speak and is said to be still weak from it."

I asked if he knew anything of the symptoms; the physician in me was too curious.

"There are tales of great suffering and woe going around Mainz. The sickness came on suddenly with fever and chills, progressed to pains in the abdomen and limbs, and ended with delirium that set in shortly before death." Gottfried took a hearty swallow from the cup Agnes had placed before him. "Only a few lucky ones recovered and returned home to report that a violent storm had broken out before the plague and went on for days, with rains that caused sewage to over-flow in the streets."

"That must have been what caused it," I said. "Plagues are brought on by miasmas from swamps, cesspits, and other unhealthy places." Gottfried's expression was anxious, per-haps due to the fact that the weather was still holding warm and it had rained heavily the night before, which gave the air a humid quality. I added, "Here in the Rhineland we are saf-er than in the southern regions, where the air is more easily corrupted in the summer heat."

He smiled apologetically but with a good dose of re-lief. "Forgive my trepidation. I trust God will protect us. Of course, even if He were to test us with a similar scourge, it would be our duty to submit to it humbly."

"Certainly." I twirled my cup in my fingers. "Though cleanliness and good medical care would not be out of place either."

He nodded absently, his mind back to the news from Rome. "Returning soldiers are talking about an alliance in the making among large cities in the north. The League of Verona and the League of Cremona are joining forces and in-viting other cities—including Venice, Milan, and Bologna—to follow suit."

I listened avidly, my mind working through possible scenarios. So far, nobody had put up a strong and organized resistance against the emperor, and if this one proved suc-cessful, it might give him pause. But there was also a good chance it would harden his resolve. "Their goal, I presume, is to repel any future imperial attempts to force them to sub-mit?"

"It is about more than just that. They want to return the north to the autonomy and its cities to the privileges they enjoyed under the previous emperors. Pope Alexander is their natural ally in this effort."

"It hasn't been a good year for him," Volmar noted.

"No, but who is to say that the next one will not be better?"

"Indeed." I realized that after the German retreat, papal supporters would not waste time restoring Alexander. The peninsula was slipping from Frederick's grasp, and as his position weakened, he might be more prone to offering peace.

My face must have reflected my thoughts, for Father Gottfried remarked, "You are finding these tidings welcome, Abbess."

"I do not rejoice at the defeat of the imperial army—it has cost lives of our countrymen and their Italian opponents, not to mention the treasure accumulated off the labor of the people," I replied. "Yet it cannot but help the cause of the Church's unity that the side that had been on the defensive for fifteen years, despite growing support around the empire, might soon be on the ascendant."

"Quite so."

Father Gottfried had reached the end of his information store, and I felt disappointed. Given the chance, I would discuss matters of state for hours without wearying. Over the rim of my wine cup, I sought Volmar's eyes. With a nod he affirmed that he would go to Mainz to find out more.

By the middle of October, the emperor's closest advisors where pushing for a new strategy, and he was rumored to be listening. "He is getting older and wiser, and perhaps tired too," Volmar opined.

"I should hope so."

"More and more German bishops are switching allegiance to Pope Alexander."

"Maybe this will spell the end of the antipopes."

"That is something nobody is prepared to guarantee at the moment, but I did see signs of optimism at Mainz, even among those sympathetic to the schismatics until recently." Volmar tried to make his tone lighter to lift my spirits. He knew how disappointed I was with the other piece of news he had brought, namely that Archbishop Christian, who had returned with the emperor, would not be lifting the music interdict for now. "It may not be what we wanted, but in practice, this changes nothing from what we have been doing since Provost Engelard took office," he had told me. "Nobody will bother us as long as we do not sing during public services."

"I know." I had waved my hand dismissively, but there had been a mounting fury inside me, and I knew one thing — there would be no acceptance and no submission. "The archbishop is no friend of Canon Walter's, yet he is siding with him. Bonds of power are stronger than the sense of justice," I had said bitterly. "He is doing this to control us."

Now, suddenly, I was out of breath. I swung my head like a suffocating person searching for an opening through which fresh air might flow, but the shutters were wide open on this pleasant autumn afternoon, letting in the crisp air full of ripe scents and golden sunshine. "They will not control us as long as I am alive," I vowed.

"Are you all right?" A shadow of concern crossed Volmar's face. "Do not let it upset you too much. You will make yourself ill."

"I will be fine." I had been experiencing these flashes of heat and breathlessness for some years now. I knew they would pass, although being in a state of agitation did not help. The real danger for me lay in inaction. I had never been able to handle it well. "I must take matters into my own hands again."

A wariness entered Volmar's face.

"I will make another journey," I answered his unspoken question. "It has been two years since I returned from Cologne, and I have a stack of invitations —"

"I would advise against it."

I knew that the look I gave him was cold. "And why is that?"

"Because" — he searched for the right words — "why double down? Despite what it looks like, we have reached a compromise, and this may make things worse."

"You see it as doubling down, and I see it as fulfilling my duty to keep people's attention on the issues that matter to the Church, and which some would like me to stop talking about." I paused, considering the lines of worry on his face. Then I added, more softly, "What else can they do to me? Excommunicate me like they did Giselbert?" I shook my head. "No. That would raise an outcry they cannot afford. They have run out of tools to silence me."

Volmar did not respond for a while, but the crease between his eyebrows deepened. "It is your decision," he said finally, but it was clear that he would not be supporting me this time.

32

November 1167

T HIS TIME I had asked Griselda to accompany me, but she had refused.

"I am grateful for your offer, but I'd rather stay at St. Rupert," she had said to me. "All those years ago, I eagerly fled to the comfort of the cloister, and this is where I belong."

I had felt a pang of disappointment, but I knew she was right—Griselda was happiest when performing her daily labors and devotions, and it would not do to impose the distractions of the world on her. Not even to assuage my own sense of guilt for having always taken her presence for granted.

It was early November and I was about to embark on a journey to Trier, the seat of Archbishop Hillin von Falemagne. He had once been a staunch imperial ally who had switched his support to the papal party after the death of Antipope Victor. After my speech at Cologne, he had been among the first high officials to invite me to speak at his cathedral.

Now my traveling party — which included Rego, his son, Gertrude, and two servants — was ready to set out.

"I will be back before winter," I sought to reassure Volmar. "The weather is still mild and dry." I looked up at the church tower, where the roof tiles reflected the honeyed tones of the autumn sunshine. Beyond the church, the trees surrounding the cemetery — where Giselbert still lay undisturbed — had lost some of their leaves, although flaming reds and bright yellows still fluttered on the branches.

Volmar frowned. "The weather is not what worries me."

"What is it, then?"

"I don't know." His eyes met mine, and there was a despondency in them I had never seen before. I found it disconcerting; after all, he was supposed to be the steady one, always ready to offer words of reassurance.

"You may be underestimating the hardships of a journey through the Hunsrück," he said, but we both knew that was not the issue. I was sixty-two and tired more easily than before, but I was lucky not to be afflicted with the joint pains and deformations that had crippled Brother Wigbert and so many of my elderly patients. The headaches that had plagued me when I was younger had all but disappeared. My determination to see this mission through gave me the energy I needed, but just to be safe, I had packed bottles of aconite oil and sacks of dried fennel and powdered oak bark to make strengthening tisanes along the way.

"I know you disapprove, but I have to do it." I took his right hand in both of mine and ran a thumb over his index finger, callused from years of gripping the writing stylus. "I hope you understand that."

He did not respond. For a moment, he looked a little lost. I had already noticed that aging had treated Volmar differently than me. There had been a decline in him in the last few months — nothing specific, just a touch of heaviness to his once agile movements or an occasional memory lapse that he tried to cover up. There were episodes of nodding off in the scriptorium in the evenings so that Johanna had to shake his shoulders gently and bid him retire to bed. He had gone to Mainz the month before, but the trip had taken a toll on him. I would have to find someone else to undertake these missions for me in the future. I would persuade him to a well-deserved retirement. When I came back.

"I will return as soon as I can," I promised. "Meanwhile, we have enough scribes to handle all of our copy work, so do rest." Then I added, with mock severity, "I asked Griselda to keep an eye on you."

He did not laugh with me; instead, a grimace crossed his face, as if from a twinge of pain.

"I will see you very soon." I let go of his hand and swallowed an unexpected lump in my throat.

He stood watching as we made our way out through the gate. When I turned for a last look, the iron-studded double door was slowly swinging closed. We held each other's gaze until the two wings came together with a dull wooden sound and separated us.

With a silent vow, I turned toward the forest as the wagon began to descend the hill. *This will be my last journey, then I will take care of you.*

At Trier, we lodged at the Abbey of St. Matthias, Abbot Bertolf's old residence. Archbishop Hillin had been held up out of town on diocese business, so I spent several days visiting parishes around the city, meeting people of all walks of life, dispensing medical advice, and holding debates with clergy. There was less appetite for reform than I had wished for, but those who shared my views were fervent about it. That gave me hope. I would add them to my roster of correspondents, and I would keep the flame alive for as long as I could.

On the morning of my planned meeting with the arch-bishop, I awoke to snow swirling thickly outside the win-dow. It kept falling and falling until the cloister garth van-ished under a heavy blanket of white powder, and even then it did not stop. It continued for three days, so when it finally ceased, only the tops of the cloister's arches were visible. It was the biggest snowfall in living memory. By the time the main streets had been cleared sufficiently to permit people and commerce to return, the month was nearing the end.

On the first day of December, frosty enough to make it possible to walk on what otherwise would have been rivers of mud, I made my way to the archbishop's palace. As I care-fully negotiated the central tract and the streams of people, carts, and animals moving in both directions, the façade of the cathedral, one of the land's oldest churches, came into my view. It was a plain and small-windowed structure, yet with two square and two round towers crowned with tall sloping roofs flanking the entrance, it projected a sense of grandeur over the clutter of flimsy wooden houses of the surrounding district.

When I arrived in the square in front of the cathedral, I was out of breath and my legs hurt so much that I was be-ginning to question the wisdom of the whole endeavor. Just then, a voice rang out near me, "That's Abbess Hildegard of St. Rupert!"

I looked around to find a man of about forty in a sol-dier's gambeson, with the hilt of a heavy sword protruding from among the folds of his cloak. He had a long-healed scar running from his right cheekbone, under the ear, and down his neck before it disappeared into his collar. My eyes were immediately drawn to it.

"I went with the last crusade in the army led by our present emperor," he explained and pointed to his back, where I guessed a cross had been stitched on his cloak.

"May God reward your service," I said. "But how did you know who I am?"

He gave a small smile, sad and knowing. "As a youth I wasn't particularly devout, but the Holy Land changed me. I fought for God, saw my companions die at Constantinople and Dorylaeum, and was badly wounded myself. When I heard you were staying at St. Matthias, I went to Mass there and heard you speak."

"And what did you think about it?"

The knight pulled on his small beard and hesitated before answering. When he did, his voice had a ring of heartfelt honesty. "God bless you for taking up a matter nobody else seems to dare approach." He shook his head ruefully. "We did not fight for a Church that's rotting from within. When I heard your words, I felt great hope that our sacrifice would not be in vain."

A small crowd had begun to gather around, intrigued by the exchange between such an unlikely pair as the two of us. Some stopped for nothing more than idle curiosity, but others listened attentively, and a few heads nodded in agreement with the knight's words. I heard voices rippling through the group.

"Who is this sister?"

"Abbess Hildegard . . . a physician . . ."

"Apparently, she preaches sermons too . . ."

"No!"

"Yes, she once spoke at the cathedral in Cologne . . ."

"Truly?"

The crusader heard those queries and turned around. "Abbess Hildegard," he spoke loudly to the crowd, even as he addressed me, "will you repeat what you said in the abbey church the other day for the people who have not heard you and may never have another chance?"

"Yes! Tell us!" Several voices called out. Careworn faces and dim eyes became animated. "Are we doomed?" Somebody started praying. A woman sobbed.

I stood uncertainly. It was one thing to speak by invitation, quite another to do so spontaneously in a public square.

Many of these people were truly desperate, and I might be accused of fomenting unrest, or worse.

But the knight's passionate plea had moved me, so I stepped to the center of the circle that had formed around me and repeated my message, choosing my words carefully. I talked about the need for the Church to return to the simplicity, honesty, and innocence that had been its strength in the beginning, before greed and power hunger had taken over.

They nodded as I spoke, but when I finished, they asked for blessings for themselves and their families. The crying woman dried her eyes, relieved that the apocalypse was not yet upon us, only a plague of corrupt priests. Then they began drifting away to the daily worries that preoccupied them more, and understandably so, than the state of the Church.

It began to snow lightly as steely gray clouds veiled the midday sun, and I bid my crusader acquaintance good day. I wrapped my cloak more tightly about my shoulders and entered the archbishop's palace.

Up in his private chamber, kept comfortably warm by two large braziers, Archbishop Hillin and I walked to the window that gave onto the square. I knew even before he told me that he had witnessed the little gathering below.

"You started something important when you spoke at Cologne," the archbishop said. He had a reputation for prudence and generosity, and his eyes were keen and sharp, unlikely to miss anything. "Something that one day may be mentioned alongside the Cluniac movement and the Gregorian reforms as one of the greatest efforts to cleanse the Church of its transgressions."

"Your Excellency is giving too much credit to my poor efforts," I replied, warming my hands around a cup of spiced wine. "I do not see how mere words can have that effect. Unlike the Cluniac monks or Pope Gregorius, I do not have legions of holy men at my command who can carry my message to all corners of Christendom."

"You may be underestimating the power of the people's desire for a change."

Below us, the square was becoming more crowded as sellers of pies, ale, and all manner of trinkets opened their stalls, despite the intermittent squalls of snow. There was something heartening about the spirit that brought them out despite the harsh weather.

"Perhaps that is because their needs are never taken into account when those who already have much are reaching for even more," I said. "Ordinary people are always the ones who pay the greatest price of every conflict."

"True," Hillin agreed. "And that is why I have hope that words like yours—directed at a problem that affects everybody, not just those within the Church who would like to see it purer and more Godlike—are like seeds thrown in the wind. It may take time, but eventually they will find a patch of fertile soil and grow to nourish and infuse the withering frame with a new vitality"—he raised his cup as if in a toast—"or *viriditas*, as you would call it."

I acknowledged his words, and we stood watching the activity in the square for a while. The season of Christmas was approaching, and I had seen several wealthier houses decorated with branches of fir and spruce. They were believed to ward off the devil and ensure health for the family in the new year. I loved the balsamic fragrance and the greenness in the midst of the season of nature's repose, but the Church disapproved of such decorations as pagan. By the time Christmas Day arrived, those branches would be torn down by the religious patrol.

I was glad of the archbishop's optimism, but the enormity of the task was clear to me. For every cleric like him, there were scores of others who cared nothing for addressing the real problems their flocks faced, or for setting a good example. Yet people thirsted after it, and as that thirst went unquenched, their discontent would grow until it forced the Church to change—or it might end it.

The door squeaked in its hinges, jostling us out of our contemplation.

"Ah." Archbishop Hillin put down his cup and rubbed his hands together. "Just in time. I have arranged for some refreshments."

I sent him a grateful look. The walk from St. Matthias and the scent of roasted meats and spices that carried from the square had made me hungry. We sat at a table by the hearth on which a young cleric arranged a tray with bread and honey, cold hams, and slices of cinnamon-dusted apples. He had also brought more wine that the archbishop poured for us after dismissing the priest.

"I have something to tell you, Abbess," he said, glancing at the door. "In confidence."

"Of course."

"I have it on good authority that the emperor is considering issuing an edict of protection for St. Rupert, which will be read during the spring audience."

My heart leaped—not a common occurrence those days—but I quickly reminded myself to be cautious. I had learned not to trust Frederick's promises, especially when they were still only gossip making rounds of the imperial court. "That would be of enormous help to us, but I have heard nothing as yet, and, as you know, my relationship with the emperor has been strained."

"I do." The archbishop nodded. "But I have reason to believe it will happen." He leaned his considerable frame back in his chair. "Despite our recent differences, I know Emperor Frederick to be an honorable man who recognizes merit and gives credit where credit is due. You may be surprised to hear it, but he has had your warnings in mind over the years, though he admits he is not humble enough to heed them. He is God's anointed monarch, after all." The archbishop crunched on an apple slice. "But—regarding the edict—I would not be surprised if you received a notification before the end of the year."

I took a deep breath, again reminding myself not to entertain hopes that could be cruelly dashed again. "It would help expedite the petition to the Archbishop of Mainz to reverse the music interdict," I said nonetheless. Archbishop Christian had only just returned home after years in the south, and although my appeal had been lodged long ago, its priority must have been low. But an imperial edict would do much more than that; it would insulate us from the canons' meddling once and for all. It would also offer greater safety from mercenary armies, for punishments for violating imperial foundations were far more severe.

"I will travel to Mainz in the new year to visit my friend the archbishop, and I will bring it up with him," Hillin offered.

"I would be grateful, Your Excellency," I said. I gazed into my cup, so his sharp eyes would not read mine. For even though I meant what I said, I also could not help wondering at this game of politics that was principle, compromise, and opportunism in equal measure, where support and alliances constantly shifted and the line between friend and foe was rarely clear. But if out of all of this my abbey would emerge safer, stronger, and more independent, then so be it.

It was past vespers and getting dark when the archbishop ordered his carriage to take me back to St. Matthias, an offer I accepted readily, for we had drained a flagon of wine between us. As we bid each other goodbye on the threshold of the palace, I invited him to visit St. Rupert and he invited me back to Trier.

As it turned out, it would remain our only meeting. Archbishop Hillin would die less than a year later, and I . . . well, I would never leave the abbey again.

I returned to St. Matthias just as compline was coming to an end. The snow had stopped, but the air remained cold, and it had cleared my head from the vapors of the wine by the time I alighted from the carriage.

I walked through the gate to the ebbing sounds of the final chant. I stopped in the middle of the courtyard and watched a dozen or so townspeople and several guests of the abbey come out of the church. It was getting colder, and I pulled the hood of my cloak closer about my head.

"At least it has cleared up," Gertrude said as she came up to me.

"Indeed." I looked up at the inky sky. There were only a few wispy clouds over the horizon, where the moon's crescent was on the rise. Bright stars had come out too, and suddenly I realized that it looked exactly the same as on the night I had discovered Jutta in the chapel, mortifying her flesh with a whip. I was only a child of twelve then, but the image of that sky had remained in my memory forever. A shiver ran down my spine, and I pulled my cloak even tighter around me. "Let's go inside."

"Archbishop Hillin is going to bring up our case at Mainz in the spring, and there is also a chance we might be receiving an imperial edict of protection," I said as we neared our guest cells. My mood lifted again. "I am going to write to Brother Volmar tonight."

I would have preferred to tell him in person, but I was also secretly happy to be held up in Trier by the snow. It gave me a chance to visit a few more abbeys where I could enjoy more debates and discussions, whether on politics, theology, or medicine. I relished those meetings; they energized and exhilarated me, even if at times I felt the same way I had as a young girl at St. Disibod when I had wished I'd been born a boy so I could enjoy the life of the mind more freely. If I were a man, who knows, maybe I would have been sitting where Archbishop Hillin had today.

"Speaking of letters," Gertrude's voice reached me through my musings, "a message arrived when you were away. From Sister Griselda."

"Oh."

"I suppose that means the roads are not in such bad shape after all," she said as we opened the doors to our separate cells.

Inside, the brazier was already lit, and I stood over it to warm my hands. I closed my eyes and imagined the first Mass after the ban was lifted, with chants soaring under the vault of the church, even higher than the swirls of incense could reach.

The door creaked open. "Here's the letter," Gertrude said.

"Put it on the table." I wanted to savor the sensation of the heat enveloping my fingers a little longer. "I wonder if St. Rupert got as much as snow as we did."

"I hope not, for the sake of the bakehouse roof." Gertrude lit more candles before withdrawing.

Chastising myself for not having seen to the roof before the winter, I walked to the table and picked up the letter. Across the corridor, I could hear Gertrude opening the door to her cell, the rusty hinges protesting loudly. I broke the seal. As I began to scan the lines, I felt all blood drain from my head and my chest, pooling somewhere low, too low to allow me to remain standing.

I remember falling and the letter slipping from my hands, sliding across the stone floor, but I do not remember feeling any pain. I must have been numb before I hit the ground.

I was lifted by a pair of arms, hoisted to a seated position with my back against the frame of the bed. Gertrude was speaking, but I could only hear some of the words through the pounding in my head.

" — ." Her lips moved. "Hildegard!" she cried. " — ?" No sound. "Are you ill?"

I tried to respond but could only manage a heave. Even breathing was becoming a struggle. I kept staring at the letter that lay between the iron legs of the brazier, and she reached for it.

The words she silently read were already burned into my memory with a searing pain, as if my flesh had been branded with them.

Beloved Hildegard,

I shudder to convey the most terrible news. There has been an accident – Brother Volmar is gravely injured after falling from his horse, and we fear he may be near death. We implore God to give you strength and beseech you to come back to us as soon as you can, for we are greatly distressed.

Your loving friend and sister,
Griselda

Gertrude sank by my side and dropped the hand that held the letter. That was when I heard the first sobs come out of the deepest part of me, somewhere I had never reached before. She wrapped her arms around me and held me until I could cry no more.

Then we were still and silent until the last embers in the brazier went out.

33

December 1167

L ATE IN THE night, I fell into a shallow and fitful sleep, waking before lauds to a feeling of an invisible band of iron crushing my chest. A single candle burned low and the brazier was full of ashes, but the room was still warm enough. Rego was dozing in a chair at the foot of my bed, and Gertrude was asleep on a pallet against the opposite wall. A rosary was twined between her fingers. Gazing at it, I realized I was unable to pray.

I rose with effort, my body suddenly heavy and old, pulling me back down against the dictates of my will. The creak of the wooden frame made Rego stir.

"Pack our things. We are leaving at first light," I said.

"The roads are frozen and slippery. Shouldn't we wait a day or two? Folk are talking about a thaw coming," he said gently, and the compassion in his voice pierced my heart instead of giving me comfort. *There is no need to make things worse,* his expression added.

I shook my head firmly. "I must go."

Rego hesitated for a moment, then nodded, realizing that nothing in the world would stop me, not a thunderstorm nor a blizzard, much less a frozen tract.

It was a slow and silent journey. I do not know what Rego and Gertrude were thinking behind their somber façades, but inside me raged a tempest. At times I felt angry; why had he gone to ride that wretched horse, at his age and during this season? But more often I was assaulted by guilt, crushing and merciless. Would this have happened had I not left St. Rupert and kept an eye on things, knowing how he had declined lately? I remembered that he had stopped riding a while before. Was it my absence that had made him do it again? Whatever it was, I had not been there to stop it. Like Jutta von Sponheim in the throes of her repentance so many years before, I took no food for the duration of that sorrowful pilgrimage home.

When the abbey finally came into view, darkly outlined against the pale wintry sky late in the afternoon of the fourth day, I reflected on the irony of it all. My insight had given me a deeper understanding of what was beyond the reach of most people—in the medical arts, in matters of faith, in the knowledge of the human soul. Yet I had not anticipated *this*. If I'd had any premonition, I had not understood it, or had ignored it.

Volmar rested in one of the private cells in the infirmary and was asleep when I arrived. In a low voice, Sister Beatrix explained how, taking advantage of the thaw that had arrived here some days before it had reached Trier, he had taken the old mare out of the stables for exercise, and she had slipped on a patch of ice that had not yet melted. Volmar could not move his legs, and the flask of poppy juice next to the cup of wine by his bedside testified to the severity of his injury. It was a draft I had made and administered countless times, yet seeing it now caused me to nearly double over, for I could not stand the thought of him in pain.

"I will make a draft of hypericum and sweeten it with honey." I began to think frantically of other ways to make him comfortable. "Did you add honey to the poppy infusion? It will taste better — " I heard my voice, desperate in its urgency, as if it were coming from somewhere outside of me.

Beatrix took me by the elbow and guided me to the bench by the window, where I slowly regained the clarity of thought. There was nothing stronger I could make for Volmar. Nothing more I could do for him. "What a cruel blow to one whose great joy in life was the ability to move through this world," I said, my voice still coming as if from a great distance. My eyes felt frozen, I could not blink, and deep under my eyelids rose the stinging pressure of new tears.

"You should rest," Beatrix suggested softly. "Brother Volmar is well cared for."

I brought the back of my hands to my eyes and shook my head. "I must stay with him."

After she had left, I sat in a chair by his bed and waited. The light of the short January day — for the new year had arrived while we were on the road — had faded, and Agnes brought candles and more charcoal for the brazier. The soft light took some of the pallor off Volmar's face and smoothed his tightened features.

He opened his eyes not long afterward. He gazed at me for a long moment, as if trying to remember who I was. I was seized by a fear that he would not know me anymore, would not know me ever again. A faint smile relaxed his lips, a shadow of the one I knew so well, yet it made my heart leap nonetheless.

"You came back . . ."

"As soon as I heard." I took his hand.

"I hoped to see you one more time." The air was suddenly heavy with the implication of the unsaid. I wanted to protest, but I did not. We had always been honest with each other, and I wanted it to remain so. "You were right about riding, as about everything else," he added, and this time he sounded a little stronger.

"It doesn't matter." I stroked his fingers. "I will take care of you now. I will not leave you again. Will you take more wine with the poppy juice?" I added, seeing a grimace of pain.

"No, not now. It clouds my head, and I want to be here . . ."

We remained silent for a long time, then he spoke again, slowly. "All those years I rode because after giving up so much, I couldn't bear to lose more." He closed his eyes. "But I should have been able to renounce everything. I was weak, and I hope God will forgive me."

"You made great sacrifices. Greater than most. You could have done anything you wanted and earned great esteem from your scholarship—here or in France. You could have been the abbot of St. Disibod, the best they ever had." I laughed, though my tears were flowing freely now. "But you chose a small place where an unlearned woman needed you."

"And I would do it all over again." He returned my caress so that our fingers were now intertwined like those of two lovers on the cusp of fulfillment. On impulse, I pulled off my veil and lowered my face to kiss his hand, letting my hair spill around my head. And just like on that distant summer day in the orchard of St. Disibod, Volmar buried his fingers in it and slowly traced its length. "It is still like burnished sunbeams, after all this time."

I turned my head so my cheek rested on his hand. "But for the accident of our birth, we could have had a different life, different choices before us," I spoke fiercely, even though emotion was threatening to choke my voice with a sense of double loss, past and impending. "But would it have been better, or has this been the most meaningful way we could have lived?" Questions I had kept at bay for a lifetime came flooding in.

"I had a wonderful life." I heard the smile in his voice. "And I found a way for you to be in it. I have no regrets."

I lifted my head. "Then neither do I."

"We have never lost what we had. We have not been broken by storms or disappointments." He cupped my chin, wiping away my tears with his thumb. "You were right about that too."

Before I had a chance to respond, there was a knock on the door. I sat up and called out to come in, and Agnes stepped in with a supper tray.

"My only hope is that I will not be a burden to you," Volmar said when we were alone again, and I helped him to a few spoonfuls of broth.

"There is nothing more important to me than to be with you now, for as long as it takes."

I ate my supper afterward, and as the night fell, we reminisced about St. Disibod, our secret trips outside the abbey, the hunting, and the herb-gathering. "That was my happiest time," I said. "Even though I am proud of everything I did later, those are the days I go back to in my memory when I feel nostalgic or in need of comfort."

"I am glad I have been there to see it all."

"I would not have done it without you."

Volmar shook his head. "You would." He paused. "But it is better to have a companion along the way."

The morning after a sleepless night I had passed in the empty cell next to Vomar's, Griselda brought me a letter bearing the imperial seal. I asked her to read it to me. It confirmed the rumor Archbishop Hillin had shared with me — Emperor Frederick would grant the order of protection to St. Rupert, elevating our status and opening the way for the termination of the interdict imposed by the canons, from whose jurisdiction we would be removed. It was the measure of my current misfortune that the news, while welcome, elicited only a nod on my part. I had no strength to comment on it.

Griselda read the rest of the letter, in which the emperor invited me to an audience he would be holding in May at Ingelheim. "Will you go?" she asked.

My gaze wandered to the window. It gave onto the church, on the other side of which was the abbey cemetery. "No."

Volmar would remain here forever, and so would I.

I spent the rest of the day and the following morning with Volmar. In the afternoon Abbot Gottfried arrived from St. Albans.

I left the two of them alone and waited in my parlor with refreshments laid out by Agnes. When the abbot joined me, his small eyes, set in a pudgy face that usually beamed with cheerful goodwill, were rimmed with red. I suspected mine were no different.

"I will pray for his peace—and for yours," he said, sympathy coloring his voice.

"I thank you. It will be much needed."

"The world will be bereaved of a fine spirit, but the rest of us must carry on."

I studied him. On the surface, it sounded like a platitude one would offer to those who grieve, but something told me there was more to it.

He must have read the question in my face. "I hope that despite this tragic turn of events, you will continue to show the persistence and courage that led you to establish St. Rupert, and now to save it."

So Volmar had told him of the imperial order.

"I will fight to my last breath for this foundation," I said.

"But even outside these walls, you have surpassed your sex to take on matters that so many others were afraid to, and have ignited a much-needed debate within the Church. Like all such debates, it will rage for years to come, but that is how change eventually comes about."

I was surprised at how his words echoed those spoken to me by Archbishop Hillin only a week before, even though it seemed like a lifetime had passed. "Neither of us will live to see it," I said, but I regretted it almost immediately. Gottfried was trying to comfort me, and I should not appear ungrateful. "But I applaud your optimism, and I hope I will come to share it in time."

"There is also talk around Mainz of the emperor preparing to sue for peace."

I could not even bring myself to scoff. "That would be a novelty."

"Nothing concrete yet, but he is said to mention your name and your desire for that to happen whenever the issue is raised."

"I have heard that too. But so many years have passed since my audience with him, and there is still no sign of an end to these constant hostilities —" I broke off, feeling tired. How many times had I said that?

"When . . . it is over, you can travel again, keep these matters at the forefront so they do not fade away."

Whether he was trying to suggest that there was life after Volmar, or whether he truly believed that I could help reform the Church or persuade the emperor to negotiate a treaty with the pope, a small part of me felt the familiar thrill. Since the day I had overheard Abbot Kuno and Bishop Otto of Bamberg, I had been fascinated by matters of high politics. I had managed to become involved to the extent that my state allowed me. Now my position was such that I could do even more — go where no other woman, save perhaps a royal one like the indomitable Queen Eleanor of England, had gone before. I could arrive at a palace and be ushered into the presence of the emperor or an archbishop and debate with them, present my view and my argument. Yes, I could do that if I wanted to.

But that would mean that I would have to leave Volmar again.

I shook my head. "My place is here," I said. "I started this, but now let someone else pick up the torch. I have no doubt someone will come along with enough passion to follow in my footsteps."

"I understand how you feel at this moment," he said. "But maybe with time you will change your mind."

I did not respond. I wondered if this was something Volmar had encouraged him to say to me. Something told me he would want me to do that. But I knew I could not.

The candles were burning low when Volmar asked me for more wine, and I watched him relax into the profound, pain-free sleep that only poppy extract can bring. Then, overcome by weariness myself, I lay down next to him, wrapping my arms around him, and drifted off into a dreamless slumber.

I awoke sometime later, my arms still around Volmar. Even before I opened my eyes, I knew he was gone; something essential was missing, as if the air had thinned. From then on, it would always be like that for me — no breath would be sufficient to fill my lungs, no matter how deeply I inhaled.

The embers in the brazier were glowing faintly, and the chamber was veiled in deep shadows. I wrapped the blanket tighter around him, as if that could stop his warmth from escaping. I murmured assurances, which — if he could have heard me — I hoped would not have surprised him. Holding him like that, I waited for dawn in a silence punctuated only by the muffled sobs that came intermittently from somewhere deep inside my hollowed-out being.

When I finally rose, an invisible cloak descended on me like something made of hardened mortar. My face was dry. I opened the door to find Griselda sitting on the bench outside. "Brother Volmar is gone to God."

She took both my hands and kissed me. "Our loss is great, but nothing compared to yours."

For years afterward, the sisters would tell the story of how I had not shed a single tear in front of the others that day. In their eyes, I must have appeared like that lump of salt I had kept since I was eleven years old. I had put it into Volmar's hands to be buried with him — clear, hard, and unbroken.

If only they had known how my heart wept for him on that cold winter morning, and how it has been weeping ever since.

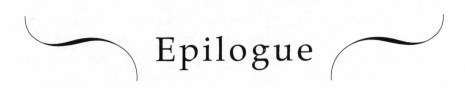

Epilogue

September 1179

I AM SITTING by the briskly burning fire in my parlor, wrapped in a woolen blanket. The night is wet and chilly. Across the chamber, Brother Guibert, a monk from the Abbey of Gembloux, is writing assiduously, the scratch of his quill and the soft patter of rain outside the only sounds breaking the silence of the late hour. I have just finished telling him my story—he had asked for it because he wants to write down "the deeds" of the foundress of the Abbey of St. Rupert. He became my secretary four years ago, the first and only one since Volmar died.

As for *what* he is writing—which you may perhaps read yourself one day—remember that he is going to embellish it; you know what these monk-scribes are like. He is going to add flourishes, perhaps make up a thing or two to make it more exciting, awe-inspiring, less mundane. Although mundane is the last thing my life has been.

But do not hold it against him. Brother Guibert is a good man, and the story of his arrival here is one that gives me hope that my struggles were not in vain.

He showed up on our doorstep one day and offered his services, and when I heard what had befallen him, I took him on at once. He was forty years of age at that time and walked with a slight limp. His long face, dominated by a prominent hooked nose, wore a monkishly serious expression, but there was a fiery intensity in his penetrating dark eyes. That intensity was fueled by a righteous outrage, as I would soon find out.

The year before, a brother named Johannes had become abbot of the house at Gembloux in an election that Guibert felt had been tinged with the stain of simony, Johannes being a nephew of a local landowner and a benefactor of the abbey. Guibert duly refused to pledge allegiance to the new abbot, a stance that earned him the status of an outcast in his community. After a few months, he left the abbey for Villiers to lodge with the brothers there, but he did not have the permission of his abbot and was therefore in breach of *Regula Benedicti*. "As long as Johannes remains in his post, I will not set my foot back at Gembloux," he told me as we supped together on that first evening.

I had already been looking for a scribe with excellent Latin skills, and had had many excellent scholars from all over the empire apply, but it was his brave stance against this abominable practice that tipped the scales in Guibert's favor. Of course, the matter of his move to St. Rupert had to be formally approved, lest his breach of The Rule put him permanently outside the Order. But that was not difficult; I wrote to my friend Bishop Rudolf of Liège—who had briefly been Archbishop of Mainz after Archbishop Arnold had been assassinated—and he gave his permission for the relocation. My satisfaction in meting out this kind of treatment to the simoniac abbot of Gembloux was unbecoming of my consecrated state. But it was, and remains, intense.

I am glad Guibert has heard my story now, as I suspect I do not have much time left. My age is a burden now—I have pains in my knees and feet that are making it difficult to walk, and I spend more time in my old chair by the fire than anywhere else these days. But sitting is exhausting too, after a life spent in throes of activity. And so, no matter what I do, I feel that my *viriditas* is leaving my body, ever so slightly each day.

It began with the news of the peace that Emperor Frederick had finally reached with Pope Alexander in Venice in the summer of the year 1177. I prayed all day after a messenger from Mainz had brought the announcement, thanking God I had lived long enough to see this fruitless conflict come to an end. Finally, Barbarossa—for that is the nickname that the Northern Italians, whom he had tried unsuccessfully to subdue for so long, had given him because of his red beard—had realized that God was not blessing his unjust endeavors. It was something I had warned him against more than twenty years before during our one and only meeting at Ingelheim.

Now, however, I hear that Frederick is up to his old tricks, and that the pope has been forced to flee Rome. There has not yet been a word of a new antipope, but if the past is any indication, he will not be tardy in arriving. In these times, more than ever before, rulers of temporal domains are locked in an ever-madder struggle against those whose remit is spiritual—sometimes committing abominable crimes, like that perpetrated on Archbishop Thomas à Becket in England a few years ago. So my optimism, like the strength in my body, is ebbing again. Now I am left hoping that if the schism must reemerge it will not happen before I depart this world, and thus I will be spared that knowledge.

I look back on my life with a mixture of pride and regret, as do most of us, but there is more pride than regret in it. For I have not spent my life merely observing events; I participated in shaping my own destiny, beholden to nobody but my own conscience and God. I fought for and established a foundation that I will leave in the capable hands of forty devoted sisters at St. Rupert and at Bingen, many of them trained as physicians, helping those who would otherwise have no access to care. They are also free to sing our *canticum laudum* again. They can do so without fear of persecution, for we are an imperial abbey now, shielded from the changeable winds of favors blowing from Mainz. Thankfully, Archbishop Christian is still at the helm, a great friend to us, and his tax concessions have greatly increased our wealth and therefore ability to extend charity to the sick and the poor.

But I grieve for the fate of St. Disibod, the place that first opened my mind and spirit to knowledge. It enjoyed significant good fortune during Abbot Kuno's long reign, producing scribes and illuminators and expanding its library collection. Those gains had been lost under Helenger, and although Abbot Peter managed to restore some of the abbey's old reputation and stabilize its income, it has, since Peter's untimely death, toiled once again under weak and ineffective abbots. There are rumors that the remaining brothers are thinking of abandoning it altogether. I have been writing regularly to Mainz and to abbeys throughout the Rhineland, urging bishops and clerics to help by sending a competent governor, but nothing has come of it so far.

I am also bereft of my oldest friends. Burgundia, Gertrude, Rego, and my faithful Griselda — only last winter, in her sleep, quietly and without fuss, the way she had lived — have all preceded me to eternity.

I am ready to join them — and Volmar, of course, whose presence, unlike that of the others, I still feel every day.

Guibert rubs his red-rimmed eyes and retires eventually, but for once I am comfortable in my chair and only ask him to add more charcoal to the fire. I close my eyes as he leaves, and I relish the heat that pervades my limbs.

I am still there as the day breaks; my niece Hiltrud comes to find me when I have not joined them for lauds. She leans over me, and I look up at her, but I cannot speak. I can hear her, however. She is asking if I am well, for I have gone so gray.

I am well, I want to assure her.

Behind her is an arched window, and the sky is gray too, with low clouds still lingering after last night's rain. But as I gaze, they part, a straight line that sends a stream of pale gold sunlight down to the earth. And again they part, another line crossing the previous one, and more light falling. The feather-like lightness that I have not felt for years returns, my body weightless once again, no longer the burden it has become.

I turn my eyes to Hiltrud, wondering if she can see the light, but she is calling someone, though now I cannot hear her voice anymore. The other sisters arrive, gathering around me, looking anxious and alarmed.

I want to tell them not to worry, that everything is well, but that comfort is no longer mine to give them.

Thank you for reading *The Column of Burning Spices*. I hope you enjoyed it. Would you kindly take a few minutes to support independent publishing by leaving a review on Amazon and/or Goodreads? I will greatly appreciate it!

If you would like to learn more about Hildegard or about my current writing projects, feel free to get in touch via my website's Contact Me form at www.pkadams-author.com. You can also follow me on Twitter @pk_adams

Author's Note

THE PIVOTAL EVENTS, as described in this story, that defined the second half of Hildegard's life are all historically true. Abbot Kuno did alert Pope Eugenius to her writing activities, which resulted in a visit from a group of envoys in order to investigate it. They took a copy of *Scivias* back to Rome, where — likely to the abbot's dismay — it was well received. After a lengthy tug-of-war — and after appealing to the Archbishop of Mainz for backing — Hildegard did manage to win independence from the Abbey of St. Disibod and establish her own foundation.

Her life at St. Rupert, while happier in many ways, was not, however, devoid of challenges. There was a period of famine and flood. The canons of the Mainz cathedral took to meddling in her affairs, and the conflict culminated with the music ban. Ricardis broke her heart by leaving St. Rupert to take a post at Bassum. It is also true that Hildegard admonished Emperor Frederick against waging wars in Italy and appointing antipopes, and that she gave an unprecedented speech (or sermon) at the Cologne cathedral.

However, in the interest of narrative flow, I decided to alter some of the timelines and to fictionalize certain events. The sisters left St. Disibod in the year 1150, and Hildegard obtained the charter for her new foundation in 1158 from Archbishop Arnold von Selenhofen (despite the fact that the charter signified economic independence from St. Disibod, Hildegard was never able to shed the abbey's spiritual authority). The burial crisis and the music interdict occurred in the final year of Hildegard's life, making it even more egregious.

The date of her famous speech in Cologne is most likely the year 1160. The speech, as presented in this novel, is not the actual text but rather a composite of her correspondence with various contemporaries on the issue of clerical corruption, simony, and the threat of Catharism. In putting it together, I used the excellent translation by Joseph Baird and Radd Ehrmann (*The Letters of Hildegard of Bingen*, vol. I-III); the chapter on the emergence of dissent in *A History of the Church in the Middle Ages* by F. Donald Logan; the chapter on Ricardis (Richardis) in *Hildegard of Bingen: The Woman of Her Age* by Fiona Maddocks; and the section on Hildegard's political mission in *The World of Hildegard of Bingen. Her Life, Times, and Visions* by Heinrich Schipperges. I refer those who would like to read the entire (lengthy) speech to letter 15r in volume I of *The Letters* (pp. 54-65).

The exchange between Hildegard and King Frederick during the meeting in Ingelheim is also based on their correspondence. In reality, that audience took place around 1150 and therefore before Frederick's ascension to the throne. It is not known what they said to each other then, but based on their subsequent (and contentious) letters it is possible to imagine both the topic of the conversation and the nature of Hildegard's arguments. I constructed two other scenes based on her correspondence: the conversation between Hildegard and Abbot Bertolf about the Synod at Trier in Chapter 15 and between Hildegard and Abbot Edmund in Chapter 30.

The scene in the papal palace in Rome is entirely fictional. Pope Eugenius did give an order to investigate Hildegard's writings, but the meeting of his advisers could not have happened the way it is described here because in 1145 there was so much political turmoil in Rome that he was not able to be consecrated in the city (that ceremony took place at the monastery of Farfa in February 1145). And while a group of envoys did visit St. Disibod, the storyline involving a spying conspiracy is also fictional.

As in *The Greenest Branch*, all the main characters are historical figures, even if some of the storylines involving them are invented. The real Abbot Helenger outlived his fictionalized counterpart and continued to be a thorn in Hildegard's side well into the 1170s. Volmar died before Hildegard (in 1173), but the riding accident is fictional.

The body of Hildegard's work and the scope of her activities were so broad that I could only scratch the surface here. She composed far more than I was able to reference in the two books. In addition to *Ordo Virtutum*, she was the author of *Symphonia armoniae celestium revelationum* (a collection of some 70 songs), as well as numerous antiphons, hymns, responsories, and sequences. The extent of Hildegard's journeys was also much larger than described here. She undertook no less than four separate tours after 1158, including to Cologne, Trier, Metz, Würzburg, and Bamberg during which she openly attacked clergy for corruption and pursuit of worldly power. In her sixties by then, she traveled by boat as well as overland on foot, on horseback, and by litter. All of that despite the limitations imposed by The Benedictine Rule and the biblical admonition against women preachers.

Finally, a note on the title. Upon hearing of Hildegard's exploits and the controversies that accompanied them (by which I mean church*men* having trouble accepting her work and her outspokenness), Pope Eugenius is said to have exclaimed, "Who is this woman who rises out of the wilderness like a column of smoke from burning spices?" (as quoted in Fiona Maddocks). I find this to be a very evocative simile, and also a metaphor. The "wilderness" could be a reference to the provincial character of that part of the Rhineland, but also to the inflexible and narrow-minded Church milieu that sought to curtail Hildegard's activities. Is that what the pope was suggesting? He did organize a public reading of *Scivias*, which greatly boosted Hildegard's fame. It is quite possible that without his support, her life would have taken a different turn. It is therefore fitting that his words should grace the cover of the second, and final, part of the Hildegard of Bingen duology.

Bibliography

In researching this book, I found following sources particularly helpful:

The Letters of Hildegard of Bingen ed. by Joseph Baird and Radd Ehrman

The Creative Spirit. Harmonious Living with Hildegard of Bingen by June Boyce-Tillman

Heretics and Scholars in the High Middle Ages by Heinrich Fichtenau

Original Blessing. A Primer in Creation Spirituality by Matthew Fox

Planets, Stars, and Orbs. The Medieval Cosmos 1200-1687 by Edward Grant

The Holy Roman Empire by Friedrich Heer

The Ways of the Lord by Hildegard of Bingen (ed. Emilie Griffin)

Scivias by Hildegard of Bingen (ed. Elizabeth Ruth Obbart)

Hildegardis causae et curae ed. by Paulus Keiser

Cambridge Illustrated History of Germany by Martin Kitchen

Medieval Thought: St. Augustine to Ockham by Gordon Leff

A History of the Church in the Middle Ages by F. Donald Logan

Hildegard of Bingen. The Woman of Her Age by Fiona Maddocks

Daily Life in the Middle Ages by Paul B. Newman

Frederick Barbarossa by Marcel Pacaut

Natural History by Pliny the Elder (Book XXVI)

Life in Medieval Times by Marjorie Rowling

The Gracious God: Gratia in Augustine and the Twelfth Century by Aage Rydstrom-Poulsen.

The World of Hildegard of Bingen. Her Life, Times, and Visions by Heinrich Schipperges

"Hildegard of Bingen and the Greening of Medieval Medicine." *Bulletin of the History of Medicine*, 1999, 73:381–403 by Victoria Sweet

"Text and context in Hildegard of Bingen's *Ordo Virtutum*." by Patricia Kazarow in *Maps of Flesh and Light. The Religious Experience of Medieval Women Mystics* ed. by Ulrike Wiethaus

Lyrics to Hildegard's chants in Latin and English can be found at http://www.hildegard-society.org

All of Hildegard's works are in the public domain, and the translations used in the text are mine.

For biblical quotations I used the New International Version translation.

 Acknowledgements

A s I REACH the end of the eight-year-old journey of
bringing this series to life, I would like to thank the
many people who have helped me along the way, whether
by reading and providing feedback, or just by listening to me
extolling the highs and complaining about the lows of being
an author. The process of writing and publishing *The Greenest Branch* and *The Column of Burning Spices* has brought me
into contact with many amazing writers and other industry
professionals, in person or via social media, whose knowledge, experience, and creativity I value deeply.

I would like to express particular gratitude to my be-
ta-readers Elaine Buckley, Pippa Brush Chappell, and Jena
Henry, who provided comprehensive and insightful feedback on the manuscript of *The Column of Burning Spices*.
Enormous thank you as always to my editor Jessica Cale and
cover designer Jenny Quinlan from Historical Editorial. Your
input made the book infinitely better textually and visually,
and any errors that remain are mine.

I am also thankful for the friendship of my fellow members of the Fearless Female Writers group and for the monthly dinners of the Boston chapter of the National Writers
Union. Both help me remember that while writing is mostly
a solitary pursuit, it is important to cultivate a community of
book lovers in my life.

Last but not least, thank you to my family for being supportive of the path I have chosen. I dedicate this series to my late grandmother — my first history teacher.

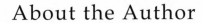

About the Author

P.K. ADAMS IS the pen name of Patrycja Podrazik. She is a historical fiction author based in Boston, Massachusetts. A lifelong lover of history and all things medieval, she is also a blogger and historical fiction reviewer at www.pkadams-author.com. She graduated from Columbia University where she first met Hildegard in a music history class. *The Column of Burning Spices* is the second in a two-book series about one of the medieval era's most fascinating women.

Made in the USA
San Bernardino, CA
14 February 2019